About the author

Born in London in 1962, Mitchell Levene travelled and lived around the world for ten years in the 1980s, with the sole intention of having a good time, perfecting the art of doing nothing and generally getting away with it. He's lived in Barcelona, Spain, since 1990, running a successful small company and is apparently still getting away with it.

He published his first novel, *Breakfast in Bombay*, in 2008, based on one of his own adventures: it's a wry and witty tale that tips its hat to Howard Marks' *Mr Nice* and Gregory David Roberts' *Shantaram*, and with more than a mere nod to *Midnight Express*.

THE NOT SO SILENT WORLD OF DANNY VALENTINE-ROCKER

Mitchell Levene

THE NOT SO SILENT WORLD OF
DANNY VALENTINE-ROCKER

Vanguard Press

A CIP catalogue record for this title is
available from the British Library.

ISBN 9781784657 27 7

*Vanguard Press is an imprint of
Pegasus Elliot MacKenzie Publishers Ltd.*
www.pegasuspublishers.com

First Published in 2020

**Vanguard Press
Sheraton House Castle Park
Cambridge England**

Printed & Bound in Great Britain

Dedication

To Alicia

My rock and the person who has come the closest to turning me into a responsible human being.

CHAPTER 1

Suzie Valentine-Rocker fought unsuccessfully to compose her thoughts, which had just gone from their usual state of idling somewhere between non-existent and mildly banal to a full-blown, head-screwing pyrotechnic extravaganza.

"Deaf? What on earth are you talking about? I mean, he's ten years old and can hear and speak perfectly, for God's sake. Of course he isn't bloody deaf!"

"I realize this must be a bit of a shock to you, but I'm afraid the results of his tests indicate Danny is indeed deaf," replied the now slightly flustered Doctor Hanks.

The slim woman with long, black hair and slightly oriental features sitting next to a fresh-faced youth, leaned far forward across his desk and fixed him with an adamant stare.

"So when you say he's deaf, you mean he's hard of hearing?"

"I'm afraid not, Mrs Valentine-Rocker. Not according to these results anyway." He spun the papers around for her to scrutinize.

"Okay, let's get this straight, Doctor. Just how deaf is he?" asked Suzie, trying to decipher the information in front of her. Though in her present state of mind she might as well have been trying to read ancient Greek.

The doctor sat back in his chair, making a steeple with his hands under his chin.

"Let's see. How can I put this? Now, technically speaking, he has a Grade 4 profound hearing impairment, 81 dB or greater hearing threshold in both ears. In layman's terms, he's stone deaf."

"Stone deaf? Here we go again. So, are you telling me my son's totally deaf as in *deaf* deaf?" said Suzie, three octaves higher than her usual voice.

"I'm afraid so, and I can understand your surprise. I myself had to run the tests three times, as Danny seemed to follow most of my instructions without too much of a problem."

Danny Valentine-Rocker sat impassive next to his mother, swinging his legs back and forth.

"But that's ridiculous. Don't you think I'd have noticed if my son was completely deaf? The only reason we had his ears checked in the first place was at the suggestion of his school. They thought that his total lack of musical ability was down to a hearing problem. I mean, Danny can be a bit distracted sometimes – he never comes when I call him, for example – but he's not deaf. He watches the telly, plays with his friends. He's your common-or-garden ten-year-old boy."

She was beginning to babble now, her mind whizzing through thousands of scenes and situations with Danny over the last ten years, but she could find no tangible evidence to endorse what the doctors had just told her. In fact, some of the memories that flashed into her head categorically disputed the doctor's diagnosis. Images of Danny as a toddler dancing to the radio, teaching him songs, hundreds of thousands of everyday normal, verbal interactions that she has had with her son.

"I need a second opinion."

"Of course, that's your prerogative, Mrs Valentine-Rocker, but I'm telling you that these tests are undoubtedly reliable. The chances that…"

Suzie interrupted him. "Danny. Stop kicking the desk!"

Danny's legs stopped swinging immediately.

Thank..." She didn't finish her sentence.

Suddenly, it occurred to her that the irrefutable evidence that indeed her son wasn't deaf was the fact that he could hear every word she said.

"There. You see? As I said: he *can* hear," she said triumphantly, but feeling like a complete idiot for not having the presence of mind to dispute the doctor's diagnosis with such obvious and accessible evidence a few minutes earlier.

The doctor smiled.

"I think I may have the answer to this mystery. Watch! Danny, can you hear me?"

Danny shook his head. Suzie sat dumbstruck.

"What's your name?"

"Danny."

"Where do you live?"

"29 Park Avenue, Crouch End."

"If you can't hear me, how do you know what I'm asking you?"

"I dunno. I just do. I watch your mouth and I know what you're saying."

"So you lip-read?"

"What's that?"

"You read people's lips when they're talking to you?" Doctor Hanks drew circles in the air while pointing to his own mouth.

"'Suppose so."

"This is an extremely fascinating and highly atypical scenario indeed," remarked Dr Hanks.

Suzie sat there listening to Danny in a daze, as if she had unexpectedly been transported to some kind of twilight zone. She was trying desperately to form a chain of lucid thoughts as images and flashes of life with a closet deaf son swirled around in her head.

Drawing a deep breath and vigorously shaking her black shiny mane, she snapped out of it.

"Atypical? Fucking mind blowing, I'd say."

The doctor raised his eyebrows at Suzie's own analysis of the situation.

"Pardon my language, Doctor, but as you can imagine, this is a real shock. I'd be less surprised if I had just found out he could walk through solid walls."

She looked at her young son, who sat quietly at her side.

Was this her son or some sort of extraterrestrial surrogate who had been switched with the real Danny while they were in the supermarket doing the Saturday morning shopping together?

"Just a minute, Danny. Are you telling me that you can read lips? You can understand everything people are saying?"

Danny nodded.

"Even me, when I speak to you in Mandarin?"

For the first time, she noticed that Danny was observing her face intensely as she spoke; or was she just imagining it? She also noticed the doctor's expression change from one of stoic acceptance of the situation, as if he had come across such cases on a daily basis, to one of genuine astonishment.

'Mandarin,' she saw him mouth to himself.

Danny nodded again. His face had changed from one of mild indifference to one of sadness.

His secret was out. It was a secret that he enjoyed. It was a secret that had been keeping his young life as it had always been before he had stopped hearing.

He knew it was all over, that it was all going to change when Miss Munster, the beaky-nosed, thin-faced music teacher that everybody called Monster, couldn't take any more of Danny's screeching attempts to make noises that even resembled music on the regulation wooden recorder. She recommended to his form teacher that he get his hearing checked.

"Everything?"

"It's a bit more difficult to understand you in Mandarin, but I'm getting better. In English I can understand nearly everything, but sometimes I can't. I need to see people's faces. I look at their mouths. If I can't see them, I don't know what they're saying. Also, when a lot of people are talking at once. There are some people who, even if I can see their faces, I don't know what they're saying, like Mr Patel at the corner shop."

"Hmmm. I Imagine that Mr Patel has a rather strong accent or doesn't have a complete command of the English language," intervened the doctor.

"Doctor Hanks. Nobody can understand Mr Patel," Suzie informed him.

Danny chuckled.

"The fact that he can't understand people if he can't see their faces is both logical and understandable. Lip-readers need to see the whole face; not only the lips, but the eyes, eyebrows, cheeks and jaws. They read their facial expressions. But what adds another dimension to your son's already considerable skills is the fact that he can lip-read Mandarin. I take it that you are of Chinese descent and you've addressed your son in Mandarin since birth?"

"My mum is Chinese and she's always spoken to me in Mandarin. And as I've always enjoyed having a secret language to speak with her in that my dad and my friends can't understand, I thought it'd be fun to have the same with my son."

"Do you only speak to Danny in Mandarin?"

"No. I used to, though, until he was a toddler, but I mostly speak to him in English nowadays. Except when I don't want his dad to know what we're talking about. His grandmother always talks to him in Mandarin, though. He seems to understand okay, but for some reason he's never spoken Mandarin very much."

"Fascinating and extraordinary. I must say your son must possess brain faculties that far exceed anything I've ever heard of or read about," said the doctor.

Suzie looked once again at her son, now practically convinced that his origins had not been her womb.

"Extraordinary?" she squeaked.

The doctor now sat forward, visibly excited.

"I know a little about this subject. Lip-reading requires extraordinary observational skills and, if we only consider lip-reading in English, it's been estimated that only about thirty or forty percent of sounds are distinguishable from sight alone."

"Really? Only thirty or forty percent?"

"Just think about it. Think about words that start with a 'b' and 'p', like 'bat' or 'pat', for example. To a lip-reader, a word on its own like 'stick', 'brick', or 'kick' is totally indefinable. They need more context to distinguish them. Then there are letters like 't', 'd' and 'n'. Really difficult to distinguish. Try miming the word 'patted' or 'padded'. Go on! Being able to lip-read is all about context."

Suzie found herself silently mouthing words, giving her the appearance of imitating a fish, and instantly understood just how difficult it must be to determine whether a speaker is pronouncing one word or another.

Dr Hanks let her carry out her practical experiment for a few moments before continuing.

"So, you see, when lip-reading, they tend to lip-read part and guess or predict the rest. Lip-reading is said to be eighty percent guesswork."

Suzie looked at Danny, wanting to say something, but no words came. He answered her look with raised eyebrows and an open-handed shrug.

"Now, I'm not an expert in languages, but if I'm not mistaken, I believe Mandarin offers an added difficulty to the art; I understand that tones tend to play a big part in any Chinese language. If you pronounce the same word in a different tone, it takes on an entirely new meaning."

Although still in the twilight zone, Suzie was now listening with a certain fascination.

Her mind shifted to analyse simple Mandarin phrases and was now doing Chinese fish impressions. She was beginning to fathom the extent of her son's skill.

"You're not wrong. Mandarin has four tones, and I can certainly see why this could make lip-reading it more complicated. I must say, you seem to know quite a lot about lip-reading, Doctor."

"I've been studying the subject a little as part of our cochlear implant treatment."

"What's that?"

"A cochlear implant is a surgically implanted electronic device that provides a sense of sound to a person who's profoundly deaf or severely hard of hearing. This is a solution that we'll discuss for Danny in a moment; but, as I was saying, as part of the UK Cochlear Implant Group, I've been reading up on the subject of lip-reading. It's felt that all patients with these implants can benefit enormously from training to develop their lip-reading skills. So can parents of severely hard of hearing children. They can be taught how to adapt or condition their language to help the child to develop lip-reading skills from an early age."

"So, if lip-reading is such a difficult task with so many influential factors, how is it that Danny has been able to master the art so well?"

"That's a good question and I can only say that your son seems to possess some outstanding and extraordinary observation and deduction skills that enable him to literally process thousands of contextually relevant factors in a fraction of a second."

Suzie studied her newly discovered child prodigy once again. That morning, she had an ordinary ten-year-old who had problems in his music class. Now she was sitting next to a mini Stephen Hawking.

She was imagining her husband's face when she tells him later that evening, when they are sitting in front of the telly, watching the nine o'clock news.

The doctor, continuing with his revelations, drew her back to the present. "You'd be surprised to hear that lip-reading is important from a very young age. When babies as young as three months were shown video recordings of people speaking where the lips are not synchronised with the audible speech, they quickly lost interest. Their attention was re-established when the synchronisation was returned to normal. So even at this tender age, infants make the connection between what they're hearing and lip movements. By the age of nineteen months, toddlers can lip-read familiar words."

"That's all very interesting and you're right, I am surprised. But what I'd really like to know is, how long has Danny been deaf? I mean, he wasn't born deaf. I'm absolutely positive."

"I can only base my comments on his English speech, of course, but the fact that his speech is perfectly normal and there are no evident alterations in his pronunciation or limitations regarding vocabulary, indicates that his speech development has been allowed to follow its normal course until he was eight, which is regarded as the age when children normally complete speech development."

"So you're saying he's gone deaf in the last two years?"

"It would seem so. I must say he has done surprisingly well in maintaining such a level of voice and pronunciation control that's totally indiscernible and nobody, not even his parents, have noticed. I mean, just keeping the volume of his speech at normal levels is a feat on its own."

Suzie sat in silence for a few seconds while she tried to digest what the doctor was explaining.

"So will he always be able to speak normally?"

"Now that's a good question. I don't see why not, but just to be on the safe side I would recommend that he learns sign language."

For the first time in her life, Suzie consciously turned her face towards her son so he could read her.

"Danny, I just can't understand it. Why didn't you tell me about all this? Why didn't you tell me about your hearing? Why did you keep it all to yourself? Can you explain it to me, please?"

Suzie was now feeling a gush of guilt and self-recrimination. What sort of a mother doesn't realise her own son is deaf and, worse still, what sort of a mother is she that her son doesn't feel comfortable enough to come to her with such a serious problem?

Danny sat in silence for a few moments, and Suzie wondered if he hadn't been able to read what she was asking him.

"I don't know, Mum. It just happened that way. I like not hearing. I like knowing what everybody is saying."

A few seconds passed while he seemed to be searching for the answers to a question that he hadn't even asked himself.

"I don't want anything to change if everybody finds out."

"What do you mean, you like it? Who in their right mind can like *not* hearing? Don't you think I could've helped you? And what do you think would change?"

Suzie was now firing questions that she knew Danny would have problems answering. After all, he was only ten.

Danny started crying. Two years of keeping his secret, two years of isolation, two years of trying to live the life of a normal little boy had come to an end.

Like a dam bursting, all his buried and suppressed emotions of the last two years were now pouring down his cheeks.

CHAPTER 2

At eight years old, Danny hadn't had enough life experience to be able to analyse if his childhood was happy or not. As with all children, his state of well-being, if he was feeling okay with the world or not, was determined by emotions triggered by events in the present; and, in Danny's case, he generally felt okay.

He lived in a comfortable four-bedroom house with a big kitchen and plenty of room to run around in. A big garden with a slide and a swing big enough to play football in kept him entertained in the summer or when it wasn't raining. He was an only child, with his own bedroom full of toys.

He had lots of friends who lived down his street and he'd spend hours playing with them in each other's gardens or at the local park.

Being an only child, he had a monopoly on his parents' affections and attention.

Both his Mum and Dad had time to play with him and made him feel good with occasional hugs and kisses. He particularly liked his Mum reading to him at night and his games of football with his Dad in the garden, even though sometimes his Dad made him kick the ball only with his left foot, telling him that if he wanted to be a professional footballer, he'd have to know how to play with both feet.

His Dad was a sports journalist and football was his religion. He was prone to using football analogies to give him, or anyone for that matter, advice about life. Most of the time Danny had no idea exactly what advice he was being given.

"You have to decide where you want to play in life, son. Are you a defender, a midfielder or a forward?"

"You have to make every shot on goal count. You never know if you are going to get another chance."

"Remember, let the ball do the running, son," he said on more than one occasion. That one was particularly baffling for Danny.

The only blot on his idyllic childhood everyday life, the only thing that could make him feel 'not okay', was his parents' constant bickering. They would end up screaming at each other about things like dirty socks being left on the bedroom floor, about whose turn it was to do the dishes, about drinking too much, spending too much money, criticising each other's families, about who said what and to whom at a party. On and on they would go until one or the other, usually his Dad, would storm out of the house, slamming the front door, or his Mum would go upstairs to hide behind another slammed door.

However, these moments were just blips as, just when these fights had Danny beginning to feel like his world had shifted into some sort of weightless, colourless space with no solid floor, his parents would be back to their normal state of amicable tolerance. As if nothing had happened or been said and with harmony restored, he once again felt the floor firmly under his feet.

Yes, his parents' bickering apart, Danny was feeling okay until he started to notice that everybody was speaking more softly, as if the volume on the TV had been turned down.

In fact, it was the TV that had provided him with the proof and the first signs that something was wrong.

"Danny, for the last time, turn that telly down."

"But I can't hear it very well."

"I think the neighbours four houses down can hear it. Turn it down."

So he turned it down and unconsciously began to follow the people's lips to be able to understand them. *Batman*, *The Lone Ranger*, *Swap Shop*, *The Partridge Family* and *Doctor Who* all became lip-reading exercises.

It wasn't all plain sailing, though: he noticed he did have a big problem with cartoons, as the characters' lip movements provided very few clues as to what they were saying. He could only try to guess from the context what was going on, which, luckily, did not prove to be too difficult.

Jerry chased Tom, the coyote chased the Road Runner, and Dick Dastardly tried to knock the other Wacky Racers out of the race.

One day, he turned the TV on to watch *Blue Peter* and, after about ten minutes, just as one of the presenters was telling the show's pet dog

Shep to "get down" while he presented a glowing child with his 'Blue Peter badge', his Mum came in and asked him how he could enjoy his programme with the sound off. He hadn't even noticed. He'd been able to follow everything.

For Danny, this was a watershed moment. From then on, whenever he was alone he watched all his programmes with the sound off.

This is the time when he discovered the extent of his abilities, when he became conscious of a skill that wasn't normal; but Danny didn't conceive it as a gift. He only knew that he didn't have to hear people speaking to be able to understand what they were saying, hearing being something that was getting increasingly more difficult by the day. If he didn't watch people's lips, he couldn't understand the words. He still heard them, but they were now just muffled sounds.

At some moment during this learning curve, he had made an unconscious decision not to reveal his hearing difficulties to his Mum and Dad. A number of complex factors came into play for him not to own up to the demise of his hearing faculties, the first being an unusual sense of peace. The sound of silence seduced and conquered him, wrapping him up in a white, fluffy cloud.

Voices could be raised, insults exchanged and doors could slam, but Danny heard none of it. All he had to do was not look at them and, for him at least, the venom flying backwards and forward, filling the air with hate, just disappeared.

The second factor was that nobody noticed; neither his parents nor his school teachers showed any indication that anything had changed. He played with his friends as he always had. Occasionally, questions like "Did you hear what I said?" or "Are you deaf?" would be thrown his way, but he was careful enough to make sure he could see what everybody was saying to him and nobody had to ask him these questions more than was necessary, nor enough times for them to suspect.

He had become so good at lip-reading that he was even able to follow, almost perfectly, multi-party conversations and from quite far away.

Two or three of his friends could be talking at once and he found himself able to 'read' enough to follow what they were saying without any problem.

At school, he strategically made sure he sat at the front of all his classes. He had no problem following a teacher's lips from the back of the class, but he had discovered the problem that if other kids in front of him were speaking, he couldn't read them. So, by sitting at the front, he could just turn around.

As his world became more and more silent, the only thing that made him uncomfortable with his affliction was not being able to hear his own voice when speaking. Not knowing if what he was saying was coming out as it should was disconcerting and particularly worrying at first. If his secret was to be discovered, it would certainly be his own speech that would give him away; but, as time went by, the fact that his family and friends interacted with him as they always had convinced him that he was indeed speaking normally. Just how he managed to pull this off surprised even himself. The only palpable evidence he could count on to make sure sound was coming from him were the vibrations he could feel deep in his throat.

His control of his vocal cords seemed to be automatic.

He was beginning to have fun with his new skills. He enjoyed being able to know what anybody and everybody was saying if he could see their faces.

On the bus on the way to school, he would follow conversations. A lot of these conversations were like having some sort of advance life education lessons, although, for the most part, his young age and lack of experience made a lot of what was spoken about by adults sound like incomprehensible gibberish. He would read two large ladies, both with blonde hair and black roots, talk about their husbands.

"How's things with your husband?"

"Same as usual."

"Still can't...?"

"Half."

"How does he...?"

"Stuffs it in."

"Oooh, dear. But still quick?"

"Two minutes, tops. Then he's snoring his head off."

"Sounds familiar."

And they both laughed.

"We certainly picked some good 'uns, didn't we? Still, can't complain. He's a good husband, and he's good with the kids. So long as he's happy."

"Yeah, I know what you mean. You can't have everything in life, can you?"

His lip-reading also introduced him to new vocabulary, especially when he would be watching football games on the TV with his Dad.

The camera would focus on two players arguing after a nasty tackle. Joined at the forehead, locked together like two stags, veins throbbing.

"You fucking animal!"

"What? I hardly touched you."

"Fuck off, you big tosser."

"Fuck you. Wanker!"

Danny looked over to his Dad, who was frantically scribbling on a pad.

"Dad."

"Shh! I'm trying to work."

"What does tosser mean, Dad?"

"Ahem, harrumph." His Dad had just swallowed a fly "What?"

"Tosser. What does it mean?"

"I'll tell you when you're older."

"And winker?"

"Winker?" he asked, now with a puzzled look on his face.

"Or wanker?" Danny had had problems identifying the correct vowel.

His Dad swallowed another fly and then coolly added, "The same as tosser. Now shut up and watch the game."

Danny's skills and experience reading people's conversations also taught him very early that most of the time they weren't worth reading. People mostly spoke about boring rubbish, at least from a little boy's perspective.

He had stopped reading most of the conversations practically as soon as they started.

Perhaps the most common topic was the weather; or, rather, this being London, how much it had rained recently and speculation about the whereabouts of the sun.

The weather was closely followed by football, TV programmes, films, and health problems. If there was one thing that surprised Danny, it was just how much people talked about others behind their backs in social situations, usually aesthetic-related observations about the size of a nose, a backside, stomach, or a choice of clothing.

Another factor that contributed to Danny not telling anyone about his hearing was a naïve and perhaps innocent conclusion that a ten-year-old would take from watching a film about a deaf boy with his parents. He sat there watching a cheesy Saturday afternoon American TV movie which had a storyline that had some eerie, though not exact, parallels to what was happening to him. It was a CBS 1979 film called *And Your Name is Jonah.* A deaf nine-year-old boy is misdiagnosed as being mentally retarded and is institutionalised or, as his Dad explained it, put in a loony bin. When a teary, over-dedicated and smothering mother finds out, it becomes all about a deaf boy's struggle to play catch-up on all his emotional and intellectual development that he'd been missing out on all his life. Once ascertained that he was deaf, he goes to special school for the hard of hearing, where he learns sign language and struggles to live a life as normally as possible.

Danny's own mother sat crying and snivelling throughout the whole movie, saying things like, "I couldn't begin to imagine what that mother is going through", "Poor boy" or "Society can be so cruel and unfair".

Danny's father contributed with exclamations like, "What a load of crap! The boy's a poof."

All Danny could do was imagine his own life being turned upside down if anyone found out he couldn't hear. 'I could be stuck in a special school,' he thought. 'They'll take me away from my friends and people will think I'm some kind of loony.'

Even if the film did have an inspiring ending, with the boy proving to all and sundry that, with the love and support of loved ones and gritty determination, he could live something resembling a normal life, Danny was now sure he had to keep his mouth shut.

What Danny wanted to avoid losing was exactly that: something resembling a normal life.

CHAPTER 3

Although Suzie's thoughts were still engulfed in self-recriminating turmoil, the tiny, and in the most part considerably inoperative, pragmatic part of her mind began to kick in.

A gush of questions came to her at once and she knew that she had to ask them all at once, before they disappeared like sand through a sieve.

"So, what would you say was the cause of his losing his hearing?"

The doctor opened his mouth to begin his explanation, but, before he could emit any sound, he was hit with the rest of Suzie's interrogation.

"What are our options?"

"And what made him go deaf?"

"Is there an operation to fix it?"

"What is this cold cheer thingy you were talking about?"

"Is he going to be deaf forever?"

He held up both hands, palms out, as if he were trying to protect himself from a physical projectile.

"Slow down, please. One question at a time, Mrs Valentine-Rocker."

"I'm sorry, Doctor. It's just that..."

"There's really no need to apologise. Your questions and your anxiety are perfectly normal, given the unusual circumstances. Let's take them one at time and I'll try to answer them as best as I can."

He stood beside a large poster depicting the intricate workings of the human ear. "Now, a good place to start would be to explain, as simply as I can, how we hear and the basic workings of the parts of the ear. Your ears pick up sound which travels in invisible waves through the air. They travel down the ear canal and hit the eardrum in the middle ear. This causes the eardrum to vibrate."

Taking a pen from the top pocket of his white coat, he pointed to the middle ear.

"These three tiny bones link the vibrating eardrum to this snail-shaped thing we call the cochlear, which is in the inner ear. The cochlear contains a liquid that carries the vibrations to thousands of tiny hair cells, which, in turn, fire off tiny electrical signals that send messages to the brain."

He paused to check for signs that his temporary student was understanding or following his explanation. Slow nodding indicated that she was.

Although not academically bright, Suzie was able to follow without a problem. Her parents and teachers had been sure that she suffered from some kind of ADD, but tests had proved negative.

Suzie's was a clear case of selective ADD. When something interested her, or perhaps more important was in her interest, she was able to concentrate one hundred percent.

"So the answers to most of your questions would depend on what actually caused Danny's hearing loss. It could be due to any number of things. I doubt that it is due to earwax. My initial examination showed no excessive build-up and, what's more, wax is not a cause of total deafness. My examination also discounted the possibility of him having a ruptured eardrum. I think the most likely scenario is he may have an abnormal bone growth in the middle ear, the tiny ones I told you about, or he may have damaged or affected nerve hairs found in that snail, or cochlear."

Once again, Suzie was nodding, showing that she understood, so he continued. "May I ask if he was a premature baby? I'm talking about seven months. A premature baby's auditory system is not yet mature when born and consequently is susceptible to damage."

"Nope, he was born a very healthy eight-pound boy."

"Did you have any problems during pregnancy?"

"Nothing that I can remember, unless you call turning into a whale, excessive flatulence and weak bladder a problem." She was about to add that they didn't make any socially acceptable clothes for expectant mothers, then thought better of it.

"Has he had any serious ear infections?"

"Nope."

"Well, for the moment, the actual cause of Danny's hearing loss will remain a mystery. We can only monitor him and see what develops. It isn't that his affliction is irreversible; however, due to the unexpected and unexplainable way that Danny lost his hearing, it isn't inconceivable that one day it might return."

"Is there any kind of exploratory operation he can have?"

"We could go in to see if he has otosclerosis, an abnormal bone growth. Those tiny bones I told you about in the middle ear. If this is indeed the problem, the operation to correct this condition has a very high success rate. Children normally develop this problem around the age of puberty, which doesn't mean that Danny doesn't have this problem, but it does suggest that it's unlikely."

"So you don't think this operation is an option?"

Doctor Hanks had obviously been weighing this up as he sat back in his chair, crossed his hands at the back of his head and looked at an imaginary spot in the far corner of his office.

"My professional opinion, based on my instincts gained by twenty-five years' experience as an ear specialist, is that Danny doesn't have otosclerosis. And if I were wrong, I'm afraid a Stapedectomy, the operation to correct the problem, would not result in improved hearing, as Danny is technically deaf. Maybe, and it's a big maybe, if I had seen Danny while he still had some hearing capabilities, we could have considered this option. It is definitely an operation to improve hearing and not to cure deafness."

Suzie sat in silence for a moment while she digested the doctor's explanations. He seemed to be an extraordinarily competent professional, and she could find no reason why she shouldn't respect his opinion.

"Okay, that kind of makes sense. What about the cold cheer thingy you spoke about?"

Doctor Hanks smiled. "Cochlear." He wrote it on a notepad for her to see. To save prolonging any embarrassment, he didn't hesitate with his answer. "Okay, now, the cochlear implant doesn't cure deafness or restore hearing." He paused and appealed to the ceiling for inspiration. "How can I explain it? It allows the patient to have the sensation of sound. I don't want to get too technical, but the implant kind of does the work of the hair cells that stimulate the auditory nerve."

Noticing that Suzie now had a very confused expression as she forced herself to follow him, he paused a moment. "Look, the bottom line is that having this implant would mean that Danny would have to go through an operation to implant a receiver and electrodes. The former goes just under the skin and behind the ear and the latter will be surgically inserted into the snail-like cochlear in the inner ear. These electrodes stimulate the fibres of the auditory nerve and sound sensations are perceived. Then, externally, the patient will wear a microphone, a speech processor and a transmitter."

"My goodness!" was all Suzie could say. She looked at Danny, who sat there stoically swinging his legs. She wasn't sure if he had been reading any of this and, if so, if he'd been able to understand the half of it.

"What do you think, Danny?"

"About what?"

She didn't know how to elaborate on her question. Perhaps she just needed to ask somebody the question instead of herself.

"It doesn't matter, precious." She stroked his black shiny hair and smiled. "So, Doctor Hanks, would you recommend that Danny has a cold... cochlear implant?"

"Once again, I feel I must give you my honest opinion. As Danny can quite clearly defend himself, and his hearing loss doesn't seem to affect his daily life or impede him from actively participating in any normal functions or activities, I don't think we should subject him to an operation carried out under general anaesthetic. Nor to a lifetime carrying around all that electrical paraphernalia. Quite frankly, I don't think the implant would improve his quality of life. Of course, he'll never be a disc-jockey or an air traffic controller, but I'm sure he'll do just fine. He's a very talented and special little boy. You should be proud of him."

"Believe me, I am. I can't wait to see what my husband thinks of all this."

"If you want to bring him along, I'd be happy to go through it all with him."

"Thank you."

"So, to conclude, I think we'll just see how Danny develops and we can see each other again in around six months."

CHAPTER 4

Suzie, immersed in an introspective daze, walked to the car, oblivious to what was going on around her.

Although not raining hard, tiny drops fell intermittently from a gloomy, dark sky, but she didn't feel them as they pinged her face. She felt as if her life had just been simultaneously turned upside-down and inside-out. She was desperately trying to assimilate all that she had heard and learned at the doctor's surgery.

Danny walked silently by her side. That suited her just fine. She was sure that Danny's own instincts were telling him that now was not the time for conversation. Besides, he probably had his own deliberations to contend with.

Just an hour or so ago, in another lifetime, Suzie had been like just any other mother going to see a doctor with her young son for a routine hearing test, and she had left with a prodigious anomaly. What happened? What should she do now? What will all this mean to their lives?

Suddenly, she became aware of the spots of rain hitting her face, and, as she looked up at the sky, as if God was offering her a kind of tangible metaphor, a ray of sunshine pierced through a diminutive gap in the heavy-laden clouds and, just for an instant, lit up the world.

As the muddy-coloured trees became green and all the colours around her radiated their true and bright natures, it dawned on her that what she had always considered a dull and grey life full of disappointments and unfulfilled expectations was about to obtain a little spark.

From a very young age, Suzie had been convinced that she was not like other people. That she was special. She was sure her life would be special, one full of glitter, fame and recognition.

Born in 1950, an only child to an English father and a Chinese mother, she had been brought up in a nondescript semi-detached house in one of London's equally unremarkable northern suburbs.

It was a childhood full of under-achievement, dissatisfaction and, according to Suzie, humiliation. One of the earliest indications of her discontent with what life's circumstances had dealt her was when she was old enough to appreciate just how close she had come to having what she considered to be a cool name.

Her mother's maiden name had been Wong, so although now not technically possible, if her mother had had her out of wedlock, she could have been Suzie Wong, the mythical and legendary main character in one of her favourite films, *The World of Suzie Wong*, starring Nancy Kwan and William Holden.

Inappropriately, her father, an accountant in a large car parts factory, had the most unfortunate surname of Higginbottom, a name which Suzie despised with a passion from the moment she was old enough to comprehend just how regrettable it was to be named Suzie Higginbottom. She could only hope that one day her mother would come to her senses and leave her dull and boring father and revert to her maiden name, allowing Suzie to follow suit. This was a desire that she'd later in life regret having, when her father was killed by a drunken driver who had lost control of his petrol tanker.

From an early age she adopted a disdainful attitude towards her parents and all that surrounded her. She spent almost all her youth dreaming or fantasising about how she would become famous. She was desperate to stand out among her boring grey and unadventurous family and peers. She devoured glamour magazines, romantic novels, and movies, filling her head with all that they portrayed and often supplanting herself in the position of her favourite heroines or movie stars.

She was determined to make these musings a reality. She didn't care how or what she would do to achieve her goal, be it become a pop star like Lulu, or an actress, or an Olympic medallist.

Unfortunately, Suzie lacked the one essential and definitive ingredient if anybody wants to succeed in any of these areas – a minimal amount of talent. She discovered this the hard way. Not for the want of trying, though. She convinced her parents to enrol her in drama school, but she was never given anything but a few lines to say in every play they put on.

Her biggest speaking part was a talking tree.

She wasn't at all musical, unable to master even the most basic skills in guitar or piano. As for her singing voice, there were throttled pigs that could hold a note better. On the sports field, she proved to be dismally average and was never picked for any of the school teams.

Having no academic aspirations, she left school at sixteen and went to work in a clothes shop in the fashionable King's Road. She felt that by this means, it was as close as she could get to being chic and glamorous, this being where the rich and famous came to buy their clothes.

She did, in fact, sell Marianne Faithfull a pair of leather trousers. Well, at least she thought it was Marianne Faithfull, which was good enough for her.

She frequented the chic night clubs of the West End and Soho, like *The Marquee* or *The 100 Club*. If her own talent, or lack of, couldn't catapult her to the life of the rich and famous, then perhaps she could get there on the back of someone else's. She was on the hunt for footballers, actors and rock stars.

Her parents tried to keep her in, but she always managed to escape as soon as they had gone to bed, which, fortunately for her, was around 10pm. She undoubtedly had a good time in the clubs, dancing until the early hours on amphetamines like Black Bombers, but the closest she got to catching her glamorous prey was when she went out with a secondary actor who had a bit part in the popular soap opera *Coronation Street*. He wasn't too good-looking, being short, with wispy blond hair and an overly narrow face, but she didn't care; he was on TV and sort of famous.

Their relationship lasted as long as his part on the soap opera: about three weeks. The writers killed him off, along with Suzie's dreams.

At twenty, she was still living at home, still working in the same shop in the King's Road. She was frustrated and depressed. Doomed to grow old, having led a boring and anonymous life. One day, she was watching a report about The Beatles in India on TV, and she was inspired. It was to be a catalyst for her to take a risky and brave decision for perhaps the first time in her life.

She gave up her job and went to stay on an ashram in the hills of Northern India.

Although she knew this wouldn't directly get her to where she wanted, she had this romantic idea that spending time with a Yogi in places that The Beatles had made fashionable, she could write a best-selling book based on her adventure, or at the very least add a little colour to her life.

The first days of her stay, although she found it difficult to adapt to the extreme poverty and total lack of any form of hygiene or basic amenities, for the first time in her life she felt euphoric. She was at last an independent woman. From her fellow spiritual junkies she received something she had never received: admiration and recognition.

Her ego-fest was only to last five days. She came down with acute dysentery.

What started as what seemed to be a mild case of Delhi Belly quickly accelerated to a full-blown emergency. She spent five days passing blood and mucus. A doctor was called, but he was unable to calm her severe abdominal pain, the loss of fluids, and a delirious fever that caused her to lose consciousness.

The doctor's prognosis was ominous: if she stayed in the ashram a few more days in that condition she may well die, or at the very least damage her colon and intestines for life.

Her parents were contacted, and she was almost immediately airlifted to Delhi and put directly on a hospital plane back to England. Three hours after landing, she went into emergency surgery to correct a perforated colon.

It took her six months of rest and following a special diet of lukewarm barley water, chicken broth, diluted milk and her mother's Chinese herbal remedies for the first weeks to get back on her feet, and another six months to be well enough to consider going back to work. She never quite recovered the two stone in weight that she had lost in the first week and now looked better than ever.

This brush with death didn't calm her quest to make some kind of impact on society, but it did exclude adventurous travelling as a means to achieve her goals. The India trip was to be the first and last foreign excursion she was to have in her lifetime.

She met Johnny Valentine-Roca at a party in 1971. At first, he made very little impression on her. He had average looks with no real distinguishing facial features, was of medium build, but sported the beginnings of a paunch; however, he did have a luscious, premature mane of white hair that gave him an air of maturity and sophistication, and it was only this feature that made Suzie invest any time on him.

After a few minutes chatting, Suzie's interest began to grow, and two facts made her mind up to take the possibility of going with Johnny seriously. The first was that he told her he was a writer, a journalist for a well-known national newspaper. The second, and perhaps the definitive one that really made an impact on her frivolous sense of values, was his name. Johnny Valentine-Roca; the Roca pronounced as in 'Rocker', which was what Suzie understood it to be.

She silently pronounced in her head, while he continued chatting about his job, the name Suzie Valentine-Rocker. Wow! She loved it. Even better than Suzie Wong, she mused excitedly. She later learned that the origins of the name were that Johnny's father was called David Valentine, and he married Anna Roca, a young Spanish student.

As in Spain, the wife doesn't automatically and legally adopt her husband's surname, and Anna didn't want to lose her family name, so it was agreed and, in the eyes of the law, arranged for her to adopt both surnames with a hyphen.

Yes, that name was enough to convince Suzie. She was tired of chasing rainbows and practically made up her mind that very night that she would become Suzie Valentine-Rocker.

Johnny seemed pleasant and, what's more, he was a writer for a national newspaper. That certainly had a glittery feel to it. What she hadn't heard while she was fancifully renaming herself, was his telling her he was, in fact, a sports journalist.

What may have sealed the deal for Suzie was when he drove her back to his own bought and paid for bachelor's flat in a fashionable part of the city. Later, as she lay in his bed, she was overcome with a warm and fuzzy feeling, and she whispered to herself, "Yes, this will do nicely", before dozing into a contented and profound sleep.

Eight months later they were engaged, and before the first year was up they were married. On Suzie's insistence, they had their honeymoon in Scotland.

Although Suzie had now discovered the correct spelling of what was then her new surname, she insisted on spelling Roca as Rocker, and some years later convinced Johnny to get the surname officially changed to Rocker.

Like nearly all marriages, they got on well for the first years, their different characters and interests taking a back seat, or at least remaining on another untouched and unanalysed plane, while they built their nest together.

Johnny was constantly away working and, when he was home, they were content enough to watch the TV with supper on trays. He was a simple man in the sense that as long as his basic needs were satisfied, he needed no further cultural or social stimulation, as Suzie was soon to find out. Johnny's life was football, football, and more football. If you gave him the choice between hot, passionate sex and football, he would probably wonder why you should even consider offering him an alternative to practising his religion. Suzie accepted this as Johnny accepted her constant need to banter on about show business gossip. Both reached a sort of tolerant *status quo* for the sake of a peaceful married life.

At the start of their second year together, Suzie became pregnant, and Danny Valentine-Rocker was born in 1972, the Chinese year of the Rat, according to her mother. And despite the unattractive connotations of the name, it was apparently a strong and positive sign.

It didn't take long for Suzie to convince her husband to put down a deposit on a big four-bedroom house in the leafy suburb of Crouch End in North London. Suzie's life as a young parent was traditional: feeding, changing and entertaining the young Danny, some housekeeping and cooking. Johnny's life didn't change all that much. Gradually, Suzie's dreams changed from being of an excited expectation to a distant hope, then, finally, up to her eyes in dirty nappies, a mere whimsy.

CHAPTER 5

The sun disappeared back to its place behind the clouds in what must have been a nanosecond and sucked up all the colours along with it; but a nanosecond was all Suzie needed to realise the immense possibilities that having a child prodigy opened up for her and, what's more, one that could lip read. She took Danny's hand and squeezed it, before opening the car.

As they pulled away, the drops of rain turned to a fine drizzle, and for a while they drove in silence, the only noise being the intermittent squeak of the windscreen wipers.

Suzie was concentrating just enough to go through the motions of driving. Her mind had gone into scheme, plan, and dream mode, and she was wondering if it might be possible to get a story about Danny into her husband's newspaper. She pictured a photo of them together, right next to a story about another of her heroines, Princess Grace of Monaco, who had just died in a car accident in Monte Carlo.

Busy thinking about what she should wear for the photo, she cut up a blue Volvo and was instantly hooted.

"Oops, sorry," said Suzie to her rear-view mirror.

At the next set of traffic lights, the Volvo drew up alongside and hooted again. Suzie looked over Danny to the irate face screaming at her. The windows being up, she didn't get a word of it.

"He said 'Fucking women drivers. Shouldn't be allowed on the road', Mum."

"Oh, he did, did he?"

Suzie stuck her middle finger up at him, holding it up just behind Danny's head and out of his field of vision.

"And up yours, too, you fucking stupid bitch," relayed Danny.

"Okay, Danny, thanks for that. But if you could just look away and stop reading that moron's lips, please."

The light changed and the Volvo shot off. Danny was about to repeat his parting shot when Suzie thrust up a flat hand.

"Thanks again, Danny, but I think I can imagine what he said."

At the next lights a car with two women pulled alongside. Suzie gave them a quick glance. They were busy chatting away.

"Danny, what are they talking about?"

"I can't read the other one very well; I need her to turn her head a little bit. But the one driving is saying, *I'd like to lose a bit of weight off my hips and backside before we go to Magaluf. If I put last year's bikini on now, it'd ping off in five minutes.*"

Suzie was dumbstruck.

"Oh, come on, Danny. Did she really say all that? You read every word? She actually said ping?"

It was almost a rhetorical question, as she knew that a boy of ten years old couldn't even begin to invent that speech. She silently mouthed the word bikini, concentrating on how the word would look without sound.

"I'm sure that's what she said," said Danny confidently.

"Danny, you're a genius, you know that?"

He smiled. "Mummy?"

"Yes, Danny?"

"What's going to happen now?"

"What do you mean?"

"I mean, are you going to send me away to a special school like in that film?"

"What film?"

"You know, we watched it with Dad, the one about the woman who has a deaf son that everyone thinks is a retard, but it turns out he was deaf and they send him away to a special place. You cried."

Suzie took some time to remember the film. "Oh, yes. Oh my God. I can't believe you even remember it. But this isn't the same, darling. What happened to the boy in that film has nothing to do with what's happened to you. And what's more, you don't honestly think I'd send you away, do you?"

"But I'm deaf."

"So?"

"Won't I have to change schools because I'm deaf?"

"Don't be silly. The only thing that we might have to do, though, is learn sign language."

"We?"

"You don't think I'd let you learn sign language on your own, do you?"

"What's sign language?"

"You know. What deaf people use to speak, making words with their hands."

Danny watched the windscreen wipers for a moment. "But why sign language?"

"The doctor thinks it would be a good idea in case you lose the control of your normal spoken voice."

Throughout the conversation, Suzie was aware that she was turning her head just enough for Danny to read her, whilst at the same time keeping her eyes on the road.

"You and I are going to have some fun together."

Danny smiled. Perhaps one of the biggest smiles he'd ever made. At that moment, he felt safe and secure. He had a warm, fuzzy feeling in his stomach. At that moment, he stopped feeling something that he had felt for a very long time. Alone. Though he did wonder what his mother meant by 'you and I are going to have fun together'.

When they got home, Danny put the TV on. Suzie put the kettle on, then went to stand behind him. She was curious to witness the extent of Danny's skills again.

He was watching *Newsround*, a news and current events programme aimed at kids.

"So you can follow every word they're saying?"

Danny didn't answer.

She was about to repeat herself when she mentally kicked herself – she was standing behind him. She gently tapped him on the shoulder so as not to frighten him, and asked him again.

"Of course I can. Well, not every, every word, but more or less. If I can see their faces, I know what they are saying."

"What's he saying now, then?" She leaned over and hit the volume button on the TV remote.

John Craven, the presenter, was talking about a baby panda that had just been born at London Zoo.

"Today, Mimi the Giant Panda at London Zoo is now the happy mother of a 3½oz, six inches big, baby girl called Foo Foo. Both mother and daughter are said to be doing well. This is only the second baby panda to be born in captivity in Britain, the first being Mimi herself in 1970."

If being able to repeat the bikini conversation in the car had left Suzie with her bottom jaw on the steering wheel, this nearly blew her off her feet. Not only was he able to read what John Craven had said, but he repeated it as if giving a simultaneous translation a split second after it was said, almost as it was said.

"My goodness, Danny. How and when did you learn to do that?"

Danny then recounted his story, telling her about when he first noticed he was losing his hearing and how he first noticed that he could understand people on TV by watching their mouths and faces. He told how he would practise every day at first with the sound on and later with it off.

"And at school? How on earth did you manage to get away with it in class?"

"I always sat at the front, so if anybody was speaking in the class, I just had to turn around."

"Mind-blowing. That is absolutely mind-blowing. Just wait till your father hears about all this. He's going to flip."

Johnny Valentine-Rocker came home about 6pm, announcing his arrival in the usual way. The door slammed, followed by the clang as he dropped his keys into the bowl in the hallway and the customary shout, "I'm home."

He found Suzie and Danny sitting at the kitchen table. This threw him a little, as this wasn't the usual domestic scenario he found when coming home at 6pm. Danny was always either watching TV or playing with friends in the street.

"All right, Danny? Why aren't you out with your friends? It's not raining." He ruffled Danny's hair as he walked around to give Suzie a peck on the cheek.

"I've been talking to Mummy."

"Oh, yeah? What about? What's going on? Anything wrong?"

"I think you'd better sit down, Johnny."

"This must be serious. Has someone died?"

"Just sit down and hold onto your hat, because you aren't going to believe this."

Johnny did as he was told and had already gone a bit pale in anticipation.

"You're not pregnant, are you?"

"Don't be daft. Listen. Danny is deaf."

Johnny looked at his wife and son for any signs of jest and found none.

"Yeah... and? So what's new?"

"No, I don't mean he doesn't listen. I mean he can't hear a thing. He's stone deaf."

"What the hell are you talking about? I've just been speaking to him. He's sitting there, listening to this conversation."

"Hmmm... How can I explain this?"

Johnny's face was a picture of defiance.

"You know he had an appointment with the doctor today because Danny's music teacher had suggested he get his ears checked? She felt that his total absence of musical skills was due to something other than just a lack of talent."

"Uh... Oh, yes, that's right, he did, didn't he?"

Suzie knew that he hadn't remembered, but there were more important things to talk about than her husband's total lack of attention to the day-to-day logistics of the Valentine-Rocker household. Suzie went on to recount as best she could all that had gone on at the doctor's that afternoon. Every so often, Johnny looked at Danny and would vigorously rub his face with the palms of his hands, as if this would bring him back to reality.

When Suzie had finished, Johnny sat back in his chair and looked at the kitchen ceiling, as heaven wasn't immediately at hand, then leaned forward, placing his elbows on the table and resting his chin in his hands.

"Jesus, Danny. Why didn't you tell us? I mean, don't you think it's something we ought to know"

He was now kneading his temples with his middle fingers.

Danny didn't try to give any explanations; he just said, "I'm sorry, Dad."

"Sorry? That's it? Sorry?"

Danny lowered his head.

"I mean, why the hell didn't you tell us? And the lip-reading thing?"

"Okay, Johnny, that's enough. He's had a tough enough time as it is. Danny, go and play or watch the telly."

"So, let me get this right. Danny can read lips?" asked Johnny, when his son had skipped out of the kitchen.

"He can't just read lips, Johnny; he's a lip-reading genius, a bloody freak of nature. He can practically understand exactly every word that people say, so long as he can see their faces. And get this, he can even lip-read Mandarin. Do you realise just how difficult that must be? Think about it. Have you noticed anything out of the ordinary? Have you noticed anything wrong? Haven't you had a million conversations with Danny these last two years?"

"Fuck me."

"Johnny, is that all you can say? Fuck me?"

"What do you want me to say? I'm in shock. How in hell didn't we notice? Why didn't he tell us?"

"It's complicated to explain and I'm still not sure about the whats, hows and whys. But right now it's not important."

"So you're telling me we've got some sort of bloody genius on our hands?"

"Something like that."

"Bloody hell! Well, how did that happen? I mean, as far as I know there are no Nobel Prize winners on either side of the family."

"Really Johnny? That's what most bothers your tiny brain?"

He shrugged and swept some invisible crumbs off the table.

"You're right. It's just…" Suzie was now glaring at him with dagger eyes. "So, what are we going to do?"

"Nothing. We just carry on as we've always done. Danny's a perfectly normal boy. He's already proved that he can lead a perfectly normal life."

"You can say that again," interrupted Johnny.

"He can go to school, play with his friends, just carry on doing what he's always done. The only difference is, we've got a son who is not only very special, but just think about the possibilities. Danny can lip-read."

Johnny sat for a moment, biting his bottom lip.

It came to him in a flash. Having a lip-reader around at a football match could be very useful indeed. What if he could know exactly what everybody on the bench was saying and, more importantly, what the manager was saying? Bench conversations could be very revealing. Game plans, who's unhappy, who gets on well with the manager and who doesn't. Of course, not to mention the referee and the chats he has with the players. Johnny could know the exact reason a foul was given or a penalty denied. It always frustrated him, having to wait until the end of a game to understand the reasons behind a controversial decision, and that was only if the ref was even willing to go public about it.

Oh, yes. Johnny could definitely see where Danny could be of use.

"Hmm, I'm beginning to see where you're coming from," he said, rubbing his hands together in excitement."

"Johnny, I couldn't even imagine what's going on in your deranged mind right now, but I'm sure it's got something to do with your bloody football."

"Oi, don't knock it. It's what pays the bloody bills in this house."

Suzie ignored the reproach. It was Johnny's favourite speech. It was how he always justified constant trips away from home and the fact that when he was home, all he'd do was watch games on TV, and ninety-nine percent of his conversation was related to football.

"The important question, Johnny, is if we should let everybody know about all this – his school, the family... you know, everybody."

They sat there for a while in silence while they contemplated the dilemma. At least, Suzie was contemplating. Johnny was just waiting for his wife to come up with the answer and make a decision, as was the norm regarding anything to do with the house or the family.

After a while, Suzie got up to put the kettle on and complied with Johnny's expectations.

"Okay, I think as far as the school is concerned, the music teacher is bound to ask about the results of his hearing test. We should say that yes, he's lost some hearing, but we're not going to say that he's totally deaf.

That way, he won't have to do music and the school can make some concessions regarding helping Danny adapt. With the family, we can do a bit of the same. We can tell them he's lost a bit of hearing as a way of explaining why he's learning sign language."

"Suzie, you really are a scheming little cow, aren't you?"

"I think we know each other pretty well by now, Johnny. One thing is clear, though. However we have fun with Danny's talent, his well-being is first and foremost."

It was felt that it would be a good idea if at least one of the two knew sign language and, as the only signs that Johnny would ever dominate involved one or two fingers, and the fact that Suzie was so excited about acquiring a talent that might make her stand out from the crowd, it was agreed.

CHAPTER 6

Six months after that conversation, Suzie and Danny went to their first class. They were held in the local civic centre, where they would share the installations with the cooking class, the local bird preservation society and an amateur theatre group. A poster with a big 'Welcome' in sign language greeted them at the door. Inside, they found a semi-circle of chairs that had their own built-in table that had to be lifted to sit down, and an easel holding a huge pad of white paper. On each table they found a little booklet titled *Sign Language Book 1*.

Their fellow students were all women of between thirty and fifty years old who had probably signed up for at least two of the other activities on offer at the centre.

When all were comfortably settled into their seats, a woman of about forty, dressed in faded blue jeans and a big black roll-necked sweater, came in and placed herself in the centre of their semi-circle.

Without further ado, she started signing to them. First, with an open hand, she traced a large 'n' shape in front of her. She then touched her forehead with two fingers, then held them out, a sort of two-fingered American army salute; then, pointing to her chest with one finger, she proceeded to make shapes with her two hands.

"*Hello. My name is Katy.*" She repeated it five times while also repeating the hand gestures.

"As you see, this is how we introduce ourselves in British Sign Language. I need to point out something very important. I'm not signing that sentence in the order I'm saying it. I'm signing name, me and last, I'm spelling Katy with my hands. Get used to it. Sign Language is a different language." She paused so this could sink in.

"Now, our first class will be for all of us to learn how to introduce ourselves using Sign Language. To do so, you'll have to learn how to spell words with your hands. The books in front of you contain the whole alphabet. I'm warning you all now that from the second class onwards you won't be allowed to use your voices; you'll have to sign everything. What you don't know the sign for, you'll have to spell, so make sure you learn how to spell in Sign Language before you come back for the second class." She paused again, before continuing. Perhaps she expected half the class to get up and leave. As nobody moved, she said, "I'm very glad to see we have a young student here. How old are you?"

"Nearly eleven."

"And you understood every word you've just heard?"

"I understood it, but I didn't hear it."

"He lip-reads," interjected Suzie proudly.

"Do you indeed?"

Danny nodded.

"Well, this is going to be interesting. Something tells me you are going to pick this up very easily. Probably a lot faster than anybody else in this room."

Danny looked at Suzie. She had a very worried look on her face.

"Don't worry, Mum. It'll be a piece of cake. I'll help you."

Suzie smiled, but it wasn't a happy smile. More like a 'I'm in deep shit and I don't know how to get out of it' smile.

"Okay, well, before we start, I'd like to give you a little general information about British Sign Language. It's not just making shapes with our hands and waving our arms about. The important thing to remember is that the grammar used in BSL is completely different to that used in everyday English. Imagine a language that you get right inside of. Until you learn it, it's hard to describe the feeling, but when you use sign language, you don't just speak the words; you become them, you are them. Sign languages can say anything a spoken language can, from translations of Shakespeare to the works of Plato and more.

"The face is extremely important. If you've ever wondered why deaf people are so animated, why they make some pretty crazy faces when they're signing, it's because they use facial expressions the way hearing people use tone of voice and inflection to communicate additional meaning in conversation. For example, elevated eyebrows when signing means one is asking a question.

She looked at Danny, wondering if she should use language more suited to a child, but he was smiling. Then she looked around at everybody else and, satisfied that nobody had fallen asleep yet, she concluded her introduction. "So, welcome to the fascinating world of Sign Language."

Katy smiled. Most of the students let out a slow breath with puffed cheeks.

Danny was already trying to spell his name using the book. As Katy had predicted, and as often happens with all children, Danny was quick to pick it up and in a short time was way ahead of Suzie, but she persisted and was able to keep her selective ADD in check just enough to progress.

They would practise at home and often sign each other, making fun of Johnny in front of him. One morning, he came into the kitchen and they greeted him with a flurry of hand movements.

"Oi, you two, what are you saying now? Don't you think I've had enough with the bloody Mandarin?"

"We're saying you look particularly smart today."

"Yeah, and that we think your hair looks good, too," added Danny, chuckling.

They had actually said that his belly looked bigger than ever and that his hair, which was all over the place, made him look like a mad professor. Danny added that he was more like a pot-bellied scarecrow.

Johnny then made his own sign and went off to have a quick look in the mirror, leaving Danny and Suzie doubled up, laughing.

When there was a family event like a wedding or a Christmas get-together, Suzie would keep Danny by her side. From the very beginning, Suzie's expectations were fulfilled. At one of Johnny's cousin's wedding, held in an elegant ballroom of a top London hotel, Danny, Johnny, and Suzie Valentine-Rocker stood together at the welcoming reception. People mingled, kissing and shaking hands with relatives they only saw on this type of occasion.

"Okay, Danny, do your stuff. What are they talking about? Those two scoffing canapés and guzzling champagne over there."

Danny followed his mother's gaze.

"The one in the black dress with sparkly things down the front is saying, *I really can't see it working, they've only known each other a year.*

"The other one is saying, *I can't see what she sees in him: he's thin as a rake and he's going bald.*"

Danny continued to relay the conversation as they spoke.

"*It's obvious, isn't it? He's loaded.*

"*Must be it. And what about her? She looks pregnant in that dress.*"

"*Maybe she is.*"

"*She could have found something a little less tight.*"

"Okay, Danny, you can stop reading now." But he kept relaying as the bride and groom approached the two ladies.

"*Aunty Vivien, Aunty Daphne. How are you? Thank you so much for coming.*"

The bride kissed them both on the cheeks. The groom followed suit.

"*Yes, thank you, you both look radiant.*"

"*How could I miss my favourite niece's great day? You look stunning in that dress, and you make such a lovely couple.*"

"*Thank you. You don't think it makes me look fat?*"

"*Fat? Come off it. It really flatters you, love; shows off what a lovely figure you have.*"

"My God. Talk about being two-faced," said Suzie.

"Wow, Danny! That was brilliant. But what a couple of witches," exclaimed Johnny, putting his arm around Danny's shoulders.

As the bride and groom walked away from the aunties, Danny focused his attention on them and read the groom. "*Man, those two are like a cross between Tweedledee and Tweedledum and Danny La Rue.*"

Suzie and Johnny clinked champagne glasses.

"Fun, isn't it?" said Suzie, laughing.

She loved going to these events with Danny, but it did have its downside, as sometimes she was the target of gossip and comments that Danny was reading and didn't come out exactly smelling of roses, despite Danny's attempts to dilute the slander.

Apparently, she dressed like a hippy, she was superficial, she thought she was better than anyone else and was married to a slob.

She'd always make sure she bumped into the perpetrator of these comments a little later on and drop a relevant comment like, "Do you think this dress makes me look a little too much like a hippy?" or "Don't you just hate condescending, superficial people?" and then watch their faces as they fought a squirm, or blush while they wondered if Suzie had perhaps been standing behind them.

In a year, she practically knew who was being unfaithful to whom, which men were the best and worst lovers, whose business was in trouble, and a million other trivialities; but, perhaps more important, who her real friends were.

When their sign language skills improved, Danny and Suzie could communicate with each other from across quite large distances, which, apart from being fun, was quite practical.

Danny's life had markedly turned around since his secret had been discovered. He was happier than ever. He was happy at school, where they now always put him at the front of class so he could hear the teacher. The fun part was knowing that when people spoke to him they practically shouted to make sure he could hear. The tricky bit was when they felt that the best way to get their message through was to get their mouths as close to Danny's ear as possible. This had two problems, the first being that this made it almost impossible to read their lips, and the second being he would often get sprayed with saliva in the process.

What especially made Danny happy was the amount of time and attention his parents were giving him, especially his father. Johnny would take him along to work, which meant going to football games at least once every few weeks; and when he didn't go to the ground, he would watch a game with his father on TV.

His mission was to read any conversation he could. Although going to the games was fun and exciting, even if he couldn't hear the crowd sing and shout, his father would give him a pair of binoculars, which effectively restricted his ability to observe and feel the game as a whole. He was always scanning and focusing on people's faces and sometimes came home with circular red rings around his eyes from having the binoculars glued to them for such long periods of time.

Watching the games on TV was far more comfortable and, more often than not, produced better lip-reading opportunities, as the cameras did the work of his binoculars and to better effect. Whenever the camera director deemed it interesting to focus on any on-or off-pitch conversations, Johnny would tap his shoulder and say, "What? What?" Occasionally, in his excitement he would forget to tap him on the shoulder and Danny wouldn't hear his commands; but most of the time it wasn't necessary, as he instinctively relayed simultaneously all the conversations that the camera focused on.

"Take him out. Take him out, he's a ponce."

"Go on. On your own, son."

"What a fucking prat."

"What? I never touched him, ref; I went for the ball."

"One more and you're off."

"My granny could've stopped that one."

Generally, these were the sort of comments that Danny relayed, not to mention the slew of profanities that contained every known variation or use of the 'f' word.

After a few months of this, Johnny showed signs he was seriously beginning to feel that he had overestimated the depth and importance of football match conversations that would be of any use to him as a journalist, when out of the blue, in one TV game Danny began relaying an interesting conversation indeed.

Stephen Pyke, a player recently bought for a record transfer fee, began an exchange of words with his manager while he was still on the pitch. Luckily, the cameras had captured the manager screaming and gesturing wildly at his star player and had decided to follow events, taking advantage of the fact that play had been stopped to treat a player who seemed to be about to die as he rolled around on the pitch.

"*Stevie!*" shouted the manager when his player was close to the touchline to hear him.

"*Stevie!*" he shouted again. The player was clearly ignoring him.

"*Stevie, you're coming off.*"

"*Fuck you!*" responded the player.

"*A one-legged blind man could do a better job than you're doing today. You're coming off now.*" His substitute had already taken his tracksuit top off and was vigorously warming up next to the manager.

"*If you take me off, gov, I'm putting in for a transfer.*"

"*Never mind a transfer, you're out, mate. It's over. Kaput.*"

A few seconds later, the player's number was held up, signalling his imminent departure from the pitch. The crowd obviously agreed, as when they saw the number a huge cheer went up and the player commenced his slow walk towards the bench, shaking his head and letting loose a slew of insults related to the manager's relationship with his mother, which Danny continued to relay.

"Yeah, all right, Danny, I get the idea. Just pay attention to the moment the player passes in front of the manager," said Johnny, hoping the camera would do the same.

Still mumbling insults, the player passed close enough for the manager to spit out a venomous death sentence. *"I've had enough, Stevie... enough of the drugs, the booze, the birds. You're out!"*

The player just gave him the finger and disappeared down the tunnel.

"Bingo!" shouted Johnny. He immediately filed the story with his editor.

"Johnny, are you sure about this? I can't go with it if it's just a load of bollocks that you made up," said the excited editor.

"Have I ever made anything up?"

"No comment," came the reply.

"I'm telling you, this is legit. I can't reveal my source, but I can guarantee that that was the conversation word for word."

The next morning, Johnny got a back-page exclusive. The headline read in bold black letters:

ON YOUR PYKE, STEVE!!!

STEVE PYKE KICKED OUT OF UNITED FOR DRUGS, BOOZE AND BIRDS.

The club denied everything, of course, but a week later Pyke had left, apparently to play in Italy, and Johnny got a pay rise and was promoted to senior writer. The story had a massive backlash at the club, and they launched an internal enquiry to discover who was leaking dressing-room information.

Yes, Danny was really enjoying himself, as was his family. By the time he reached his teens, it was clear that the chances of him recuperating his hearing were slim and getting slimmer as time passed. Actually, he never thought about it. He was even beginning to forget what some noises sounded like. He continued to improve his lip-reading skills and, according to his mother, was still able to control his voice volume and pronunciation; though he knew that at some stage it was probable that his speech would be slightly affected. So, for the moment sign language was just a tool to have fun with and a means to get some extra pocket money.

In fact, Danny had fallen in love with this elegant and beautiful way of communicating, and he had quickly surpassed the level of his fellow civic centre students. He was recommended by his teacher, Katy, to enrol in an official BSL interpreters' course.

In record time, around his sixteenth birthday, he was able to reach the required level to first get his CACDP, then the recognised MRSLI, which would permit him to work as an interpreter. In fact, nobody had ever reached an official interpreter's level in so short a time and at such a young age. He was certainly the most precocious member they had ever had at the Association of Sign Language Interpreters (ASLI).

He had reached such a level that he was now able to give a simultaneous account of someone speaking with the most complex vocabulary and grammatical structures. His sign language had been described as unique, pure, crisp, and elegant at the same time. He was first asked to sign at a lecture that an important history scholar was giving at a London university, thanks once again to Katy, who had recommended him.

The university was somewhat dubious at first, given Danny's young age, but a quick check on his credentials was enough for them to contract him. He did such a good job that he immediately gained a reputation that would in turn give him a continuous string of assignments in schools, colleges or universities, health centres, residential homes, local government offices, hospitals, law courts, and prisons.

Despite his growing reputation, whenever he turned up at universities or courts presenting himself as the SL interpreter, he was still often met with such incredulity that he had to wait while his credentials were checked out.

Not one of these institutions were aware that Danny himself was deaf and would be lip-reading what he was contracted to interpret.

The pay wasn't too bad for a teenager either, anywhere between £15 and £20 an hour, which was way more than his friends were getting for car washing and babysitting.

Danny's achievements in this field were extraordinary, taking into account he not only had to relay complicated discourses and lectures with sign language, but he also had to lip-read them. This experience gave him the opportunity to hone skills in both reading and interpreting the most complicated of structures in such specialised areas to such good effect that it would have a major influence on his future and become relevant to how his life would play out. In the meantime, he had other more natural, down to earth developments in line with puberty to contend with. True to the laws of human biology, his body began producing copious amounts of testosterone, one of the consequences being a heightening, if not obsessive, interest in the opposite sex.

He still found time to help his father with his football reporting and was responsible for several more minor scoops. In fact, Johnny had obtained a certain reputation as a football journalist, often being invited to TV shows to participate as a pundit. This notoriety pleased Suzie no end, and she was quick to drop her husband's name whenever possible. It didn't do their marriage any harm either, as Suzie was willing to tolerate far more than she had before.

Danny also still kept his mother happy, relaying what he considered to be ever more stupid and trivial nonsense. Any spare time he had now was dedicated more and more to the pursuit of girls. By now he had revealed his lip-reading skills to his closest friends, and although he'd always been popular among his peers, this talent had elevated him to a certain star quality and near hero-worship status. As a friend, Danny offered some interesting added value. His snazzy name only enhanced his legend. Everybody wanted to know Danny Valentine-Rocker.

At parties and clubs, he and his friends took advantage to read what girls were saying. Armed with this information, they could ascertain if there was any interest, or, for that matter, any lack of interest, thus influencing the amount of effort to invest in going in for the kill.

The drawback to possessing such information was the risk of being on the receiving end of a major ego bashing.

Comments such as, *Oh, he's cute, the one in black on the left*, or *I hope he asks me to dance*, or *Let's go and stand near them, they might start talking to us* were positive enough, but *Ew no, I wouldn't touch him with a barge pole*, or *His eyes are too close together*, or *Where does his mummy buy him his clothes: the Oxfam shop?* certainly weren't.

Danny tended to tone down or even not relay some of the more damaging or cruel comments to avoid any suicides among his friends. If boys often wondered what girls spoke about, for Danny this was a real eye-opener.

Apart from the usual banal conversations about clothes and shoes, he also read conversations about preferred sexual positions, if they liked giving oral sex and, if so, if they swallowed, and some real gems like the width and length of cocks and tongues and, to top it all, how to fake an orgasm, apparently a frequent occurrence. The purpose of this last topic baffled Danny then, and would do so for the rest of his life.

In clubs, Danny faced the added difficulty when lip-reading of a distinct lack of light and, perhaps even tougher, the presence of flashing lights. This made life a little more difficult, but he enjoyed the challenge. Talking with a girl in these circumstances allowed him to employ every one of his skills to the limit. He had to raise the volume of his voice without knowing just how high he was raising it, but, on the plus side, his intended partner's words weren't drowned out by loud music either. He could read them perfectly.

Dancing was another challenge. He couldn't hear the music, so he preferred to wait for the slow dances that always played at the end of the evening. With the slower tempo, he could take cues from the body movements of the girl he was dancing with.

Danny had inherited his father's mane of thick hair, though for the moment it was still black. Unlike his father, he wasn't prone to bad hair days as it always seemed to lie perfectly groomed. A quick rake through with his fingers was enough to maintain its form.

His mother's genes just topped up the film-star looks by giving him blue eyes. Danny had no problems finding partners to improve his sex education from early on in his teens, even without the help of his lip-reading skills.

In fact, it was perhaps a bit too easy for him, which resulted in a constant flow of girls passing through his life without ever having the urge or need to have a steady relationship.

Danny was conscious of this and, in some way, was hoping that sooner or later he'd find that girl who would blow him away. He tried hard to treat all the girls he met with the utmost respect and was careful to let the serious ones down as gently as he could, but it wasn't always possible. He was young and girls came easy. He had no choice but to go with the flow. With so much going on during his teens, he had little spare time to dedicate to one of his passions: books and literature.

This was his island, his space, his private world. It was the only entertainment that didn't require him to employ his lip-reading skills. When Danny read books, he used a part of his brain that wasn't busy analysing and processing the enormous amount of information needed to understand just one simple sentence. This part was where his imagination and his fantasies swirled freely, fuelled by the written word and the author's will. To sit immersed in a book was like being driven on a straight and empty country road surrounded by rolling green hills laced with clear fresh-water brooks, as opposed to driving a geared car through traffic-filled city streets using every sense and faculty just to arrive at a destination in one piece.

The walls of his bedroom were floor-to-ceiling bookshelves filled with everything from Kafka to Tolstoy, stopping off at Cervantes and Dickens on the way. Like most avid readers often do, he would spend a few minutes running his fingers along the rows of books, stopping occasionally to gently stroke those he was particularly fond of. He could instantly remember their plots and characters and, for a moment, he was transported to relive the emotions he had felt when reading them.

His family and friends all knew that when Danny had his head in a book, it was the only time he could genuinely be considered well and truly deaf. His books were his real lovers and the one that satisfied all his needs more than any other was *The Count of Monte Cristo*. Perhaps subconsciously, his life was to play out as it did thanks in part to that book.

CHAPTER 7

With five A-levels under his belt, Danny applied for and got into Manchester University to study political science and English literature. The university was particularly interested in his sign language capabilities and interpreter's credentials and offered him reduced fees in exchange for interpreting some lectures when attended by other deaf students.

In September 1990, the three Valentine-Rockers, with two suitcases full of books and one of clothes, set off in their car for Manchester. Suzie sat in the back so Danny could chat to his father, but most of the journey was spent in silence, each submerged in their own thoughts as they sped up the M6 under a low, multi-shaded grey sky.

The Owens Park student hall complex is on the Wilmslow Road in Fallowfield, North Manchester, a twenty-five-minute bus ride from the university campus. They pulled into the small car park feeling as if they had just arrived on another planet.

The student hall complex was made up of several narrow, six-storey blocks clearly built in the 1970s. The nondescript buildings of grey and white breeze blocks and large oblong windows were a tribute to an architecturally starved decade when the need for economical and practical solutions to housing outweighed any aesthetic or longevity issues.

As instructed, they left the luggage in the car and headed to the front office situated on the ground floor of one of the blocks. It was easy enough to find, as several signs indicated the way.

A sandy-haired man in his twenties leaned across a low counter with his hand out.

"Welcome to Owens Park Student Complex. I'm Stewart, your student rep," he said in a distinct Manchester accent, confirming that they were now in a foreign land.

He didn't wait for an answer and went straight into a well-rehearsed welcoming speech, telling them all about the installations, the student cafeteria and bar, the grounds and what he seemed to think was the most important information, that there was a great kebab shop and convenience store just over the road.

After going through a few formalities, he gave them a key to 6G and indicated which of the blocks was Danny's. Danny's tower was imaginatively called Block 4.

"You're on the sixth floor, and you're the last in." He checked a list he had in front of him. "Danny Valentine-Rocker. You're one of the deaf students, aren't you?" He asked this raising his voice as if, although deaf, Danny just might be able to hear him if he spoke loud enough.

"The one with sign language, aren't you?" Danny wondered why the guy even bothered to form a question structure, as once again he didn't wait for an answer. "Declan McCracken, the other deaf student, is already installed in the flat, and I can tell you he's going to be very happy to see you, as he can only communicate with sign language and we are all getting a bit tired of having written notebook conversations with him." He paused, then added a question that, this time, he clearly needed answering. "Just a minute. How come you can hear me?"

"I can lip-read."

"Aah. That explains it. Well, you're bloody good at it, if you don't mind me saying."

Another pause preceded another logical question. "And you seem to speak like a normal person."

Danny decided instantly such a politically incorrect observation was probably due to a lack of having a better way to express himself and politely informed him, "Yes, I seem to have no problems in that respect."

"Wow, the other guy only makes noises. Impossible to understand him. Anyway, forgive me if I don't take you personally, but I've got a couple of urgent things to attend to. You can't miss your block; it's the only one with a broken front door. We had to kick it in a few days ago when the lock got jammed."

After thanking him, they took the key and went to get the luggage from the car.

"What a dick-head!" remarked Johnny.

"Yeah, not your most tactful of student reps," agreed Danny.

Luckily, Block 4 was only a short distance from the car and they were soon through what was left of the front door.

"Where's the lift?" asked Johnny.

After navigating the entrance and ground floor hallway twice just to make sure, Suzie came back with the answer. "Bad news, I'm afraid."

"Fuck me! You've got to be kidding."

"Johnny!"

"Sorry, but Danny's unit is on the bloody sixth floor."

Fifteen minutes later, they arrived at Danny's floor. With Suzie marching on in front, calling out the numbers on the identical red doors, Johnny and Danny lumbered with two enormous suitcases, puffing and panting down the narrow corridor.

"Jesus, Danny, what have you got in this case? An anvil?" spluttered Johnny, but he was behind him, so he got no answer.

In fact, he was carrying all the books Danny could fit in one case.

"Here we are. 6G," announced Suzie triumphantly.

A narrow hallway led them to an open living area, and they gladly relieved themselves of their luggage burden, dropping them into the nearest available space.

"You can bring up the other, Danny," said Johnny, breathing heavily.

They all stood in silence for a moment as they took in what was to be Danny's home, at least for the immediate future, and waited for Johnny's blood pressure to come down by half.

"Well, this is it, eh? Home," said Johnny, hands on hips and still panting.

They looked around at the sparse furnishings. A pale green Formica table with matching chairs littered with dirty tea-stained mugs and plates with leftover crusty rice and caked brown sauce took up most of the living space.

A three-seater couch, once gold velvet, lined the wall. Each of its worn cushions were shaped like a bird's nest. The floor was covered in square, grey, industrial carpet tiles often seen in offices, and the walls were off-white and bare.

"Nice!" exclaimed Suzie ironically, and walked into the tiny kitchen to find at least a week's dirty dishes, cups and glasses piled up in the sink. A row of empty wine bottles filled the space between the sink, and a gas cooker decorated with spaghetti added a splash of colour to the décor.

Danny and Johnny followed.

"Welcome to student life," said Johnny, chuckling.

The next step was to find Danny's room and get him installed. The narrow hallway had four doors down one side. Only the last one had a key hanging from the lock, indicating which was his.

A single bed, a small desk, and a standing wardrobe occupied about eighty percent of the space. The floor-to-cciling window that flooded it with light, and offered the same views of Platfields Park as the living room, saved it from being considered not far off a claustrophobic prison cell.

A short while later, when Suzie had cleared the table, washed up all the dishes with the three drops of Fairy Liquid left in the bottle, and put clean sheets on Danny's bed, all three were in the car park ready to say their farewells.

Suzie and Johnny had decided to head straight back to London and stop off on the motorway to have dinner. They all felt uncomfortable and a little anxious, knowing that this was a significant moment in their lives. All three wanted to say their goodbyes as soon as possible, but at the same time, they didn't want that moment to arrive at all.

As if to help them along, it started to rain. Suzie opened her arms for Danny to hug her. It was to be their last hug as mother and baby boy. They embraced in silence, Suzie's head laying against Danny's chest, as he was by now at least a foot taller than her.

When they finally broke away, Suzie grabbed both of Danny's hands and mouthed the words, *I love you. Take care, my baby.* Tears welled in her eyes. If she had used her voice, she would have broken down completely.

Johnny followed suit and, in true man-hug style, the two repeatedly patted each other on the back. Leaning back so Danny could see his face, he said, "Look after yourself, son. Keep your eye on the ball, work hard, but play clean and you'll be scoring goals in no time."

Causing Suzie to raise both eyebrows and look up to the sky.

"I will, Dad. You look after yourself and Mum," said Danny croaking, and he kissed his father's neck.

"In the meantime, if you watch a game and see anything juicy for me, be sure to give me a call."

"Er. . . Dad." Said Danny pointing to his ear.

" Oops, right. Sorry.

It was raining harder now, and all knew the time had come. Another back-patting hug with his father and a kiss for his mother and they were getting in the car. At that moment, he felt so much love for them that it caught him by surprise. An arterial surge originated in the pit of his stomach and gushed throughout his whole body, making him sway on his feet.

"Love you. Safe journey," he shouted through the closed window. Rain was now dripping off his nose.

He waved as their car pulled away. His mother's hand was now waving back and didn't stop until they had turned the corner and disappeared temporarily from each other's lives.

He went back up to the flat and sat in the middle bird's nest in silence. He was alone now. Truly alone. Melancholy engulfed him and made him sink even deeper into the faded gold velvet. A few minutes passed when what he presumed were his three flatmates appeared in the living room.

Two were talking, and it took a few seconds to focus on their faces to understand them.

"Jesus! Are we in the right flat? Look, the table's been cleaned. I didn't know it was green."

Danny was probably sunk so far into the couch that they hadn't seen him.

"Ah, so this must be the other deaf bloke," said the big one with cauliflower ears and a broken nose.

"This is going to be fun sharing with these two. I've never written so much in my life. We'll have to stock up on more writing pads," said the skinny one, leaning on a sticker-covered skateboard and wearing clothes that hung off him like he'd been shrunk while wearing them.

The third one, with red hair and large bright green eyes, greeted Danny with a timid, "*Hi, I'm Declan*" in BSL, and Danny responded the same way. Declan smiled. It was a sincere smile. A smile that lit up his face, radiating happiness and speaking a thousand words.

Danny then quickly signed. "*Watch their faces.*"

"Hi, I'm Danny," he said, struggling to free himself from the grips of the couch. "You won't have to worry as I can understand every word and don't have any problems speaking."

The other boys exchanged glances and made "oops" faces. Declan stepped forward and took Danny's hand in both of his, and shook them vigorously. The other two took a second to react, then offered their hands, giving Danny an opportunity to break Declan's bone-shaking grip, which was showing no signs of coming to an end.

"Sorry, mate. I'm James. I thought you were supposed to be deaf. At least that's what they told us, that we'd have two deaf flatmates," said the big one as he gripped Danny's hand in his enormous paws.

"Mike. But just call me Baggy. Yeah, sorry about that," said the other.

"No problem. Well, the truth is that I *am* deaf, but I can lip-read." He signed this simultaneously to Declan, who signed him back. "*Why are they sorry?*"

"*I'll tell you later.*"

"Bloody hell!" said James. "You're bloody good."

"Yeah," said Baggy. "Just as well you told us or we could've really put our foot in it."

Declan signed to Danny that he wanted in on the conversation, so Danny positioned himself so he could sign at the same time as he lip-read.

"So, you know how to use sign language? I'm impressed," said James.

"Yep. Any time you want to speak to Declan, you can do it through me."

"Brilliant, man, this is wild," said Baggy, shaking one hand in the air above his head. "How come you can speak properly then? Declan just kind of grunts."

Danny diplomatically only signed the question.

"I didn't go completely deaf until I was about ten, so I'm somehow able to control how loud I speak and my pronunciation. At least I think I can, so if I start grunting, it'd be good to know."

"*You can't imagine just how glad I am to see you*," signed Declan. "*Life has just got a whole lot better.*"

He caught Danny off-guard when he hugged him. It was a heartfelt hug and Danny reciprocated.

"*Anything you want to relay to these clowns, I can do it.*"

Declan laughed. "*They're not so bad when you get to know them. Their spelling and grammar have got quite a lot to be desired, though.*"

"Hey, you two! What's with all this man-love and what are you saying?" asked Baggy.

"Yeah, this isn't fair," said James.

"Well, now you know how Declan felt," Danny said, winking.

James and Baggy exchanged a look which confirmed that they had got his point.

"You boys want a hug, too?" asked Danny, arms outstretched.

"I'm good," said Baggy, taking a step backward.

"Me, too," said James.

They spent the rest of the afternoon chatting and drinking tea.

James Smith-Johnson spoke about his rugby playing, his passion for the sport, and the beer-swilling, song-singing social life that went along with it. Despite having general thuggery as the main ingredient on the pitch, he considered it a gentleman's game played with courage, but, above all, honour. His goal was to be a professional rugby player, but his parents, both barristers, insisted on him getting a university degree first.

Mike Bagg talked about his home in Birmingham, in the Midlands. His parents had both died of cancer in the same year when he was twelve and he'd been brought up by his grandmother. The money from the sale of the family home helped towards his upkeep.

The last thing his mother had said during her final days in hospital was that he make them proud and that he would work hard to go to university. His grandmother's neighbourhood wasn't the ideal place to grow up and fulfil his mother's dying wishes, and there had been times when he just felt like dropping out of school, signing on the dole, taking copious amounts of drugs and being a general nuisance to society; but, true to his mother's memory, he did none of those things, except for taking copious amounts of drugs.

He spoke with such a thick Brummy accent that Danny had to step up his concentration to read him.

Danny then went on to speak about his parents and give a shortened version of when he lost his hearing, the consequent quest to learn and then perfect his lip-reading skills. This left his audience open-mouthed and in awe.

Declan's contribution had remained relatively passive throughout, mostly just watching Danny sign everything that was said. He couldn't help but marvel at the speed and elegance of his new flatmate's signing. It had been Declan's sole means of communication since birth, but he felt that he'd never been able to express himself as well as Danny, nor had he ever seen anybody do so, perhaps with the exception of his sister.

"And you, Declan. What's your story?" signed and said Danny.

Until now, Declan had only been able to exchange parts of his story with James and Baggy, due to communication limitations. Now, with Danny's help, he could fill in the gaps.

"*I was born in Glasgow, but my dad, who's a welder by trade, got laid off when we were seven.*"

Danny signed him to stop for a moment. "When *we* were seven?" he signed and spoke the question.

"*Yes, sorry. I have a twin sister called Molly.*"

Something about the name inexplicably stirred Danny's emotions. He'd recently reread *Great Expectations* and Molly was one of his favourite characters. He felt a sort of pang in the pit of his stomach.

Molly. He said the name in his head and the sensation repeated itself.

"*Anyway, when he lost his job, we moved down here to Manchester.*"

It took Danny a couple of seconds to notice that Declan had resumed his story and he had to play a little catch-up when relaying to James and Baggy.

"*Losing his job was a real blow to our father, but in the end it turned out to be a Godsend. If you've ever been to Castlemilk, our neighbourhood, you'll know what I'm talking about. Immigrants and refugees from the poorest and roughest parts of the world have been known to get right back on the boat after a month in the place. Castlemilk*" *has only had two days of sun in a decade and boasts deep-fried Mars bars and pizza as their local culinary delicacies.*"

They all laughed.

"*Both my sister and I have been deaf from birth...*"

"Sorry to interrupt you again, Declan, but both of you are deaf?"

"*Yes. I know, it's pretty rare, even in identical twins. My parents were devastated. They thought they had had two seemingly healthy babies, until a routine check-up with the paediatrician at eleven months revealed the problem. Eleven months of singing us lullabies and nursery rhymes and calling us by the names we never knew we had. Apparently, we were good sleepers, though! By the time we were three, our whole family was signing. Our mother had no problem, but our father to this day still finds it difficult to express himself. He even reduces the most basic and simple phrases to monosyllable signing. Our mother says that he has difficulty expressing himself with normal speech, so no one was really surprised. According to him, he signs with a Scottish accent. We went to special schools for the deaf, so for most of my life my best friends have also been deaf. The person closest to me on the planet is Molly, my sister.*"

There goes that pang again, thought Danny. Is it possible to fall in love with a name?

"*As you can imagine, when it comes to finding girlfriends, the field is reduced drastically, so it's been a challenge, to say the least. If it weren't for a few trips to Amsterdam, I'd be a deaf virgin to this day.*"

"Love Amsterdam," said Baggy. "Europe's most educational city."

Everybody rolled their eyes.

"And Molly?" asked Danny.

But before he could complete his question, Declan piped up, "*Is she a virgin? I honestly wouldn't know; you'd have to ask her.*"

Danny didn't detect any signs of annoyance or offence on his new friend's face.

He laughed. Realising he'd stopped relaying Declan's signing, he repeated the answer to the other two, who laughed, and he resumed his simultaneous interpreting.

"No, I didn't finish the question. Does she go to university here in Manchester?"

This time they all laughed.

"No, she's on a mission. Totally dedicated to improving the lives of Manchester's deaf population; working with the Manchester City Council's programmes that help young kids and adults learn sign language, whilst teaching at the very same school for the deaf that we attended."

"So, why are you a resident student here at Manchester University if your family lives here?" asked James.

"Simple. The university works closely with the school for the deaf and my sister's programmes. When they told us about you and your collaboration with them, we felt that it would be productive for my integration and adaptation to university life if we shared accommodations. I have to admit that I was a little dubious myself, but now that I've met Danny, I'm beginning to see the advantages."

"And your sister?" piped in Baggy. "Is she a bit of all right?"

Danny signed the second question, but adapted it to a more tactful *"Is your sister pretty?"*

"Molly is gorgeous. All the guys go crazy for her. That is until they discover she's deaf, and then any long-term interest usually fades away."

"You said you were identical twins," said James. "How identical are you?"

Declan had called her gorgeous, but the fact that Declan didn't exactly have film-star looks, with his wispy red hair, prominent nose, thin lips and an all-round unhealthy look, made all three wonder if his description had been slightly biased.

"We're technically identical twins, but I was just unlucky enough to accumulate all the ugly genes and Molly the attractive ones. We do, in fact, share the same green eyes."

"In that case, we'll have to meet her one day," said Baggy.

Declan laughed.

"I'm serious!"

They all laughed, but Danny was somehow hooked on a name with bright green eyes.

It was now dark, and they decided to have dinner in to celebrate Danny's arrival and the completion of the group. Baggy offered to go over the road to Gaffs, the convenience store that sold everything from cigarettes to curry powder, to buy some beer.

"Right," said James. "The choice is spaghetti with tomato sauce, spaghetti with no tomato sauce, tuna pasta, or baked beans. We might be able to rustle up some bread and butter if you don't mind clipping off the bits of blue mould."

"Mmm. Yum, yum, it all sounds so deliciously mouth-watering. I'll leave it up to you guys," said Danny.

"*That's just about all we eat around here, although sometimes we get a bit decadent and splash out on takeaway kebabs from over the road*," signed Declan with an expression depicting resignation.

Four hours later, with dinner finished and the table returned to its familiar chaotic state of plates and empty beer bottles, they were still chatting. Despite their different backgrounds, they all got on well and seemed to be enjoying one another's company.

For James, Baggy and Declan, it was a huge relief to be able to sit and chat without the aid of a notepad and pen. All their past conversations had been conditioned by and limited to the amount of words each one would be prepared to write, so elaborate sentences to describe complex and detailed stories were avoided. The fact that Baggy's handwriting resembled a cross between Arabic and that of an overworked doctor didn't help.

James recounted his rugby stories, which mostly contained copious drinking, singing and naked frolics, and Baggy talked about street life in Birmingham. He confessed to having a criminal record for breaking and entering and theft. He'd been more than a little drunk and high one night and decided it would be a good idea to kick in the local video shop's window. Once inside, he grabbed as many videos off the shelf as possible and, loot in hand, turned around to face two patrol cars with blue lights flashing, blocking his escape.

In the interrogation room a little later, two officers were laughing their heads off when they informed Baggy of the charges. He was being booked for stealing *Dumbo*, *Snow-White*, *The Jungle Book* and other assorted Mickey and Donald tapes. In his haste, he had looted the Disney section.

Danny was also enjoying himself with his new friends, but after several hours of lip-reading, signing everything, and speaking practically simultaneously, he was ready to give his now beer-soaked brain a rest and headed off to bed. The others quickly followed, as no one felt like getting the notepads out.

He was so tired, he didn't have the energy to hunt for his toothbrush among his luggage, which still sat largely untouched where he and his father had dropped it. Only the small bag containing the bedding had been unpacked by his mother.

As he lay in his new bed, he thought about the new people in his life, especially Declan, whose well-being and adaptation to university life, and perhaps even life itself outside of deaf institutions and his family, seemed to have been placed squarely on Danny's shoulders. Thankfully, he liked him a lot. He shuddered to think just how unbearable his life could have been if he'd been hooked up with someone he didn't. He was sure they would be good friends. He could see it in his eyes. All the years of lip-reading and communicating with sign language had given him a sort of sixth sense about people's characters. The eyes were his gateway to their souls. Observing the face in both cases was of the utmost importance to capture not only context, but the mood and emotions of the person he was reading, but it was the eyes in particular that gave him the most information. He'd read somewhere that the human was the only animal on the planet with white surrounding their pupils. The theory was that in the time of prehistoric man, when they lived in caves and hunted to eat, language didn't exist. Their only means of communication was with signs and with their eyes. Their eyes were an integral part of the way they transmitted emotions like fear, surprise, anger, puzzlement and love.

Danny found Declan's eyes to be particularly expressive and very informative. Bright green and almost the colour of a new leaf, they were full of passion, intelligence and sincerity. He then wondered if he would find the same in his sister's eyes.

It was with these thoughts that Danny nodded off to sleep.

***

Declan lay in his bed feeling very happy indeed. In all his silent life, he'd never met anyone like Danny. He had come across some good signers before, but none who compared to Danny. The detail he relayed and the speed and elegance that he executed it with were astounding.

What's more, he was one of his own. He belonged to the very same silent world as his, but with a big difference: he hadn't been born deaf; he'd known sounds. He probably remembered what people's voices and music sounded like. He could use his own voice like any normal person, something extremely rare for a deaf person; and, in a way, he could hear every word that people said just by watching their faces. Until now, his sister Molly had been the most competent and capable person he'd ever met. She had always taken care of him; she was his rock and, if it hadn't been for her love and dedication, he wouldn't be about to start university. He had been petrified about not being able to fit in, about not having Molly around to help him.

Incredible, Declan thought. He thanked the higher powers for Danny's presence in his life. He now felt as though a whole lot of loose communication cables that had been flapping about in the air for years had just been plugged into life, along with the rest of him.

CHAPTER 8

Molly McCracken yawned as her bus threaded its way through the morning traffic.

She leaned her head against the steamy, rain-splashed window as if it weighed too much for her neck to sustain it upright.

Oblivious to the cacophony of sounds that surrounded her, the chatter on the bus, the deep, throbbing roar of the bus engine, the tinny beat escaping from someone's Sony Walkman, she enjoyed the vibration of the window and her mind was free to wander without distractions.

She thought about her brother Declan and how he was getting on during his first days at university. She made a note to visit him soon to see for herself. For obvious reasons, they hadn't been able to speak on the phone. She wasn't overly worried about him, but this was the first time in his life that he had stepped out from the protective skirts of his family and the relatively insular world of the deaf education system.

The fact that the university had assigned him a sign reader gave her some assurance that he had access to all they could offer him academically. What worried her was her brother's character. He had always been the vulnerable one. Hyper-sensitivity and anxiety made him overly self-conscious and, instead of facing the world, he tended to face himself. Full of self-deprecation served with huge dollops of self-pity.

Growing up, she had always been the stronger of the two twins, having been dealt the best part of the gene pool while developing by his side in the womb. She had been by far the quicker of the two to learn how to communicate with their mother and father using sign language. In fact, Molly's learning curve had been steep and premature, while Declan's had been practically flat.

Both had received the same love and attention from their parents, but perhaps Declan's ineptitude in acquiring the necessary communication tools to process what was being said, and, more importantly, to express himself, had a direct relation to his insecurities.

This became particularly evident when the twins had reached three years old; an age when it is thought that all toddlers make the transition from only being able to passively absorb emotions and sensations to obtaining the power to analyse and express their needs through words or, in the twins' case, sign language.

Molly had no problem understanding or making herself understood by her parents, friends and teachers, but Declan remained an island; a victim to unexplainable emotions and a prisoner to his inadequacies. Unlike Declan, Molly was aware that she was different from the other kids and why. Her mother was able to explain it at an early age and, opposed to understanding her handicap as something negative, she embraced it. She liked being different and relished expressing herself with her hands.

Molly was also able to appreciate her father's limitations when communicating with sign language. He expressed himself with the simplest of structures, but what he lacked in articulation skills, he more than made up for with his eyes. Green and alive, perspicacious, astute like her own, and his natural propensity to show his love and affection through physical contact.

Perhaps this was why Declan was so close to their father. He communicated directly to Declan's emotions. No words or explanations were needed to transmit what Declan craved more than anything else: to feel loved. He only needed to see his father's eyes and feel his kisses to achieve this.

Molly had also been luckier than Declan regarding their physical appearance. She had a wild mat of unusually natural dark red ringlets that framed a seemingly pore-free alabaster complexion. A small, unremarkable nose sat between a voluptuous mouth and those large green eyes. Everybody's attention was instantly drawn to the better-looking twin, practically ignoring the one with the wispy bright red hair, huge nose and freckle-covered skin.

At quite an early age she became conscious of her brother's belated development and its consequences. She dedicated hours and hours to helping him with his sign language, and instinctively gave him as much love and attention as she could.

He would often run to her crying and struggling to express what was the cause of his distress. She would calm him down with hugs and kisses, then take the time to help him express his feelings with his hands.

Naturally, Molly excelled at school and she was quickly able to read, which opened up a whole new world to her, books feeding her imagination and quenching her thirst for knowledge. Learning to read for a deaf person is far more difficult than for a hearing person.

If born deaf, the only language they know is Sign Language which is completely different to spoken or written English. When introduced to the written word, it's like learning an entirely new language from scratch. The hours her mother spent with her signing bedtime stories with the books open to provide visual references gave her a good solid base to start from.

Eager to introduce this world to her brother, she replicated her mother's methods and carefully chose the right books with plenty of illustrations or photos to help establish context, and would sit patiently with him for hours on end while she prised the world open for her brother. Although this took a long time and an infinite amount of good-natured tolerance, she was largely responsible for her brother at least reaching the same level as his peers at school, and was wholly responsible for instigating Declan's passion for literature.

It was this experience with Declan that helped establish Molly's vocation quite early in life. She had a natural gift for teaching, which she was passionate about putting into practice, and, from around fifteen years old, she knew what she wanted to do for the rest of her life: teach and train the deaf.

Molly was unaware that someone was talking to her on the bus, and only a tap on the shoulder alerted her to the fact. A young man with long, lank hair was asking if she could move her bag from the seat next to her so he could sit down. The fact that he was pointing to her bag told her what he was asking. She put it on her lap and went back to leaning on her vibrating window. Right away, she got another tap on the shoulder and the guy was talking to her again.

She had no choice but to point to her ear and vocalise the word 'deaf' – one word that she could pronounce nearly one hundred percent correctly.

"Yeah, right," said the guy, nodding and squinting. "If you don't want to talk, just say so."

Molly repeated the gesture of pointing to her ear and the word 'deaf', but he carried on speaking. By now, Molly detected anger in his eyes and she gave up with a shrug, turning her palms up and turning back to the window, unable to hear his "Stuck up bitch" as he went to sit somewhere else.

CHAPTER 9

Danny found Declan in the kitchen, hunting for a clean cup.

"Good morning."

"Good morning. I can't find a clean cup."

"I don't mean to insult your intelligence, but have you thought about washing one of the dirty ones?"

Declan laughed. *"It's Tuesday."*

"So?"

"Washing-up day is Friday."

"Well, that settles it, then. I suppose we'd better go out for breakfast."

They went over to the student cafe, a short walk from their block, and found the place practically empty. Danny grabbed some toast and jam and a cup of tea and went with his tray to a corner table by the window. Declan joined him a few minutes later with enough food to solve a famine in Ethiopia: fried eggs, bacon, beans, tomatoes and mushrooms formed a glistening, multi-coloured mountain in front of him which, after smothering it all in ketchup and HP sauce, he hastily began shovelling into his mouth.

"Where do you put it all?" Danny asked, observing his skinny new friend. At first Declan didn't respond as his head was down and he hadn't seen the question. Danny waited for Declan to come up for breath before repeating himself.

"My Mum says I've got hollow legs, but I guess it's down to my metabolism. I'm a nervous kind of guy; I worry about everything."

"I think pretty soon you can add heart failure to your worries."

Declan smiled and went back to his shovelling. Danny now knew that he had to choose the right moment when wanting to converse with him. Not only did he have to have his full attention, but chatting in sign language also required the use of both hands, and Declan's were busy stabbing and cutting at his grease mountain. So, he sipped his tea while observing the most impressive display of gluttony he'd ever seen. Declan didn't seem to chew his food, as great quantities disappeared down his gullet. It reminded Danny of the way a snake swallowed entire animals whole, to be digested later.

"So, are you just doing English Lit?" he asked three minutes later, when Declan finally placed his knife and fork on a squeaky-clean plate with a contented grin.

"Yes, and you?"

"I'm doing English Lit as well, but I'm planning to do a one-year MA in Political Sciences. I have to check my timetables to see how I'm going to go about it."

"How many classes do you have to interpret?"

"In theory, it's been agreed that I do twelve hours a week, a couple of which will be for my own course."

"Can I ask you something?"

"Shoot."

"Is it difficult to interpret normal speech to sign language? I've often wondered."

"Difficult? How do you mean?"

"I mean, how it compares to a sign language conversation with a deaf person, for example?"

"Now that's a tricky question to answer. In fact, they're two different questions. Give me a minute to think about how to answer the second question. The first one is easy. No, it's not difficult, unless you are relaying a particularly specialist subject."

Danny sat back and looked at the white cork-tiled ceiling for inspiration. Surprisingly, he had never considered this. It took a few minutes to decide *how* to answer the question. He had concluded in seconds that it was comparable.

Declan sat patiently sipping his tea.

"As you well know from your experience reading normal speech in books, sign language is an entirely different language with its own grammatical rules regarding things like syntax and phonology. It's not a word-for-word translation. People often mistakenly ask what's the word for so-and-so, looking for a word equivalent. When we sign things like context, concept, and time, they must be established visually, so sentence

structure doesn't follow normal speech rules. 'What's your name?' becomes 'Name you what?'. Topic first and then comment. If we want to talk about an action in the past, 'I ate apples' becomes 'past apples I eat', establishing time then topic and finally comment.

"Some people are surprised at just how articulate and expressive you can be in sign language. They think you're exaggerating when you interpret a particularly complex or abstract idea that's been signed. When we sign, we use our hands, bodies, head and face to emphasise or embellish a sentence, express a negative or generally express intangible concepts. Our eyes are tremendously important when indicating emotions, and even our eyebrows come into play when we want to indicate a question."

He paused for a moment, wondering if perhaps he was over-explaining himself, but Declan seemed to be following him with interest, so he continued.

"Okay. So when interpreting sign language to normal speech, I'm basically translating one language into another. Now when it's the other way around, and especially when interpreting a complex or specific topic with its own particular jargon, like anything medical or legal, it's no different, but I also become a sort of verbal editor. I have to analyse and process the normal speech in a fraction of a second and then relay the basic concept, editing nuances and subtleties. This is probably more difficult for me compared to a non-deaf interpreter, as I also have to lip-read simultaneously. So, it doesn't matter if I'm interpreting word to sign language or sign language to word, it's equally difficult, as they both involve translating.

"However, a direct sign language conversation with a deaf person is, of course, a case of speaking the same language, thus making it by far the easiest of the interactions; and, in my opinion, sign is far more beautiful, more expressive and more all-round enjoyable than the spoken word. But that's beside the point. The same question could be how I would compare a conversation in a foreign language, like Chinese, with one with someone in your own language. Does that answer your question?"

Declan was smiling and shaking his head in disbelief and wonder.

"*Wow. Now that's what I call an answer. You're certainly not one for holding back, are you? So, the short answer would be no, but it can be difficult when relaying specialist subjects, and you can compare it with translating a foreign language and a conversation in your own language.*"

"*Okay, no, but it can be difficult when relaying specialist subjects, and you can compare it with translating a foreign language and a conversation in your own language.*"

They both laughed.

"*Okay, Danny. I must say that you explained that perfectly, although a little long-winded; but how would you know what translating Chinese is like?*"

Danny raised his eyebrows and smiled.

"*No! Don't tell me you speak bloody Chinese.*"

"*Well, Mandarin actually.*"

"*Jesus, Danny. Can you walk on water, too?*"

Danny laughed and told Declan all about his family background and his relationship with his grandmother.

Time quickly slipped by, and a few students observed Danny and Declan's animated conversation with fascination.

Danny noticed them as well and was able to read comments like, 'Man, look at those two. I wonder what they're talking about', and one that he'd often read, 'I'd love to be able to do that'.

"*Do you like reading?*" asked Danny.

"*You mean books, as in literature?*"

"*Yes.*"

Declan smiled. "*Books are my life. Books are my teachers, my friends and my lovers. If I didn't have books, I'd be both deaf and very much dumb in every sense of the word,*" he said, his eyes more alive than ever. "*The only time I'm really happy is when I'm reading.*"

Danny couldn't help grinning, not only because his new friend seemed as passionate about books as he, but also the way his enthusiasm for the subject was clearly reflected in his signing. His whole body moved as if it had just been injected with rocket fuel.

"When I read, I'm no longer deaf. I feel in contact with the world. A world that's anything but silent and full of the one thing I'll never have: words."

"My turn to say wow. So, the simple answer would be, 'Yes, I like reading'."

They both laughed again.

"But you know what I'm trying to say, don't you?"

"Declan, if you could see my book collection at home, you'd understand that I know exactly what you mean."

Another huge smile spread across Declan's face. *"My sister Molly would like you, I'm sure of it."*

Danny felt a tiny flutter in his heart at the mention of her name, and it caught him a little unawares.

Why is it that every time I hear that name, something stirs in me? he thought.

"She taught me to read and introduced me to all kinds of literature. She's always had this knack of knowing exactly what books I'd like, or what anybody would like, for that matter. Books are one of her main tools to stimulate and educate the deaf whom she works with. According to Molly, anyone who doesn't read books is indeed deaf, dumb and blind."

"From the sound of it, I'm sure I'd like her, too."

"If you want, we can arrange to all go out some time."

"Sure, that would be great."

Danny would have loved to suggest that some time would be like as soon as possible, as he was curious to meet the person whose name seemed to affect him so much.

As if Declan had read his thoughts, he added, *"Don't get your hopes up, though. Molly isn't really interested in boys."*

"She's a lesbian?" Danny squeaked as well as signed.

"No, no, nothing like that. As far as I know, she's only been out with a couple of guys, and I'm practically sure she hasn't seen anyone for the last two years at least. Perhaps she's just too dedicated to her work, but she's repeated more than once that she'll never go out with anyone again, much to our Mum's disappointment. She hasn't said so, but I'm sure she sees Molly as the only road to having grandchildren."

"Why's that?"

"Danny, look at me. I'm not exactly James Bond, am I? Who in their right mind would want a skinny, big-nosed, freckly, deaf red-head?"

Danny laughed. *"Oh, I don't know. Perhaps we could find a skinny, big-nosed, freckly deaf red-head."*

"Thanks, mate. You're a real friend."

Danny saw that Declan had taken his quip humorously. *"No, seriously, have you ever been out with a girl?"*

Declan lowered his gaze. *"Apart from that trip to Amsterdam?"*

"That's not going out with a girl."

"I've never even kissed a girl."

"Right, that's it then. I'm going to make it my mission to fix that."

"I don't doubt that you're a man of many talents, but I don't think doing miracles is among them."

"We'll see. We'll see."

They went back to talking about books they'd read, and their friendship was well and truly sealed when they discovered that their favourite book was *The Count of Monte Cristo.*

A glance at the clock told Danny they'd been sitting chatting for two hours.

"Are you ready to go?" asked Danny, getting up.

Declan grabbed the half a slice of toast that Danny hadn't eaten and signed, *"Let's go"*, with toast sticking out of his mouth.

"Just one last question, Declan," Danny signed, making Declan sit down again with a worried look in his eyes.

"Is there anything you don't eat? And I'm referring to food, not inanimate objects like furniture."

He laughed.

"Octopus," he signed immediately without the need to ponder.

"Octopus?"

"Are you deaf or something?" Declan signed with a big grin.

"Have you ever tried it?" signed Danny.

"Nope."

"So how do you know if you've never tried it?"

"*I've never sucked a cock or shoved a red-hot poker up my arse, either. Let's go.*"

And he headed towards the door, leaving Danny laughing his head off.

"*I love this guy.*"

CHAPTER 10

Classes started a few days later, and Danny found himself pretty busy, combining attending his own classes and interpreting an equal amount. Every week he was given the list of classes and subjects he was to interpret and he had to spend some of the little spare time he had swatting up on specific and relevant jargon pertaining to each one.

When interpreting, he was strategically placed to be able to read the professor and sign to the deaf student, which, on a good day, didn't surpass two or three students.

Although he was able to sign the lectures without any problems, he sometimes felt it necessary to employ a bit of artistic licence just to avoid putting everyone to sleep.

Whenever he thought a sentence or explanation to be over-complicated or particularly long-winded, he'd often interpret it in his own simplistic or abbreviated version.

Occasionally, he'd make some derogatory remark about the professor that would make his students giggle. After some weeks, he'd only have to sign '*Bullshit*', arms folded at an angle in front of him, with the top hand making a bull horns sign and the bottom hand waving all the fingers pointing downward. This was a signal to his students that the professor was going on about something uninteresting or irrelevant.

Quickly, Danny became the students' favourite interpreter on campus and sometimes deaf students would even attend lectures that weren't even on their course. Not only did he make lectures entertaining, but it was widely commented that the fact that Danny was deaf made him a far better interpreter than the others, none of whom were deaf.

The class he interpreted on Sex and Salvation in Medieval Literature quickly became a legend on campus.

Any spare time he did have he spent either chatting with Declan or reading or drinking beer with James and Baggy at the Queen of Hearts, a sort of club housed in a converted church just over the road from the student halls complex. James and Baggy had been quick to catch on to the advantages of having a lip-reader in their midst, and Danny was often implicated in their quests to woo the opposite sex. Unfortunately, the disadvantage of having Danny around was that he seemed to attract most of the attention, leaving the others trying to pick up whatever was left.

Manchester University boasted one of the academic world's most outstanding libraries, housing over four million items. Built in the mid-1800s, its Gothic cathedral-like halls and reading rooms offered students and scholars access to everything from ancient medieval manuscripts to contemporary literature. Lush red carpets, statuettes and ornate stone-carved arches gave the building a distinguished aura of majestic grandeur.

The moment he set foot in the place, Danny felt that he had found his heaven on Earth. A place where he could revel in the written word. A place to soak up knowledge and nourish his imagination. Where everybody was expected to share what he experienced every day: silence.

He would spend as many hours as possible secluded in one of its alcoves, either reading for pleasure or swatting up on a specialist subject that he was soon to interpret.

From time to time, Declan would come to keep him company and they would chat away about literature and life without disturbing other students or visitors.

Apart from chatting with Danny, what really drew Declan to the library was its considerably advanced area for technology. He had become fascinated by computers and their capabilities. Here was a world that, for all intents and purposes, was not reliant on the spoken word. He saw it as a new world. A silent and accommodating world with its own languages. If he had been wondering what he was going to do with his life, he was now pretty sure.

He taught himself to program in languages like Basic, C and Clipper and was now learning HTML. Although he was a fan of Microsoft Windows, his real passion was for Apple Macintosh, and he would spend hours on the library's Macs.

"*Internet,*" Declan exclaimed to Danny, James and Baggy on one of the rare occasions that they all coincided around the green Formica table in 1991. It took Danny a few signed exchanges with Declan before he could relay the word to the others, as the word was entirely new to him.

"What about it?" asked James, whose attention span and interest in anything that didn't have to do with rugby were limited.

"Mark my words. It's going to change the world."

"I don't even know what it is," said Baggy.

"It's simply a network that connects all the computers to one another that's been around since the late 60s, but it was an English computer engineer called Tim Berners-Lee that invented the World Wide Web two years ago in 1989 to help scientists at CERN, a European research organisation near Geneva, to exchange information on a global scale. Internet became accessible to the world's public last year. Anyone can create a website that can be accessed by everyone connected to the worldwide network just by typing in the web address."

"Wow," exclaimed James.

"The idea is that you can do a search for any subject you're interested in and you can find a website about it."

"Extraordinary.," said Danny, who was already contemplating just how useful such a tool would be.

"I want to try it," said Baggy.

"Just come to the library and I'll show you."

"Is there any porn?"

Danny had to pause his relaying of the conversation. It took a while to think about how to transmit 'porn' in Sign. Declan screwed his eyes up as Danny repeated the gestures three times.

He laughed and nodded. *"I'd say there's more porn than anything else."*

"I'm in, then. Shall we go now?"

"It's ten o'clock at night, Baggy. The library is closed."

"So you're really into all this computer stuff in a big way, aren't you?" asked James.

"I'm telling you, computers are the future. Now would be a good time to put your money on companies like IBM, Microsoft or Apple Macintosh. You'll clean up."

"Oh, right then. I'll call my stockbroker the first chance I get."

"You may jest, my skateboarding, hedonistic, Disney-loving friend. But you'll see."

CHAPTER 11

Molly sat at one of the long reading tables in the library. She had always been moved by Robert Burns' 'Ode to a Field Mouse' and its clear and simple message of the importance of living your life in the present.

But, mousie, thou art not alane,
In proving foresight may be in vain, The best laid schemes of mice and men,
Go oft astray,
And leave us nought but grief and pain.
To rend our day,
Still though art blessed, compared with me!
The present only touches thee, but oh, I backward cast my eye
On prospects drear,
And forward, though I cannot see, I guess and fear.

She was writing out a more contemporary version to use with her students at the Deaf Centre.

'Thou art not alane' and words like 'nought' and 'timorous' were a little beyond her deaf students' learning-to-read capacities.

Normally, Molly would sit in this doubly silent world that she so enjoyed, oblivious to all that was going on around her; but suddenly, out of the corner of her eye, she spotted a young man with glossy black hair at another table about halfway down the hall.

What had caught her attention was that she was sure she had seen him sign. She focused a moment on his hands, and he was indeed signing.

He was at least a hundred and fifty feet away and turned sideways, so it was a bit tricky to pick up the thread of what he was signing, especially without being able to see his complete face, but in a few seconds she realised he was talking quite explicitly about a sexual encounter.

She was aware that she was blushing, then a wave of indignation overcame her.

'*What a pig,*' she thought, but continued to follow his signing, now leaning forward a little to see if she could see who he was signing to. She was unsuccessful, as he was behind one of the big stone pillars.

She then realised that she had been observing for some minutes now and, although she found the content of what he was signing offensive and clearly showed that he didn't have an ounce of respect for women, she couldn't help admiring the elegance of his movements.

In fact, she found herself transfixed and had to shake her dark red curls to snap out of it; and then, gathering her notes, she promptly left the building.

As she walked to the bus stop, a sensation that had long been dormant was stirring in her body.

***

Danny concluded giving Declan a crash course in sex education without having noticed the girl who had just left.

"*So, Declan. I think the time has come for us to go out and see if we can get you a girl. Tonight, we're going to the Hacienda. I've heard it's the place to go in Manchester.*"

"*I'll go with you, but I can assure you I won't be finding any girl. I wasn't only born deaf. I was also born invisible.*"

That night, after Danny had negotiated their entrance, they stepped into the main room of the Hacienda. They were immediately hit with the raw energy of the place and, for Declan, who had never set foot in a club like this in his life, he felt like he'd just landed on another planet.

The electric atmosphere was palpable, if not audible, and it drew them into its bowels with such a force that they both felt as if they'd been swept up into a hurricane of lights and colour.

They signed each other their first impressions and agreed that a drink was in order.

They were perhaps the only two people in the whole place who could converse normally.

When they approached one of the bars, they spotted Baggy screaming into a girl's ear. They knew he was screaming, because he had a vein the size of a rope running down his scrawny neck and she was wincing. Danny positioned himself to read what seemed to be so important to Baggy that he needed to risk giving himself a stroke.

It was no easy task, as lip-reading different accents always proved a challenge and Baggy had a thick Birmingham one. Danny was just getting used to it, as he was with the Mancunian accent.

"You've got the kind of face I'd like to come across every day," shouted Baggy.

"What?" she screamed back.

Baggy repeated it.

Her bored expression quickly changed to one of anger. "Fook off, moron."

Baggy hadn't heard it, as he was shouting back, '"What?", and was cupping his hand to his ear.

"Baggy! She's telling you to get lost," shouted Danny, alerting Baggy to their presence with a friendly punch on the shoulder.

"Hey, guys. What's up?" he shouted, as he led them away from the girl, giving her the middle finger.

She reciprocated. "Dickhead."

"This place is fantastic. And Baggy, you don't have to shout. I can read your lips, remember?" said Danny, as Declan man-hugged Baggy.

"Easy, boy. Not in front of the ladies. Sorry. Sometimes I forget you're deaf. Do you guys want to drop an 'E'? Dance the night away, eh? Great music."

Danny signed Baggy's offer to Declan, making him laugh.

"Baggy, you know very well that we can't dance, nor can we hear the music."

"Come with me."

He led them down to the dance floor and they followed as he threaded his way through the gyrating, hand-pumping mass of bodies over to the huge stack of speakers that towered over the dance floor.

It was Declan's turn to use sign language. He was wind-milling both arms and mouthing, *"Can you feel that?"*

Declan and Danny's bodies shook and pulsated to the beat that was thumping out of the speakers.

"Wow," signed Declan. *"This is incredible."*

Both stood spellbound by the rhythmic pounding they were feeling in their bones.

Bodies all around them moved in sync to the rhythm they could feel.

"So, you want that E or not?"

Danny shook his head. "I think this is enough sensation for me."

Baggy shrugged. "Fair enough. Enjoy. I'm off back to the bar."

They spent the next two hours moving their bodies with the beat that shook them.

They may have looked like two idiots, but they didn't care.

As they moved, they signed to each other, which seemed to catch the attention of some of the people around them. Danny managed to read a couple of encouraging comments like, "Very cool" or "Go for it", but what he found really amusing and bizarre at the same time was that some people were mimicking their signs as if they had invented new dance moves.

Then he caught a comment made by a girl dressed in a stretchy white mini-dress with big black dots, standing just off the dance floor. She was speaking to her friend, who wore the same dress in negative: white dots on a black dress.

"The one with the black hair is cute. Are they using sign language?"

The friend responded, *"You know what, I think they are. And I think it's dead sexy the way they move their hands, don't you? His friend isn't bad, either."*

Danny had to do a double-take, because the friend was skinny with bright red hair, and, it had to be said, a rather large nose. If Declan had introduced this girl to him as his twin sister Molly, he wouldn't have doubted it for a moment.

"Come with me," he signed to Declan, who was moving his body as if he were receiving electric shocks.

"Where are we going?"

"We're going to complete your sex education course with a practical exercise that doesn't include handing over any money."

A short while later, the four were in a taxi on the way back to the student complex, and, after a couple of beers around the table, they took their dotted girls to their respective rooms. Danny signed some last-minute advice, just before a decidedly nervous Declan was pulled inside to fulfil what he had thought was an impossible dream.

"*Well?*" asked Danny, when the girls had left the next morning.

"*That was, without a doubt, the best night of my life.*"

"*Everything all right, then?*" asked Danny, not wanting to ask for details.

"*I repeat: that was, without a doubt, the best night of my life.*"

"*Oooh, who's Mr Cocky now, then?*"

Declan laughed.

"*Well, she must have liked you, because she told me to tell you to give her a call.*" He handed Declan a scrap of paper with her number on it, which he grabbed and kissed.

"*Danny, I owe you one, and big time. Just ask me for anything you want. Just name it.*"

"*How about arranging for me to meet with your sister Molly?*"

"*Done.*"

"*Done? I'm being serious, Declan.*"

"*Done. Whenever you want.*"

"*Well, thanks, buddy. By the way, Declan, it's just a thought, but have you thought how you're going to call this girl?*"

"*A minor detail, my friend. Any girl who leaves her number for a deaf guy to call her can only be considered nothing less than a one-night stand.*" He turned on his heel and headed off down the hall and back to his bed. Danny was sure he looked like a man who had grown a little taller overnight.

CHAPTER 12

True to his word, Declan arranged for them to meet Molly at the Manchester Deaf Centre in Cheadle, where she worked, a few days later.

Danny woke that morning with a feeling that this wasn't going to be just another day in his life. Something was going to change, and it was all down to how he felt about a name.

He found it difficult to concentrate on his studies and less so on the one lecture he had to interpret: Power and Gender in Early Modern Literature. Which was unfortunate, because it pertained to his own course.

Time passed slower than it had ever passed. So slow, in fact, that Danny was sure his watch had stopped. At last he found himself on the bus with Declan, threading their way through the early evening traffic. When his friend signed that theirs was the next stop, Danny felt his throat tighten and his mouth go dry.

They found Molly in one of the classrooms, signing with a couple of students. The very moment he saw her, he felt something change in him, something physical. As if some kind of chemical or biological reaction were taking place throughout his body.

He felt dizzy and unsteady on his feet. As they stood, unnoticed, he had the opportunity to study the owner of the name that had stirred such strange feelings in him for so long. Her face exuded compassion, love and enthusiasm, as did her signing. Her students' faces responded with an obvious admiration and respect, and Danny's reverie was only broken when Molly, somehow sensing their presence in the doorway, briefly turned her head towards them. When their eyes met, Danny felt he had just been filleted on the spot, as his entire body turned to jelly.

It was obvious that these sensations were clearly not reciprocal, as Danny, being considerably sensitive to reading people's emotions expressed through their faces, picked up a tiny but unmistakable flash of anger, which left him surprised and perplexed as he stood next to his friend.

When he was sure her full attention had returned to her students, he signed, *"She's absolutely incredible. I can see now that you weren't joking when you said she didn't look anything like you."* He was conscious that although one could express anything one wanted in sign language, it was impossible to discretely whisper anything.

"As I told you before, don't get your hopes up. Our Molly is a tough nut to crack. Manchester is littered with potential suitors with flat noses or broken hearts."

That flash of anger that he had caught and so confused him seemed to confirm the fact. Molly said goodbye to her students and gave them her full attention.

"So, this must be the famous Danny that you're always going on about."

Danny felt himself blush and hoped it hadn't looked too obvious.

"Molly – Danny. Danny – Molly," signed Declan, spelling out their names.

Danny remained a little disconcerted, as her face was still showing anger, and he desperately wanted to be on the receiving end of the same enthusiasm, compassion and love that had first moved him some moments ago.

"Pleased to meet you at last. Declan's told me so much about you that I feel I almost know you."

"I could say the same, but Declan told me you were gorgeous and I have to say I disagree."

That flash of anger again made Danny pause before adding, *"You're absolutely stunning."*

Now her eyes were flashing all kinds of signals, like traffic lights changing from red to amber, then green in a loop.

"Quite the ladies' man, I see. In fact, now I come to think of it, you look vaguely familiar. Do you spend much time in Manchester University's library?"

If Danny was slightly disconcerted before, now he was completely off-balance.

"Yes, I do, as a matter of fact. Have you seen me there?"

"Let's just say I saw a guy very much like you signing some very interesting things about... let's say his personal life, the other day at the library."

It took a few seconds for the penny to drop, but Danny was pretty sure what conversation she was referring to and felt himself blush the mother of all blushes this time.

"Are you sure it was me?"

"Just how many deaf people do you think are busy signing away about explicit sex in Manchester University library?"

So there it was, the reason for those flashes of anger.

Before he could react, Declan thankfully came to the rescue, having quickly joined the dots as to why he had detected such unfamiliar animosity coming from his normally placid sister.

"Molly, if you saw Danny, then you must have seen me, as I was with him."

It was Molly's turn to blush. She started to sign and then stopped, clearly not knowing how to continue. Declan sensed that both his friend and his sister were feeling more than uncomfortable and diplomatically interjected.

"Molly, why don't you give us a tour of this Centre of yours where you seem to spend most of your life?"

She flashed a sort of puppy dog look at Danny, which he quickly responded to with a warm smile. No more words were necessary.

"Yes, of course... I... Come this way."

They walked along the fluorescent-lit, narrow hallways, occasionally stopping to enter classrooms. Some clearly catered for children, with neatly spaced mini-desks and chairs and walls covered in large posters depicting hand shapes and arm movements, alongside colourful paintings of animals, houses and families.

Other classrooms had a more academic air to them, with shelves full of books and walls covered in maps and diagrams.

As they went from room to room, Danny was delighted to note that Molly explained what activities were carried out in which room and for what purpose with the same passion and love he had seen earlier. All traces of that antipathy that had so thrown him had all but disappeared.

As she stood signing to them in her faded jeans, white T-shirt and grey cardigan, Danny took the opportunity to scrutinise what he considered to be every perfect inch of her.

He couldn't find anything he didn't like. That pale, flawless skin, framed by that wild mass of kinky dark red hair, the colour of a deep red mahogany, pulled back and loosely tamed by a black hairband rested below her shoulders, had such an effect on him that, for the first time in many years, he actually lost the gist of what somebody was explaining to him.

"If I'm boring you, please let me know." He was suddenly aware of Molly signing, but this time he was relieved to pick up that her eyes were only showing humour.

"I'm sorry, I was just thinking what a great place this must be to work. How satisfying it must be to actively participate in improving these people's lives."

Even though it wasn't the real reason for his temporary lapse of attention, Danny sincerely meant what he was saying and was pleased to see from Molly's face that he was pushing all the right buttons.

***

Molly was momentarily lost for words, or rather signs, as she was once again mesmerised by the same beautiful signing she had first appreciated and which had so affected her in the library. It wasn't just his hand movements; it was his elegant use of the rest of his body; and now, up close, everything else that comes into play when signing, like his eyes and his facial expressions. Molly often thought that some people, when signing, looked like really cheesy mime actors who have drunk too much coffee, but not Danny. Every movement, every expression, everything seemed... Molly struggled to find a word. Seemed... well, it just seemed right.

***

Several seconds passed before Declan broke the silence, so to speak.

"You know, you couldn't do any worse than to get Danny to work with you here part-time. He's the best there is. He got his advanced interpreter's qualifications at seventeen and faster than anybody else has ever done in the country."

Danny blushed. *"Thanks, Declan, but first, I can't remember offering my services, and secondly, who told you that I was the fastest to get the interpreter's qualifications in the country?"*

"Sorry, Danny, but that's what the university told us."

Danny shrugged. This was news to him, but now wasn't the time to dispute the matter. He wanted to take advantage of Declan's subtle way of opening the door for him, and he wanted to make sure he could slip through it and thus make sure he saw Molly again, the sooner the better.

"I'm afraid there are no jobs here at the moment, not even for part-time staff. You know, funding cuts and all that."

Well, that door didn't stay open for long, thought Danny.

***

Molly couldn't help noticing Danny's disappointment, and she surprised herself by immediately opening it again. *"We are, however, open to volunteers."*

"Okay. When do I start?"

Molly almost jumped back with surprise at his quick-fire answer.

"What? You're interested?"

***

"More than you could ever imagine." As he said it, Danny had the sensation that he had just jumped out of a plane without a parachute. His adrenaline was pumping; he was in no doubt that he was in for an exhilarating experience. He'd just have to worry about the landing part when it came. He had no idea how he was going to fit this voluntary work into his already overloaded timetable.

***

Molly looked at Danny and wondered if this enthusiasm to volunteer was based on a sudden burst of altruism or he had ulterior motives. This led her to rapidly examine her own motives for mentioning the volunteer option in the first place. It was obvious. She liked him and she wanted to see him again, whatever his motives may be.

She noticed Declan's face with what could be described as hero worship all over it, as he waited in anticipation of her answer.

"Okay. Come along next Friday evening at 6.30pm. You can help with the sign language class that we have for students who have lost their hearing late in life."

***

"Done," responded Danny, ostensibly calm, but on the inside he was jumping up and down and punching the air. He was in freefall.

Molly walked them to the main entrance and hugged her brother, telling him to go and visit their parents more often. She then held out her hand for Danny to shake. The moment their hands touched, both perceived the softness of the other's skin, followed by an intense sensation of familiarity, a warm sensuality; as if they had known each other all their lives.

"I'll see you on Friday, then," signed Danny, reluctantly letting go of her hand to do so.

"Okay, nice to meet you," responded Molly.

Declan gave his sister another hug and they parted company.

"So? What do you think of Molly, then?" Declan asked Danny a few minutes later on the bus. They were lucky enough to get the back seat all to themselves and so sat at either end, providing them with enough room to face each other and express themselves freely.

"Declan, I know this is going to sound crazy, but I think I'm in love."
"With Molly?"

"No, the bus driver. Of course I meant Molly. I've just met the person I want to spend the rest of my life with."

"You know what, Danny? You're absolutely right. That does sound crazy, and I think you'd have a better chance with the bus driver. You've only just met her."

"I'm telling you, Declan. I've never felt like this before. I feel dizzy just thinking about her, and I have this massive urge to go back and see her right now. Just hearing her name does something to me."

"Easy now, Romeo. I mean, on the one hand I can understand: Molly is a fantastic woman, and I don't mean just her looks; but on the other, I think you should get to know her a little before declaring such emphatic undying love for her, or any girl for that matter. As I told you before, Molly isn't interested in men. The only thing she's interested in is her work at the Deaf Centre and an international charity that she's just become involved in."

At that moment, two elderly ladies sat between them on the back seat, blocking their conversation. Danny leaned forward as much as he could and signed, *"I'm willing to take my chances."*

Declan did the same. *"Listen, if you two hit it off, I'll be delighted. You know I would. You'd honestly make a great couple. I'm just warning you. I wouldn't want you to get hurt, that's all."*

The two old ladies looked at each other and shrugged.

***

Molly walked back to her classroom, still thinking about how the touch of Danny's hand had affected her. She hadn't been interested in anyone for quite some time now. She could safely say that none of the few men she had been out with had made her feel anything remotely similar to what she had just experienced. It was precisely the lack of any emotions that had made her decide that relationships were not for her. She was convinced that she lacked whatever it was to be capable of feeling anything more than cosy comfort with a man.

The whole relationship thing for her was just an inconvenience; something that everybody else seemed to want to impose on her, as if it were one of the items on a list of things everybody should do in life if they want society to consider them as normal.

Molly knew she wasn't normal, nor did she care much for society's expectations. She knew that what made her happy was her work and she was determined to dedicate her heart and soul to it. There was no room in her life for what she considered to be useless distractions such as men.

Yet now, with just the touch of his hand, Danny had managed to turn her inside out.

She stopped in the hallway just outside her classroom and shook her head.

No... Stop it, Molly. It was just a handshake. Okay, so he's good looking, extraordinarily talented, your brother's god – and to top it off, he's got one very important thing in common with you... he's deaf. 'What's so special about that?' she asked herself.

She walked into her class and answered herself in sign language. *"Everything, Danny Valentine-Rocker. Everything."*

She smiled. *"My God, even his name is great."*

***

For Danny, Friday couldn't come soon enough. He could only think of Molly's touch. The softness of her hands, that feeling of it just being right. He could close his eyes and relive all those sensations that had come to him when they shook hands. He knew that Molly had felt something similar. He knew that one way or other, his feelings about her were reciprocated. He had felt it through her hand and unmistakably seen it in her eyes.

His timetable was so full; he wasn't sure if he could spare even one evening to volunteer at the Deaf Centre; but he didn't care. One evening might be all he needed.

That week, his classes seemed to be longer and less interesting than ever. His days felt like they had forty-eight hours in them. He simplified his interpreting of classes and discussion groups so much and so blatantly that more than one professor was made dubious by his following a particularly long and complex sentence with just a few succinct signs, often causing them to wait unnecessarily for more, before resuming their lecture when none came.

***

Friday came and Molly found herself doing something that she had never done in her life – clock watch. There was a huge one on the wall at the back of her classroom, with diagrams to show how to tell the time in British Sign Language. She watched the hands agonisingly make their way so slowly around the clock that several times she thought it had actually stopped.

By four o'clock in the afternoon, she could take no more of it and took advantage of a small break between classes to take the clock down.

***

In another part of Manchester, Danny's day was dragging by with more or less the same nerve-grinding slowness. He was interpreting what was, even in normal circumstances, a tedious lecture on Chaucer: *Texts, Contexts, Conflicts*, to only one deaf student, who seemed to be more interested in carrying out a full nostril excavation than English literature.

Ironically, the rest of the hearing students watched him sign as if they understood every hand shape and movement.

At 6pm on the dot, Danny appeared at the door of her classroom. Thinking that his arrival had gone momentarily undetected, he stood for quite a while, contemplating her profile, with which he could find no fault. Even her ears seemed perfect to him.

Molly broke his reverie by turning her head and smiling. *"Hello, I'm sorry. I didn't see you standing there. Please come in. Come in."*

"Hello, Molly. I would've knocked, but..." He shrugged and held both palms out.

"Very funny," she signed, clearly smiling.

"Sorry, a somewhat childish and insensitive joke. Are you busy? Am I disturbing you? I can come back later."

"No, not at all. I've been expecting you."

He stepped into the class, and she came to meet him with her hand outstretched.

As soon as they touched, both felt those same sensations as the last time they had shaken hands. Blue eyes met green eyes, and instantly neither of them had any doubt that any feelings they were experiencing were mutual.

"Okay," signed Molly, once they broke contact, *"are you ready to go to work?"*

"*I can't wait.*"

She stood looking at him for a few seconds. "*If you're not interested in volunteering, this is the time to tell me.*"

"*I am. I'm very interested. I mean it. I'm really looking forward to it.*"

A few more seconds ticked by. The truth was that Danny hadn't even thought about the work he had committed to do; he had only been thinking about seeing Molly again.

He could sense her reservation and insisted once again, "*I'm telling you, this means a lot to me.*"

"*Okay, I believe you, but you need to know something about me before you start. I hate lies, and, above all, I hate being lied to. Do we understand each other?*"

"*Molly,*" signed Danny, staring her straight in the eye, "*you need to know something about me. I never lie.*"

Another few seconds passed, and Danny was relieved to see her expression change. Her eyes told him she was convinced. "*That's good to know. Now, you're going to be giving quite a challenging class. I think it's an ideal class for you to start with. All the students are adults and have gone deaf later in life, so the principles that apply to teaching children who are born deaf are not applicable to this group. If you're born deaf, learning sign language will be a similar process to natural spoken language development. However, for these people it's like learning an entirely new language.*"

"*That sounds familiar.*" He thought of one of his first conversations with Declan.

"*Exactly. It's one of the reasons you're ideal for this class. You've had to do precisely the same. Another reason is that some can still speak normally, so your lip-reading skills may be very useful.*"

"*What level have they got to?*"

"*They are all beginners, so you should start with the basics: the alphabet, finger spelling and simple greetings.*"

"*Sounds pretty straightforward.*"

"*We'd better get you started. Come with me.*"

Danny saluted and then signed, "*After you.*"

He followed her down the corridor, staying two steps behind, which made communication impossible but allowed him to appreciate Molly's back.

They stopped outside a classroom with eight students of ages varying between twenty and fifty years old, all sat quietly studying their text books.

"Okay, you can leave them to me now. What time does the class finish?"

"7.30."

"Will you still be around? Perhaps we could go for a quick drink."

The invitation caught Molly off-guard, and Danny, picking up on it quickly, added, *"If you want to, that is."*

"No, no. Sure, that would be nice."

"Great, I'll see you at the entrance when I've finished, then."

Danny entered the class without watching her leave.

"Good evening, ladies and gentlemen. My name is Danny and I'm deaf. For those of you who can speak, I'm able to lip-read you perfectly," he both signed and spoke. He noticed more than one face light up with a mixture of relief and joy.

He then repeated his introduction using only sign, then repeated it several times.

He quickly remembered his first class in the local centre with his mother and started the class by getting the students to finger-spell their names and the names of the others in the class.

A large poster with the alphabet was pinned up next to the blackboard.

He was pleased to note that his group seemed like a nice bunch of people, and they could all, without exception, pick up what was taught relatively easily. He was also surprised to discover that he was genuinely enjoying himself. He had become so used to using his skills to make a living or keeping his parents and friends happy, that he found it refreshing and gratifying to feel like he was being instrumental in helping people improve their lives. These students were highly motivated, driven by the knowledge that learning sign language was as important to them as breathing.

In fact, he became so wrapped up in the class that he didn't pay attention to the clock, and it was only when one of the students, a young man who could still use his spoken voice, told him that it was 7.40pm that Molly flashed into his head and he became panic-stricken.

He quickly wrapped up the class and was surprised to see most of the students were saying good night and thank you using sign language.

As he rubbed his diagrams off the blackboard with such a speed that his hand became a blur, he almost sensed Molly standing at the door. She wore a simple floral printed dress, flat shoes, and held her coat folded over one arm. His heart missed a few beats.

"Hello," she signed when their eyes met.

"Sorry, lost track of time."

"No problem. I've been watching you. You certainly have a natural talent for teaching."

"I bet you say that to all your teachers. I had fun, though. How long have you been standing there?"

"Enough time to see how your students respond to you."

"Flattery will get you everywhere. Shall we go?"

"Are you always so humble?"

"Only on Fridays. The rest of the week I wholly deserve every kind of praise or accolade thrown my way."

"I'll have to remember that."

They crossed the road to the Lame Duck, a pub right opposite the day centre, and almost got hit by a motorbike as neither had been able to hear it approach.

Still a little shaken, Molly placed her hand on Danny's arm, signalling him to stop and face her.

"Did you know that three of our students have been run over in the last three years? Thankfully, none were seriously injured; just broken bones and bruises."

"You should try to get the town hall to create a new traffic sign like 'SLOW DOWN. DEAF PEOPLE CROSSING'."

"Now that's actually a good idea."

They found the pub quite busy, which was to be expected on a Friday evening. When they approached the bar, Danny was surprised to see that Molly and the barman exchanged greetings in sign language.

96

"*He can sign?*" asked Danny.

"*No, I just taught him the basics: 'Hello'. 'How are you?' and 'Fine, thanks'.*"

Danny didn't tell Molly that, in fact, the barman had signed "*Hello, how are you?*" but his lips had said, "You're looking just as fuckable as ever."

He did get a certain satisfaction by then ordering the drinks in a normal speaking voice with a big wink, then watching the barman's face turn an ashen-grey.

"No harm meant, mate, just a little fun."

"I won't tell her if you promise a little more respect in the future."

"Sure, mate. These drinks are on the house."

When they were sitting at a corner table, Molly asked what they had spoken about.

"*Just a bit of friendly banter; you know, football, the shitty weather.*"

"*Declan told me you were a good lip-reader, but I have to say I'm impressed. I wouldn't even take you for being deaf. I'm sure I'm not alone.*"

"*It happens quite often, I suppose.*"

"*It must be amazing to know exactly what people are saying and to be able to have a normal spoken voice.*"

"*It has its ups and downs.*"

"*Oh, I forgot, it's humble Friday.*"

"*No, I mean it. Take this pub, for example. When I look around, I can read practically everything that people are saying, except for the people with their backs to me, of course, but even then I have a good idea just by reading the people they're talking with. It's all about context.*"

"*So what's wrong with that?*"

"*Think about it. A dozen not very interesting conversations and some of them positively banal, all coming at me at once.*"

"*I think it's brilliant. What are they all talking about, then?*"

"*Do you really want to know?*"

Molly lifted her eyebrows to signal "*Please.*"

"*What everybody is talking about?*"

Molly raised her eyebrows again, this time as a way of confirmation.

Danny started to relay some of the conversations around the pub. Molly's expressions while he signed went from shock to wonderment.

"*Wow, I've sat here many a time wondering what all these people were talking about and you're right, most of it seems to be absolute rubbish.*"

"*One thing you might be interested in knowing, though.*"

"*What?*"

"*At least three people in this pub have said what a beautiful woman you are.*"

Molly blushed. "*Now you're making fun of me.*"

"*Well, their appreciation of your beauty wasn't always phrased using politically correct language, but I promise you it's true.*"

"*Yeah, sure.*"

"*Now look who's the humble one. But I have to agree with them one hundred percent. You're an extremely beautiful woman.*"

"*Very smooth, Danny. Very smooth.*"

"*I mean it.*"

Molly laughed.

"*What's so funny?*"

"*Is this a line you've used before? I've got the feeling it is. Remember, I saw your conversation with Declan at the library. You were talking about one of your sexual conquests, and it wasn't exactly a fairy-tale romance you were describing.*"

She had unconsciously placed her hand on his when she signed. It was only a moment, a few seconds, but Danny was sure she had captured his reaction in his eyes. She withdrew it with as much stealth as she could.

"*Ah, yes,*" responded Danny. "*I wanted to talk to you about that.*"

"*You really don't have to defend yourself.*"

"*But I feel I do. I realise that that was probably why you didn't have such a high opinion of me when we first met. Or at least that's the feeling I got with your killer looks. But you have to understand the context of the conversation. I've been helping Declan with the whole meeting girls department. He was asking me for explicit details, and I obliged.*"

Molly was clearly pondering on his justification, then a smile spread across her face, telling Danny she was satisfied.

"I flashed you killer looks?"

"Let's just say I was expecting laser beams to shoot out from your eyes and blow my head off any minute."

They both laughed.

"Talking about Declan," signed Molly, *"I'd really like to thank you for taking him under your wing. I've never seen him happier than in the last few months. He's somehow changed. He's more confident... I don't know how to explain it... he seems stronger, more mature, decisive... more capable about making his own decisions. It's like he's taken his destiny into his own hands for the first time in his life."*

"I have to agree. He's a different man to the one I first met – what? – seven months ago. Wow, seems like a lot longer. But you don't have to thank me. I think you're exaggerating my part in his development."

"Your humble Friday thing is getting a bit boring, Danny."

"No, I mean it. Declan is a capable guy. He just needed a little push in the right direction, to break away from being under the safe and protective skirts of his family. I hope you don't mind me saying that he's literally been Molly-coddled for too long now."

Danny had to finger spell the word 'Molly-coddled' for her to appreciate his clever use of a homonym which kind of got lost in translation.

Molly smiled. *"Perhaps you're right. We did protect him, or rather, do protect him a little too much. We obviously underestimated his potential. Something that you haven't done, and for that I'm grateful."*

"As I said, I really haven't done anything but spend time with him. Declan recognised his own potential."

"Okay, Mr Humble, let's just say that if you hadn't dedicated so much time to him, he might not have been able to do so quite so easily."

"Look, I have to admit that when I was told that I had been assigned to help a deaf student, I wasn't too happy about it. But the moment I met him, I felt guilty for even contemplating the arrangement as being a burden. I consider Declan to be my closest friend. I enjoy every minute I spend with him."

This time, Molly placed her hand on Danny's intentionally, and he responded by flipping his over to gently squeeze hers, then caressing it with his thumb. Their hands being occupied, they sat in silence for a while, enjoying the affectionate contact and the unspoken exchange of warmth. Now each knew where their relationship was going, conscious of the inevitable, and each was pleasantly surprised at just how right it felt.

It was Molly who finally and regretfully withdrew her hand to break the silence. *"So, Danny Valentine-Rocker, tell me all about yourself."*

"What do you want to know?"

"Everything. About your family, about when you went deaf, how you learned to lip-read, girlfriends, everything."

"I don't think we have enough time."

"Just start at the beginning. I have the feeling we have all the time in the world."

Danny smiled and began with his earliest childhood memories. He spoke about his zany mother and her obsession with fame and the famous, about his football-crazy father, and about his friends and school before he started to lose his hearing. At this point, Molly interrupted him.

"Do you remember what sounds sound like?"

"That's an interesting question. I can sort of remember some sounds; the ones that are related to emotions. Well, actually, it's not the sound I remember, but the feeling."

Molly's frown told him he needed to elaborate. He sat in silence for a moment as he searched for an example.

"A dog barking, for example. I can't actually remember the sound, but I do remember how I felt." Encouraged by the fact that Molly's scrunched eyebrows had relaxed a little, he tried another. *"A scream. I can't remember what it sounds like, but I can remember what it feels like... What I felt like. Do you understand what I'm saying? A door slamming is another example. Oh, here's one I've just thought of. Running water. When I'm in the shower, I can remember the sound through what it feels like."*

Molly was now nodding.

"Okay, I know it sounds a little abstract, but it's the only way I can explain it."

"I think you explained it perfectly. Now go on with your story."

Danny resumed his autobiography by recounting his earliest memory of when he first noticed he was losing his hearing, doing his best to explain how he felt, and as he was telling her how he discovered his talent for lip-reading, Molly interrupted him again.

"*Sorry, Danny, but what I can't understand is why you didn't say anything to your parents. I mean, it's the first thing any frightened child would do.*"

"*I know. I know. The truth is, I can't really explain it. I never have been able to explain it. Not even to myself. I suppose I had been such a happy kid, I just had this feeling that if everyone knew, my life would change. Everything would change: my friends, my school. I didn't want anything to be different. **I** didn't want to be different. So, when I realised that by reading people's lips nobody noticed anything different, I could see that nothing had to change and I decided not to say anything. I wasn't sure how long I could get away with it, but I hoped it would be as long as possible.*"

"*It must've been hard on your parents, the fact that you hadn't gone to them with your problem.*"

"*I'm sure it was at first, especially my Mum, but they adapted quickly once they saw that far from having a handicapped son, they had a gifted one.*"

"*If I were your mother, I would have been very hurt that her own son hadn't come to me with something so serious.*"

"*As I said, I'm sure my Mum was very hurt at first. I can remember her tears when the doctor told us I was deaf; but you'd have to meet her to understand why any feelings in that respect were short-lived.*"

Another minute of silence followed as Molly sat digesting Danny's story.

"*Would you like me to go on?*" signed Danny.

"*Yes, please do. It's a crazy but fascinating story.*"

He then told her about learning sign language, at first with his mother, and then his expeditious rise to interpreter's level.

"*So Declan wasn't exaggerating about your precocious achievements?*"

"*I was young when I got my MRSLI qualifications, but I don't know about being the youngest ever.*"

Molly just smiled and gave his hand a quick squeeze.

He went on to tell her about helping his father out by lip-reading football games, and Molly laughed when he told about his mother's insatiable thirst for gossip and how she'd make him lip-read everything and everyone at family parties.

When he told her about his passion for books and what they meant to him, he wasn't surprised to find that Molly enthusiastically mirrored everything he had to say about the subject, and their conversation quickly digressed to talk about literature, which only came to an end when Molly signed that she had to go to the bathroom.

"*I'll get us another drink, then,*" Danny signed.

When Molly returned, she raised a question she had probably thought about in her absence.

"*And girlfriends? Anyone special in your life?*"

"*Until now, no one, but I've got a feeling that that is about to change.*"

He slipped his hand behind her back and drew her close. He held his breath, knowing that this was a defining moment. He had taken a calculated risk that she wasn't going to react negatively to this clear and tangible announcement of his intentions, and only let it out again when she didn't resist and nuzzled up close to him.

Both now knew that things were moving quickly. They hardly knew each other, but it all felt right. It all felt good. Danny brushed an escaped crazy curl behind Molly's ear, and her head turned just enough for their eyes to meet, then their mouths.

Soft lips gently brushed at first, then parted as they melted into a slow and sensual kiss. After a minute or two, softly exploring each other's mouths and savouring the texture and taste of each other's tongues, Molly's hand came up to hold the back of Danny's head, and he reciprocated. Soon they were both pulling the other closer, and the kiss became more passionate, their mouths opening wider and their breathing getting deeper.

They didn't need to hear the guy on the next table telling them to get a room, as they both realised that the corner table at a pub called The Lame Duck was not the most romantic of settings, and reluctantly broke the kiss.

"*Come on. Let's go,*" signed Danny, before grabbing her hand and standing up.

"*Where?*"

"*The Student Complex?*"

"*And Declan?*"

"*What about Declan?*"

"*What if he sees us?*"

"*Then he sees us.*"

Danny studied her face while she deliberated, and she got up. "*You're right. Let's go.*"

The bus ride seemed interminable as they sat side by side under the harsh fluorescent lighting, holding hands. Not even the gloomy yellowy grey faces of their fellow passengers could put out the fuse that had been lit in the pub. Danny's heart was pumping so hard he could feel it beating in his ears. In fact, he was almost sure he could actually hear it. Molly's pheromones filled his nostrils, and he squeezed her hand even harder.

Is this what love feels like? he asked himself.

When they finally reached Owens Park Student Complex, they ran up the six flights of stairs, laughing, each mentally counting off the floors as they went. Puffing and panting, Danny opened the door to the flat, and they saw a light was on in the living room. If Declan was home alone, they knew that they didn't have to worry about any noise, but as Danny's was the first door in the hallway, they were able to just step inside without having to meet anyone. He slid the bolt lock on the inside, and at last they stood facing each other.

They obviously had different ideas about how they wanted to go about this. Danny wanted to move slowly, and pulled Molly towards him gently, and was eager to resume the soft and sensual start of the kiss in the pub; but Molly surprised him by going straight to the way they had finished it, opening her mouth wide and pressing her lips hard against his and thrusting her tongue in to wrap it around his. She pulled his hips closer and he was sure she could feel just how exited he was. They pushed against each other and embraced while they kissed.

Danny was soon aware that Molly was fumbling with his belt buckle, only pausing long enough for him to lift her dress up and off over her head. His excitement and surprise were raised another notch when he discovered Molly wasn't wearing any underwear.

Without breaking their kiss, he kicked off his trainers and then took over the task of removing his jeans. Molly then gently guided him back onto the bed and was quickly on top of him.

"Easy, Molly. Easy," said Danny out loud. "We've got all night." But even if she had seen his lips move, she didn't respond. Now was not the time for signing.

While she moved at an ever-increasing pace, he watched her face, her eyes fixed on his, occasionally closing them for a few seconds and biting her bottom lip. When she lifted both hands to run them through her thick and wild mane, her breasts rose and were the most perfect Danny had ever seen.

Her rhythm was now driving him to the brink of climax, and he was glad to see in her face that she was also close. Her eyelids were now starting to flutter, and her mouth was wide open; then, as he felt her knees grip his sides, he knew they were going to reach the end together. He lifted his hips and felt a surge of pleasure start as a tingle in his toes, then quickly travel up through his body to his head, making it spin. Molly's knees gripped him even more tightly and then her whole body froze, her back arched and she threw her head back.

Danny felt her spasms for a full minute before she flopped forward onto his chest, her face buried in the pillow.

They lay like that for a few minutes, their breathing slowly coming under control, until Molly flipped over to his side, snuggling up to him and settling her head in the crook of his arm. They lay in silence, both aware that signing pillow-talk would break the moment.

Nothing needed saying, anyway. While he stroked her shoulder, he felt a wave of contentment wash through his body. This was it. He felt that everything was all right in his world. This was the happiest he'd ever felt.

***

Molly lay there feeling much the same way as she stroked Danny's chest. Tiny spasms continued to flutter deep inside her. For the first time in her life, she was experiencing emotions that she'd only read about; emotions that she had always felt incapable of feeling, that she had been sure she never would.

***

They made love one more time that night, but this time it was slow and sensual, with no urgency, just the sheer pleasure of moving together, each aware of the warmth of the other's skin, taking in their aroma and the softness of each other's lips.

Sleep came easily to both of them.

Danny was first to wake in the morning, and he looked over to see a mass of dark red curls splayed on the pillow next to him. He brushed a few aside, hoping to find Molly's face in among them, but all he found was more curls. He gave up and, his bed being single, which made lying there without disturbing her too much of a challenge, so he got up, grabbed his clothes and went down the hallway to the living room.

He found Declan at the table with a cup of tea and buried in a book called *Object Orientated Programming.*

"Good morning, Declan. Interesting breakfast reading?" he signed, when Declan finally noticed him and looked up.

"Good morning, Casanova. And who was your lucky victim last night?"

"How do you know I was with someone? Even if we did make any noise, you wouldn't have heard it."

"Your door was locked when I tried it this morning, and that usually means only one thing. Anyway, I thought you were working at Molly's Deaf Centre last night."

Danny thought for a moment how he was going to tell Declan about Molly.

"How can I explain this?"

The fact that Declan's eyebrows suddenly shot up to join his hairline, and his eyes had widened to the size of plates, told him that his friend had just put two and two together and no explanations were necessary.

"So you were... with...? Declan managed to badly sign.

105

Danny nodded and made a face like a five-year-old who knew he had been naughty.

Declan's eyes had now glazed over, as he was clearly processing what this new scenario in his life would mean.

"Danny! If you hurt her..."

"This is different, Declan. I promise. I actually..." – he quickly turned to make sure Molly wasn't standing behind him – *"think I'm in love."*

"Strong words, my friend, and ones I never thought I'd see you sign."

"Well?"

"Well what?"

"What do you think?"

Declan closed his book that had lain abandoned in front of him and placed both hands face down on it as if it were a holy bible.

"I think if Molly deserves anyone in this world, it's you. I think it's fantastic."

"Really?"

Declan removed any doubts Danny could have by getting up from the table and giving him a warm hug, which he, surprised by this spontaneous sign of affection, duly reciprocated. At that moment, Molly came in and, on seeing them, signed, *"Make up your mind which one of the McCrackens you're interested in"*, and promptly joined them, throwing her arms around them both.

A few minutes later, they were all three sat at the table, drinking tea and signing away, when Baggy came in.

"Man, that's what I call keeping the noise down," he said, grabbing a chair, turning it around and straddling it.

"Good morning, Baggy," said Danny. "This is Molly, Declan's sister."

"Ah, the famous Molly. Pleased to meet you at last," he said, raising his voice.

"Baggy, when are you going to realise that it doesn't matter how loud you shout, deaf people can't hear you?"

"Yeah, I know, but I can't help it. Anyway, tell Declan he wasn't exaggerating; she's a babe."

Danny signed to Molly that Baggy was pleased to meet her.

"What are you doing up this early on a Saturday morning anyway, Baggy?"

"I haven't been to bed yet. Dropped about five 'e's last night. I'm totally shagged and about to go and crash. By the way, you got a letter from your Mum. Did Declan give it to you?"

Danny looked at Declan and signed, *"You have a letter from my Mum?"*

Declan signed an effusive, *"Oh, no. Sorry, that's what I came to your room for this morning,"* and handed him a folded envelope that he had retrieved from his back pocket.

One major disadvantage of being a deaf person at that time was that the telephone was a superfluous object in their lives, and whenever Danny wanted to speak to his parents, or vice versa, the only way was either in person or by post.

"It can't be anything urgent or she'd have called the university," Danny signed and said for Baggy's sake.

He took the envelope with his mother's familiar flamboyant handwriting.

Declan signed, *"You know what? We should set up an email account at the library. That way we wouldn't have to rely on letters. We could communicate almost instantly over the internet."*

"What's an email?" signed Molly.

Declan went into a detailed explanation which was dotted with all kinds of technical terms such as SMTP Protocols, Pop3 and DNS, which left Molly looking totally baffled.

"If you think I can understand any of that, Declan," she signed.

"Pop what?" said Baggy, trying to follow Danny's interpreting.

Declan looked at their puzzled faces. *"It was difficult for me to explain that to you guys in sign. So many meaningless acronyms and technical jargon. Let me try again."*

"Please do," signed Danny. His letter was still unopened. He needed both hands to sign.

"In simple terms, you can write a message and it's sent through the internet to anybody who has access to internet. Email means electronic mail. If I wrote a message to you, you could get it almost instantly."

Molly sat pondering this information for a moment, then her face lit up like a shop window at Christmas.

"*Wow! Declan, why didn't you tell me about this before? I mean. can't you see what this means for every deaf person in the world that can read and write? This is a major development that could improve the lives of millions.*"

Baggy was getting tired of sitting around watching these people waving their arms around, and more so now that Danny was no longer relaying the conversation, as he was busy reading his mother's letter. He saluted them all with a "Good night all" and shuffled off down the hall to his room.

Molly was about to continue her enthusiastic observations about what email meant to the deaf world when she noticed that, while reading, Danny's expression had changed from one of concentration to one of major distress.

She touched his arm to get his attention.

"*Danny? What's wrong?*"

He put the letter on the table, cupped his face in both hands and sat for a few seconds kneading his eyes with the tips of his fingers.

Molly touched his arm again gently. "*Danny? What does the letter say?*"

"*It's my grandmother, my Mum's mother. She died almost a week ago. Apparently, she had been out for her morning walk with her dog in the forest near her house as she had always done, and she had a heart attack. No one found her until the early afternoon, but it was too late. They only found her because her dog, which had remained by her side, was howling like a wolf.*"

"*Oh, Danny, I'm so sorry.*" She got up and hugged him.

Declan also got up and followed suit. All three gripped each other in silence.

***

Mei li Higginbottom *née* Wong had been pronounced dead on arrival at Barnet General Hospital at about the same time that Suzie had received the news of her mother's death from a neighbour who had been found through the address on the dog's collar.

She drove to the hospital like a mad woman possessed, tears streaming down her face, feeling like she had had her stomach ripped out.

When she got there, she was asked to go directly to the morgue to identify her mother.

They lifted the sheet. The ashen-coloured Oriental woman with hollow cheeks was a far cry from the vivacious woman she had seen only a few days before when she had helped her with her groceries. She looked smaller and older. Her hair that had always been a glossy black, even in old age, was now a dull mass of dark grey and wiry fibres.

Leaning forward, she kissed a cold and flaccid cheek and silently wished her a safe journey to wherever. One of her tears fell and splashed on her mother's forehead.

Since her father had died in the car accident, she had gotten a lot closer to her mother, immediately filling the vacuum left by her father's absence. Even before the accident, her mother didn't have many close friends and, although Suzie had asked her to move in with her and Johnny, she had preferred to stay in the family house.

She wasn't short of money, as her father had always been a careful saver and had managed to pay off the mortgage in its entirety. He had also maintained a life insurance policy that paid her a lump sum on his death. Added to all that, the gas company that owned the truck that had demolished her husband's car had also settled for a considerable amount of money as compensation in an out-of-court settlement.

Not happy about her mother living alone and thinking that she would enjoy the company, Suzie bought her a Golden Labrador puppy, which was promptly named Suzie Wong and was to become her mother's passion.

Suzie decided not to call Danny's university with the news as she didn't want to cause him any distress. Besides, it wasn't as if her mother was dying and it was a matter of getting Danny to her deathbed on time.

She arranged a simple funeral attended by her, Johnny and a few neighbours, installed Suzie Wong in her house and wrote to Danny.

Her letter explained the circumstances of his grandmother's death and why she hadn't contacted the university. The last part of the letter informed him that his grandmother had left him £200,000 in her last will and testament and that she would come up to Manchester to visit him as soon as she could.

CHAPTER 13

It was Danny who finally broke the hug to sign that he was fine and that perhaps he needed a little time alone.

"*No way,*" signed Declan. "*What you need is a bit of fun.*"

"*Hey, look!*" exclaimed Molly, pointing to the huge window. "*The sun is shining. Let's all do something special today. In your grandmother's memory.*"

"*That sounds like a great idea,*" responded Declan; then, after a pause, added, "*unless you two want to be alone.*"

Danny looked at Molly, trying to read if that was what she would prefer, but all he could detect was an excited anticipation of his decision. Besides, he liked the idea of spending time with them together.

"*No, let's all three of us do something. That's a great idea. This might be one of the only two days of the year that the sun comes out in Manchester. We should make the most of it.*"

They went to Gaffs and picked up some ready-made chicken sandwiches and a couple of bottles of red wine and headed for Lyme Park, a magnificent expanse of parkland just a short bus ride away in Didsley, Stockport.

When they arrived, it was soon apparent that half the population of Manchester had also decided to take advantage of the sun's rare appearance, and they joined throngs of people heading through the gates. They passed the magnificent stately home and looked for a nice spot to place their blanket in one of the few remaining patches of green among the hundreds of fellow picnickers, kids playing football, bicycles and dogs.

Once they had claimed their territory and established its boundaries with their blanket and bags, Danny lay on his back and watched the odd isolated white fluffy cloud travel across a deep blue sky, its shape morphing from resembling New Zealand one moment to a rabbit the next. The warmth of the sun felt good as it caressed his face.

A cacophony of mayhem reigned all around them, but they were a silent island where peace and tranquillity prevailed, and, staring up at the sky, Danny could just as well have been alone in Lyme Park.

His thoughts wandered to his grandmother. It seemed almost surreal to think that he would never see her again. He tried to recall her voice that he hadn't heard since he was about nine years old. Although, in theory, lip-reading her in English should have been easier than in Mandarin, her pronunciation was so bad that Danny found he could read her better in her native language.

Their communication became even more complicated because, as he lost his hearing, he realised it was increasingly more difficult to speak to her in Mandarin as he had always done. Thanks to its different tones and intonations, it was a language that he needed to hear himself speak to be sure he could be understood, so she'd speak to him in Mandarin and he'd speak to her in English.

He would miss her a lot. He would miss her great food, her sometimes childish and somewhat simple sense of humour, and he'd miss her doses of dubious Chinese philosophy that she would always adapt to suit any occasion or circumstance. They were so cryptic and abstract that it wasn't worth trying to decipher or asking her to elaborate. They made his father's football analogies seem perfectly rational. Danny couldn't help smiling to himself as he tried to remember some of her most classic gems, such as:

"If you eat fish every day, you must expect to swallow a bone or two," or, "If your hands are hot, do not put them near the fire."

His thoughts switched to the money his grandmother had left him: £200,000!

That was a lot of money by anyone's standards. He had no idea that she had that much money.

What was he going to do with it? He certainly didn't need that much money. If he put it in a Building Society account, he should be able to get quite a good interest rate.

He lifted his head, rested his weight on his elbows and saw Declan and Molly in an animated conversation about Declan's passion for technology, and Molly was encouraging him to take up a career as a computer programmer. His friend's eyes were alive, and Molly's were proud and happy. Her hair was glowing in the sun, a sort of incandescent mass of flaming wild curls. Almost as if his grandmother was talking to him from the afterlife, one of her sayings popped into his head: "Girls with red hair put fire in your belly."

He sat up and thought, 'Wow that's one that actually makes sense'. A shudder ran up his spine and his hairs stood on end as he wondered if his grandmother's observation hadn't been some sort of supernatural premonition.

He turned back in to Declan and Molly's conversation, watching them sign enthusiastically about Declan's future. An overwhelming feeling of happiness came over him.

He was in love with his best friend's sister.

***

Molly noticed Danny watching them and her eyes connected with his. She reached over and stroked his arm tenderly. She had only known him for less than twenty-four hours, yet, as she examined his blue eyes, she felt as if she'd been looking into them for a lifetime. She felt safe and secure, as if she had just wrapped her whole life in a warm blanket; but above all, for the first time in her life, she felt like a woman.

Observing Declan pouring himself some wine into a plastic cup, she was amazed at how much he'd changed in such a short time. She'd never seen him so confident, so sure of his own capabilities and with dreams and goals that he really felt he could achieve.

During his last visit to their parents, her mother had taken her aside and asked if her brother had been taking drugs. She hardly recognised her own son.

***

The cheap red wine in plastic cups was making all three of them feel more relaxed, and they were soon talking about their respective short-term plans. Molly spoke about how she'd recently joined a new charity for the deaf that had a clear international agenda. With over two hundred million deaf people in the world, the charity aimed to set up sign language schools and professional training in those parts of the world that had no national or local government organisations that supported the deaf. They would also provide hearing aids and cochlear implants to the most impoverished deaf who qualified.

She expressed her eagerness to take advantage of Declan's information about new technologies such as email and internet.

Danny expressed his interest in contributing his services to the charity on a voluntary basis, and he also told them that, if he could find the time, he'd like to learn American Sign Language, with the aim of obtaining the ASL National Interpreters Certification. It had always bothered him that there was no global sign language, and he wanted to be able to communicate with as many people in the world as he could.

Declan spoke about taking a Computer Sciences degree at the University of Manchester Institute of Science and Technology (UMIST), probably one of Europe's most prestigious. He was talking enthusiastically about joining IBM or Microsoft as a junior programmer.

While on the subject of technology and computers, Danny told them about the money his grandmother had left him and how perhaps he'd like to invest some of it by buying technology stocks that Declan could recommend to him.

By the time they decided to have some lunch, a small crowd of girls and boys had surrounded their blanket, fascinated by the three adults talking to each other with their hands and arms.

"What are you doing?" asked a little girl of about seven, her face covered in chocolate.

Fortunately, she was in Danny's line of vision and he was able to read her.

"We're talking."

"I can't hear you."

An older boy in a Manchester United football shirt and with a big round face chimed in, "They're deaf, you daft twat. That's how they talk. With their hands."

She stood silently for a while, watching Danny relay the conversation to Molly and Declan.

"You're not deaf, are you? You can hear me."

"I am, but I can read your lips."

"My lips?"

"If I watch your lips move, I can understand everything you say."

"What am I saying now, then?" said the older boy, and he mimed something with his lips.

"I'm not going to repeat that in front of other young children," said Danny.

"You see? He can't read lips."

"Let's just say you shouldn't go around telling strangers to get friendly with farmyard animals."

The boy stood staring for a moment, apparently lost for words, mimed or otherwise.

Everybody laughed; then he turned and ran.

"Okay, boys and girls, the show's over. Off you go!" said Danny, making shooing gestures, to which the band of children quickly responded by running off, laughing.

The sun was still quite high in the sky when they packed up to leave, even though it was 8pm. They'd finished off all the wine, sat chatting for a while, then all nodded off to sleep. A park full of noisy families wasn't an issue for them.

Molly decided that she had better get the bus straight home, as she hadn't told her parents that she would be spending the night out and they would surely be worried.

Danny and Declan's bus was a different one and they waited together for Molly's to arrive. A tinge of nervous tension felt by both parts of the newly formed couple as the minutes went by was dispelled by the arrival of the bus. Molly hugged Declan, then Danny, their embrace lingering as both shared the same sensations and thoughts.

Almost twenty-four hours before, they had been virtual strangers, and here they were, feeling like they had known each other all their lives. They broke off signing exactly the same thing at the same time.

"I'll see you next Friday evening at the Deaf Centre."

As Molly boarded the bus, she felt both sad and frustrated that, in the meantime, they wouldn't be able to do something as simple as calling each other beforehand.

The week's wait proved to be interminable, as they had feared. Every waking moment was filled with thoughts of the other. Flashes of them together, their faces, their eyes, their smiles, the touch of their skin and even their smells, reverberated in their minds and produced a strange tingling feeling originating in the pit of their stomachs, spreading throughout their bodies.

They both realised that this was what love felt like; until then only a foreign and romantic concept that they had only read about in books.

As Friday evening approached, Danny was excited, yet an underlying feeling of apprehension put the brakes on him being completely euphoric. What if it was all too good to be true? Perhaps his feelings and expectations just might not be as real as he had imagined.

Molly was obviously feeling much the same, as the moment they saw each other Danny knew that not only his own feelings had been real but, judging by the other's reaction, everything was real. They embraced and kissed as if a year had gone by, and could only tear themselves apart because it was time for Danny to start his class.

The moment it was finished, they practically slammed the door after the last student to leave, who had chosen the wrong time to want to ask Danny for some advice about eyebrow raising.

From then on, Molly spent Friday nights, Saturdays and Sundays with Danny, often including Declan in any plans if he was free. He managed to solve their midweek communications problem by setting up email accounts for them so they could get in touch whenever they wanted. Danny contributed by investing some of his inheritance money in two Macs, one for Molly at the Deaf Centre and one for the Student Complex flat, which turned out to be useful for everyone, especially Declan, who would soon be starting his computer science degree.

Molly's world was totally opened up, both socially and professionally, with the help of Danny's lip-reading and interpreting skills. She had hardly ever been able to participate in conversations with normal-hearing people before. Danny often found himself recruited into meetings with material suppliers for the Deaf Centre or with bureaucratic officials who handled things like funds transfers, shipping or government permits that would allow the charity she collaborated with to plan and carry out its projects both in the UK and abroad.

The Lame Duck became their special place, and they always enjoyed signing with Bob the Landlord, who called them his favourite deaf love birds. Danny taught him to elaborate on just being able to say hello, and he soon had a grasp of basic sign language. He could even serve in BSL, which turned out to be good for business, as the pub not only became popular with students from the Deaf Centre, but also with deaf people from other parts of Manchester. There was a rumour that he was seriously thinking of changing the name to The Deaf Duck.

It didn't take too long for them to add more days to their relationship, despite their busy agendas, and it soon became obvious that the most convenient way to ensure they saw each other often enough was for Molly to move into the Student Complex flat.

She was now part of the family.

James and Baggy also started to pick up basic sign language. Not enough to join in conversations without Danny's help, but enough to have fun with Molly if they found themselves alone with her.

Needless to say, the flat began to look a bit tidier, and Molly contributed in a big way to improving everybody's diet by adding a few green items to the normal shopping list of pasta, ketchup and bread.

Most weekends they practically had the flat to themselves because James was usually playing rugby and Baggy was capable of not appearing at all when he was on one of his three-day benders.

One day, after about three months, Molly told Danny that she would like him to meet her parents. Her mother had been urging her to invite him to the house, as they were anxious to meet the person responsible for Molly's now permanent absence from home, who was also Declan's hero. McCracken family Sunday lunches, which had become few and far between, had turned into the Danny Valentine-Rocker fan club.

On the bus to the McCrackens', Danny felt a little apprehensive. A cloud of guilt hung over him, as he hadn't seen his own parents since they had come up to Manchester just after his grandmother's death. They had come for a couple of days, and Molly joined them for dinner at The French at the Midland Hotel. Danny had decided that he wanted to splash out a bit to mark the occasion.

Suzie loved the retro opulence of the restaurant, but Johnny said he'd have felt more comfortable with a curry and a pint, as he tried to work out what each of the four glasses he had in front of him was for.

Suzie took to Molly immediately, telling her she reminded her of Rita Hayworth in the film *Gilda*, and enjoyed chatting to her in sign language, despite Danny's offer to interpret.

She told her how much she had enjoyed gossiping about people with Danny at family parties and how his lip-reading skills were incredibly entertaining. At this, she urged Danny to relay what was being said by a couple at the next table.

"Mum, how many times have I told you, I'm not a circus act," he said in normal speech.

"Oh, come on, Danny, just a morsel."

Sighing, he tuned in to the couple's conversation and relayed in sign what they were saying.

"*Don't look now, but the deaf people on the next table are all staring at us.*"

"*Haven't they got anything better to do? The oriental-looking one looks like some kind of mad villain from a* Star Trek *episode.*"

"*Mad villain? I'll give her mad villain!*" signed an indignant Suzie, about to stand up.

"*Mum, don't you dare! You asked me to tell you what they were saying. You'll never learn, will you?*"

"*Yes, well, somebody should tell her that blue and green should never be seen,*" signed Suzie, gesturing to the woman's outfit.

Danny winked at Molly, and she instantly captured that he had invented the whole conversation and she couldn't help but laugh out loud. Danny would have loved more than anything to have been able to hear her laugh. It was the only vocal sound that came out of her mouth.

Suzie was anything but naïve, and she quickly picked up on what was going on and joined in the laughter. Johnny just sat through it all, oblivious of everything but the huge menu. His only contribution was to moan about not being able to decide between the tortellini of chicken with wild mushrooms and black truffles or the Cumbrian lamb. He was constantly shaking his head and muttering about how they could charge the equivalent of a week's wages for a bit of fish.

Danny couldn't help smiling to himself, remembering his parents' stay. The next day he had signed all the necessary legal documents that made him the legitimate owner of his grandmother's inheritance and once again endured the emotional farewell scene with them as they headed off back down the M6 towards London.

CHAPTER 14

As the bus approached the stop, Molly squeezed his hand, signalling that they had arrived. Declan gave him a supportive pat on the back as they walked along a quiet, tree-lined street with neat, hedge-fronted gardens dotted with roses and smiling gnomes.

The McCrackens' house was a modest semi-detached in Chorlton, about four miles from Manchester city centre. Maggie McCracken was waiting on the doorstep and hugged her children effusively; then, with a warm smile, she shook Danny's hand and gave him a peck on the cheek.

She signed, "*Pleased to meet you at last, Danny.*"

"*Mum!*" Molly signed dramatically. "*Don't forget that Danny can lip-read. You can speak to him normally.*"

"*Yes, I know, dear. When I've got something I want to say to Danny privately, I'll speak to him normally.*"

Danny laughed politely, but wondered what she could possibly want to talk about privately.

Seeing Maggie, he couldn't help feeling uncomfortable or even a little uneasy, as she looked exactly like the woman he was in love with; the same dark red mass of wild curls, the same green eyes. She even had the same dimple on her right cheek when she smiled.

He was just trying to digest this uncanny likeness and the shock to his working senses when Molly and Declan's father came down the stairs with his hand outstretched.

It was Declan, twenty years older. The same nose, the same red hair, and those unmistakable leaf-green eyes.

Now he was totally disconcerted and thrown off-balance. What were the odds that a couple could have identical deaf twins, one looking exactly like the mother and the other, the father?

Declan must have caught Danny double-taking, as he patted him on the back and signed, "*I see you've spotted the family resemblance.*"

Danny shook Declan's 'other twin's' hand and simultaneously said in a normal voice and signed, "I think this family should offer itself to some sort of scientific research on genetic programming. I've never seen anything like it."

They all laughed.

"Yes, you could say we're a bit of an anomaly visually speaking and otherwise. Please, call me Dennis."

Danny couldn't help thinking Molly and Maggie, Declan and Dennis.

Even their names begin with the same letter.

It was the first time he had needed to lip-read either of Molly's parents' spoken voice and he immediately noticed a change in the vowel formations due to the Scottish accent. It took him a little while to adapt but he managed it in the end.

Maggie signed that they should all go straight through to the dining room as lunch was about ready to serve.

They sat Danny at the head of the table, and Maggie proceeded to serve enough roast beef, potatoes and assorted vegetables to feed the whole of Greater Manchester. It had been a long time since he had Sunday roast and it made him feel a bit homesick.

For the most part silence reigned as everybody ate their meal. It was quite impractical in the McCracken household to eat and chat at the same time. Danny couldn't help but smile when he observed father and son devour half a cow and two tonnes of vegetables without lifting their heads once and without any visible signs of any chewing activity. It reminded Danny once again of a snake's digestive process. Maggie caught his eye and made a "What do you want me to say?" apologetic expression. They both laughed.

"*What's so funny?*" signed Declan, with knife and fork still in his hands.

"*Just keep eating and I'll tell you later,*" signed Danny.

When the dishes had been cleared away, Maggie made a pot of tea.

"So, Danny, not wanting to sound like a father sounding out his daughter's boyfriend prospects for the future, Molly tells me you're studying English lit and political science. Any idea what you want to do when you finish university?" said Dennis in a spoken voice.

"Not really. I may go into journalism. I'm not sure. I can always make a good living as a sign language interpreter, though. Once I've got my ASL certification, I could pretty much name my price," said Danny, while simultaneously interpreting for Molly and Declan.

"Ah, of course, of course. That'd make sense, but would you go back to London?"

Danny looked at Molly. He wasn't sure what would be the best answer.

"*Stop giving him the third-degree, Daddy!*" Molly signed emphatically.

"*Just making conversation, Molly,*" he signed. It was the first time Danny had seen him sign, and it confirmed what he had been told about Dennis' limited signing capability.

"I haven't thought about it, to tell you the truth."

"All in good time, right?"

Danny nodded and smiled. Molly's face told him she was happy with his answer.

"I must say I'm impressed by the way you can lip-read, interpret and speak all at the same time. Extraordinary!"

"*Thanks,*" he signed.

"You see, this is a real luxury for me. As you can see, I'm not the greatest signer in the world, and to be able to sit down with my family and speak to my children in my own voice is fantastic. Don't get me wrong, Maggie has always done a fine job relaying for me when I've got stuck, but I see this as an extraordinary opportunity."

Molly's face lit up with pride.

"I was wondering if you could do me a favour."

"Of course."

"I'd like to speak to them now about their lives, their plans and all that stuff I normally struggle with to express myself. In the past, as I said, I've always had Maggie to help me out with more complex stuff I've wanted to talk to them about. But, although she's very good, I'd really like to take advantage of this occasion."

He took a moment to glance quickly at Maggie, as if looking for her silent approval and to make sure she wasn't taking offence. His wife's smile was enough to see that she knew exactly where he was coming from. Danny also picked up on this unspoken exchange with some relief.

"If it's too much trouble, not to worry."

"Sure, it's not a problem. I do it every day. I'd love to help." As he relayed this petition to Molly and Declan, they both nodded, and their faces beamed in anticipation. They, too, would love to 'hear' their father.

The conversation between Dennis and his family was soon flowing. He was able to discuss all kinds of topics with Molly and Declan and he was especially interested in their respective projects and plans. He listened carefully as Danny did his best to relay their excitement and enthusiasm and responded effusively with his advice and encouragement.

When he was telling them just how proud he was of both of them and how sorry he was that his poor signing hadn't allowed him to be more supportive when they were growing up, his voice was breaking up and his eyes welled with tears. Molly reached out for his hand and squeezed it, and Maggie came around the table to hug him.

Once he had regained his composure, the conversation turned to more general issues like politics and world events, like the Barcelona Olympics, the Rodney King riots in Los Angeles, and the possibility of Nelson Mandela ever becoming President of South Africa.

Everyone had something to say or sign and, for a moment, the McCracken family table seemed more like a stock market trading floor session than a Sunday afternoon chat.

Once they had resolved the world's problems, Dennis said he had a question that he would like Danny to help him with.

"You weren't born deaf, so I imagine you still think as I do, in English, I mean... normally. Is that right?"

For a second, Danny found himself examining his thoughts just to make sure.

"Yes, that's right."

"So," continued Dennis, once Danny finished relaying the conversation so far to his twin friends, who sat with scrunched-up eyebrows in anticipation of where their father was going with this.

"I'd like to ask my kids how they think. I know they can read normal English, so to speak, but how do people born deaf think? What goes through their heads when they think about even the most mundane things like they're tired or the things they have to do or about what they're doing?"

Molly and Declan exchanged glances, as if telepathically discussing how to answer.

Molly signed that she thought in sign language, and Declan agreed with his sister.

They thought in the same way as they signed.

Dennis sat there with a puzzled expression. Somehow he had expected a more complex or elaborate answer.

"You have to understand, Dennis, that Sign is their language, just like yours is English. You think in English, they think in Sign."

Feeling that Dennis perhaps needed more information, Danny went on to explain that for any human's development, for the brain to establish essential cognitive infrastructure, it was fundamental for children to grasp language, any language, be it English, Chinese or Sign. "They say that at around nine months old is the pivotal language phase, and the learning curve usually concludes somewhere between the ages of two and three years old. For any person to develop a normal level of intellect, he or she needs language in order to analyse, rationalise and act upon information they're receiving. They need language for abstract thinking and understanding concepts."

"Makes sense," said Dennis.

"According to research, sign language development happens in exactly the same parts of the brain as normal language development, which was a surprise, as it was originally thought that sign was developed in the parts of the brain associated with visual processing. As it happens, in the case of language development, a deaf-born baby will be able to communicate way before a normal-hearing baby, as it will be able to express basic things with Sign quite prematurely. Whereas the normal-hearing baby won't before he finds his voice and is able to vocalise."

Maggie was nodding and smiling.

"I see you know your stuff," said Dennis.

"I once had to interpret at an international conference on speech and language development, and I guess a lot of it stuck, as I found it particularly fascinating."

Declan signed to his father to let Danny continue.

"So, to answer your question, deaf-born people think in their language – Sign. It's as simple as that."

"Wow. So what happens if a deaf-born child doesn't learn Sign?"

"Then he'll surely be somewhat mentally retarded, as would a normal-hearing child who doesn't receive language stimulation during that crucial period."

"Makes you think, doesn't it?" said Dennis somewhat fittingly.

"Now that we're on the subject, I have a question for you, Dennis."

"Shoot."

"When a child is born deaf to deaf parents who sign, he'll learn sign language naturally, as any baby would learn normal speech. In fact, these babies have been known to make their first signs at only a few months. You're both hearing parents; how did you help Molly and Declan develop sign?"

Maggie answered for him. "When the twins were about a month old, we started to notice they weren't responding to any noises like music, our own voices, clapping, for example. Doors could bang, people could shout, but nothing would wake them while they slept. Dennis even bought a tuning fork, and we really started to worry when neither baby reacted to it when they should have been turning their heads towards the sound. We consulted our paediatrician, tests with an audiologist were set up, and our biggest fears were confirmed. As you can imagine, this was devastating. Our perfect world had been turned upside-down in an instant."

"Not to mention all the videos and music tapes we had carefully prepared to stimulate them into being two future Einsteins," intervened Dennis with a laugh and a wink.

"We can joke about it now," continued Maggie, after giving her husband a playful slap on the hand, "but at the time I cried for days on end. I did some investigation and found a local support group for parents of deaf or hard of hearing children, and they helped us sign up for a sign language course locally. We took it in turns to go to classes and, although Dennis struggled a bit, we were soon only communicating with the twins in Sign. Molly actually started signing back to us before she was one. She first made the sign for 'Mummy' and then 'bottle', then signs for 'milk' and 'more' quickly followed. I can remember being really excited and quickly got her signing different animals."

Molly helped her mother's account by signing 'duck', 'cat' and 'dog.'

"Thank you for the demonstration, dear. Anyway, Declan took a lot longer than Molly, and I have to say we were getting a bit worried as his sister was already starting to put whole sentences together. In fact, she was even signing to Declan; then, one day, it happened out of the blue."

"His first sign was to tell us he was hungry," said Dennis.

"His second sign was 'more'."

They all laughed. "Why am I not surprised?" asked Danny.

Declan grabbed a piece of cake, stuffed it into his mouth, and swallowed it whole.

"*That's my boy,*" signed Dennis, not calling on Danny to relay for an instant.

Declan treated them all to a big chocolate-covered toothy grin.

"Anyway," continued Maggie, speaking, "we were lucky enough to find a nursery reasonably close by that was pioneering 'nursery education for deaf children' with trained BSL teachers, and that's more or less how we managed it."

"That's fantastic. I must say, you couldn't have done a better job, and to have found a BSL nursery was a godsend," said Danny, who was now thinking about his own aversion to going to a special school for the deaf when he lost his hearing. He stopped signing the conversation to Molly and Declan for a moment while he remembered.

Maggie picked up on his pause and signed that they should all revert to talking in Sign, as Danny must be exhausted. She apologised for exploiting his talents when they could all comfortably talk in Sign. Dennis would just have to make an effort to follow.

"*I'm fine, really, it's no problem,*" he signed.

Dennis shook his hand, congratulated him, and signed, "*Extraordinary, Danny. I'm telling you, whatever you choose to do in life, I'm sure you'll go far.*"

The whole family clapped, and Danny blushed. Molly came around behind him and threw her arms around his neck and kissed the top of his head.

Later, when it was time to leave, Danny hugged Dennis and Maggie on the doorstep.

Dennis thanked him once again for relaying his words to his children, told him not to be a stranger and to come back soon. Maggie had tears in her eyes and pulled him away to say in spoken language that she was happy that her children had such a wonderful person in their lives; then, changing her tone to one of warning, that he had better look after Molly and never to hurt her or he would hear from her.

CHAPTER 15

Three men dressed in the same plain but well-cut suits sat around a huge glass table that could have easily accommodated ten. The only other furniture in the room were the deep red Persian rug on which the table sat and an enormous TV fixed high up on the wall and which was now the focus of their attention.

The usually muddy brown river Thames glistened silver under the morning sunshine outside the four floor-to-ceiling Gothic-shaped windows that lined one wall.

"I've called you in because I want to show you something extremely interesting," said Simon Grant Smith, Operations Director of the Monitoring and Surveillance section of MI6. He pointed a remote control to the TV and started the video.

They sat watching a university professor giving a lecture on *Beowulf*. After a few minutes, the elder of the group took off his gold-rimmed glasses and lent back in his seat.

"Simon, are you giving us a refresher course on Anglo-Saxon medieval poetry, or is there any other reason for getting us in here to watch this gem of TV entertainment?"

"David, I wonder sometimes how you ever became the section's top analyst. Look carefully at the guy doing the sign language interpretation."

They then focused their attention on the young man to the right of the professor, relaying various questions about how an anonymous Anglo-Saxon poet somewhere between the eighth and the eleventh centuries described Danish pagan society and Germanic warrior traditions with clear Christian undertones.

"*The question is,*" relayed Danny, "*although the pagan Beowulf's own beliefs are not expressed explicitly, he is described as offering prayers to a higher power with expressions like 'Father Almighty' or*

'Wielder of all'. Was the author depicting his hero as some sort of Christian ur-hero?"

"He's good," said Martin White, the youngest of the group and the only one who didn't have a double-barrel name.

"Good? He's better than good. He's brilliant," Simon exclaimed, and, noticing his two colleagues simultaneously raise their eyebrows, quickly added his motive for awarding such an accolade.

"He's deaf," he explained.

They all continued to watch Danny in silence for a few minutes, each man needing time to observe him through a different perspective to first assimilate, then appreciate the skills that impressed their director so much.

David was the first to break the reverie. "Now that's what I call impressive."

"So, he's lip-reading and signing at the same time? And not any old trivial conversation, at that," added Martin.

"Precisely. Think about how useful he could be to the section. He could lip-read everything from surveillance videos to actual political, diplomatic and economic summits."

He paused to observe his colleagues, both still staring at the TV and nodding.

"And you know, Martin, that we've been throwing around the idea of setting up a lip-reading team with this in mind."

"The idea has come up more than once, yes."

"Well, here's the real game changer, so to speak: I've been told this chap can lip-read Mandarin."

"Wow," said Martin. "You've got to be joking?"

"Nope. It seems his grandmother was Chinese and he was able to lip-read her."

"Okay, Simon," said David, "tell us all about him."

Simon took the remote and paused the video so he could have their full attention.

"As you know perfectly well, we have a countrywide network in place that identifies what are considered to be outstanding students in our universities, with the idea to evaluate them as potential recruits for the Secret Service."

They all nodded.

"Well, this youngster, Danny Valentine-Rocker, who's studying English Literature and Political Science at Manchester University, has been picked up by our radar."

"Danny Valentine-Rocker. What a name!" interrupted Martin enthusiastically.

"Sounds like some kind of film star."

"Quite," said Simon, visibly annoyed by his young subordinate's attention to trivialities.

"As I was saying, his background was routinely investigated, as is the procedure when a potential candidate comes to our attention, and it soon became obvious that we had an interesting case on our hands."

David Taylor-Browne sat back in his chair, interlocking his fingers behind his head, his elbows flayed open. "What was it that set the alarm bells ringing?"

"I'll come to that in a moment. Danny Valentine-Rocker was born in 1972 in London, the only child to Susan Higginbottom and Jonathan Valentine-Rocker, a sports journalist with the *Daily Sun* newspaper. Now here's a key fact. He wasn't born deaf. At the age of ten, as a result of some routine hearing tests, it was discovered that he had lost his hearing."

"What do you mean, it was discovered that he lost his hearing? His parents hadn't noticed that their child was deaf?" asked David incredulously.

"Now that's precisely where this case becomes interesting. The boy, for reasons only known to himself, noticed he was losing his hearing when, according to the report, he was about eight and decided not to tell his parents. It seems he found he had a natural talent for lip-reading and, with practice, he was able to carry on with his normal life for two years without anybody noticing, not even his loving parents. Until one day, on the recommendation of an assiduous music teacher at his school, his hearing was tested and his secret was out."

"Extraordinary," said Martin, shaking his head. "He would have to have been an extremely gifted lip-reader to have gotten away with it."

"Apart from this obvious skill, what really helped him get away with it was his capacity to control his spoken voice without being able to hear himself."

"So where does sign language come into play?"

"It was a safeguard just in case he should lose this control over his voice."

"Makes sense," remarked David.

"This is precisely where our candidate's extraordinary talents make him an even more interesting prospect. He enrolled in BSL classes at eleven years old, and he was so good at it that he progressed to be a certified interpreter by the time he was seventeen. The youngest on record.

Before going to university, he made himself a decent living in his free time as a BSL interpreter in hospitals, prisons, universities, conferences, courts and the like. Now you should consider that he's deaf to really appreciate just how good he is. He has to lip-read and relay in sign language simultaneously, exactly as we've seen him on this video."

"Incredible," said Martin, staring at the frozen image of Danny on the screen. "And Mandarin? Where does that come into the picture?"

"As I mentioned before, his maternal grandmother, Mei Li Wong, was Chinese. The full details are in these files that I'll give to you, but basically he had always spoken to her in Mandarin before he became deaf and was able to lip-read her after. That's all we've managed to find out."

"So, apart from him reading English lit and PS, what are his current circumstances?" asked David.

"Again, it's all in the file, but as we've seen in the video, he collaborates with Manchester University as a sign interpreter. He still does the odd job here and there for the legal system or medical conferences, but currently spends any spare time he has as a volunteer at the Manchester Deaf Centre teaching sign language."

"A busy boy indeed," observed Martin. "Does he get time to eat and sleep?"

"On top of all that, he's just started a course to learn ASL."

"ASL?" inquired David.

"American Sign Language. Very different to BSL or British Sign Language, apparently."

"I thought sign language was sign language anywhere in the world."

"Once again, it's all in the file," continued Simon, "but to put it simply, it's not the case. There are dozens of sign languages, depending on what part of the world you come from."

"Bloody Yanks! If they haven't done a good enough job of destroying the English language, they have to go and develop their own bloody sign language," said David indignantly.

"The point is," continued Simon, "that if Danny obtains an ASL interpreter's certification, his value to the section will increase ten-fold. I've looked into this, and most international conferences and diplomatic events have an ASL interpreter present."

"We want him!" said David, now sitting forward and slapping the table to reinforce his interest. "This guy could be a real asset to the section. Just think what we could do with him. He'll not only be able to lip-read every video we put in front of him. If we could get him into everything from diplomatic receptions through to attending every major international diplomatic event or trade conference in the world, we could literally eavesdrop on any number of conversations that might throw up useful information."

"And if he can really lip-read Mandarin," pondered Martin.

"That's precisely why I've brought you in here to show you this guy. Think about his interpreter qualifications. It'd be an excellent cover. We could get him in to most of these events as an interpreter."

"I think we can start thinking seriously about setting up this new team, Martin. And you can head it up."

"I'm flattered and grateful for your confidence, Simon. I'll put together a White Paper."

"Excellent."

They were all still looking at the paused image of Danny on screen while they spoke.

"So, gentlemen, we all agree that this young man needs to be kept an eye on. When the time is right, I want you, Martin, to make the first contact with him."

"Yes, sir. I'll do so right away."

"And before we adjourn, gentlemen, I think you both should study up on sign language."

David and Martin looked at each other with the same expression of alarm.

"You want us to learn sign language?" asked David.

"No, you imbecile. I just think that two experienced analysts at MI6 should at least know that sign language is not one universal language."

CHAPTER 16

Molly adjusted Danny's tie and stood back to evaluate her effort to make him look respectable. The dark blue suit they had bought together for her charity fundraising dinner made him look strangely out of place in the small, shabby student complex bedroom.

As she studied him, she felt dizzy, as if she were drunk with happiness. She physically shook her red curls as she fought desperately with her defence mechanisms that were trying to kick in. Life couldn't be this good to her. It was only a matter of time before some dark force came along like a tidal wave and swept it all away.

"What's wrong, Molly? You don't like the tie?" Danny had noticed the change of expression in her eyes.

"Nothing. The tie is perfect."

"So why all the head shaking?"

"I was just thinking..." She didn't finish her signing.

"What?"

"Nothing."

"You were thinking about nothing? It's impossible to think about nothing unless you're a practising Zen Buddhist, an amoeba, or an inanimate object."

Molly placed her palms together and, bringing her fingertips to touch the bridge of her nose, she bowed.

"Namaste to you, too," Danny signed, laughing.

The charity event was held in the Barnes Wallis Restaurant at Manchester University, and Danny and Molly mingled with the crowd. Four hundred tickets had been sold at no less than £1,000 each, so there was plenty of glamour on show.

They had been offered glasses of champagne on their arrival and they disposed of them quickly when they realised that communication would be difficult with one hand.

Molly introduced Danny to Jonathan Kenward, the charity's founder, a sandy-haired man in his mid-forties with no distinguishable features. They shook hands firmly.

Something about his warm smile and his eyes made Danny take an instant liking to him.

"So, Danny, I finally get to meet you," he signed and spoke simultaneously. "Molly's told me so much about you and, of course, I'd like to take this opportunity to thank you for all your help with our bureaucratic and logistical issues. The bane of our lives, I can tell you. You'd think that these bloody governments had a policy to make the lives of NGOs as complicated as possible."

"The pleasure is all mine, I can assure you. I think the work you're doing is magnificent," Danny signed.

Jonathan duly continued in just Sign. *"We do our best. It's basically all about education, awareness and support. Education, both abroad and in the UK, is the single and most critical service that determines the life chances of deaf children, you know?"*

"You don't have to sermon Danny, Jonathan. He's on our side," intervened Molly.

"Yes, I am dreadfully sorry; of course he is. It's just that I have to make a very important speech about all this later, so I guess I'm unwittingly using you to rehearse."

"Please go ahead and rehearse all you like. You know, anything I can do to help."

"This fundraiser is vital to our cause, you see. We're in desperate need of funds if we're to achieve even a small percentage of our goals. We're setting up programmes in Africa, India and South-East Asia to train teachers to teach deaf children. Ninety-eight percent of disabled children in developing countries are not in school, and half of our job is to make governments and communities aware that deafness is not only a consequence of poverty, but also a cause."

Jonathan only had to see the look on Molly's face to stop signing at once.

"Oops, there I go again."

"Well, if there's anything more I can do to help, please don't hesitate to get in touch," offered Danny.

"*I don't suppose you've got a couple of million quid tucked away somewhere?*"

"*Not quite, but...*"

"*There is one thing you could help me with, though.*"

Danny later relayed his speech to the hall.

CHAPTER 17

The new term in September 1992 started off quietly enough. Everybody in the student complex flat was soon back in their routines after a busy summer, unaware of the events soon to come.

James had been in Australia on a rugby tour, Baggy had spent his summer working in a bar in Ibiza, and Declan had completed an intensive programming course in preparation for his new degree course at the UMIST.

Molly and Danny had spent two weeks together on the Greek island of Skiathos, before returning to their respective family homes for the duration of the holidays.

Danny, to pander to his mother's thirst for gossip, watched the Olympics on TV with his father and enrolled in an introductory class for ASL. Molly read and prepared training manuals for teachers on one of her charity's projects in Kenya.

Everybody was happy to be back in the land of ketchup, pasta and dirty tea cups.

Due to their busy schedules, the group as a whole rarely coincided but, when they did, it was always fun, with plenty of banter and laughter.

One evening, they all sat around the Formica table drinking lager when Baggy asked Danny to show him how to compliment a deaf woman and ask her out for a drink in sign.

He was soon enthusiastically practising over and over again what Danny had shown him. Molly and Declan were on the floor laughing, and Declan and James laughed along with them, not knowing that what Declan was actually signing was, "*Hello, pig face. Would you like to come out for some swill?*"

"When exactly are you thinking of using that line, you dozy twat?" asked James.

"You never know, James. You never know. I could meet some gorgeous deaf girl tomorrow."

The joke kind of back-fired on Molly, though, as from then on Baggy always greeted her with the same line.

One wet and grey Saturday morning, however, Baggy found Molly, Declan and Danny drinking tea and signing. Molly was waiting for his usual porcine greeting and was contemplating letting him in on the joke, when she noticed that the expression on his face and general demeanour were indicating that he was in a state of serious distress.

"What's wrong, Baggy?" asked Danny, who had also noticed that something was up.

"It's James, he's in hospital."

Danny interpreted Baggy's words to the others, as they had also noticed that something was up.

"He tore all the ligaments in his knee playing rugby yesterday afternoon."

"Ooofff. That doesn't sound good at all," said Danny, grimacing.

"It's not. The doctor says his rugby-playing days are over, that his knee is destroyed. Something about shredding his aunty crossgate ligament."

Danny stopped interpreting. "His what?"

"Oh, I don't know. Something like that, anyway."

Molly signed to Danny, "*I think he means his anterior cruciate ligament.*"

Danny rolled his eyes and Molly smiled.

"Have you been to see him?"

"Yeah, he called me from the hospital, crying. I tell you, I couldn't understand a word he was saying at first. He wanted me to pick up some of his stuff and take it to him. When I walked into his room, I couldn't believe my eyes. You know James is a big lad? Well, he looked half his normal size. His eyes were red and his face was a greyish white."

"*The poor thing must be devastated. Rugby was his life. He only had one plan and that was to play professionally,*" signed Molly.

"*What are the visiting hours?*" signed Declan. "*Can we go now?*"

"He told me he doesn't want to see anybody, not even his parents," said Baggy.

"Has he called his parents?" asked Danny.

"No, but I have, and they're on the way up to him this morning."

"*The poor guy,*" signed Declan.

"Man, the whole situation is really fucked," said Baggy, shaking his head.

The conversation stopped there. Everybody sat, just staring into space as it all sank in.

They all knew, or at least felt, that this was going to change everything and could be the beginning of the end of their time together in the student complex flat.

***

A few days later, James' parents passed by the flat to pick up all of his things while everybody was out. They left a note telling them that James would be spending the rest of the term recovering at home.

From then on, their sensations about life in the flat coming to an end were confirmed when a situation with Baggy arose that not only accelerated the process, but put a definitive end to it. He'd been taking more and more drugs and had practically given up going to classes.

If this was a direct result of what had happened to James, they would never know, but the final straw came when people started to turn up at the flat at all hours of the night to see Baggy.

One night, Danny got up to open the door to some persistent banging, but Baggy had got there before him. A greasy-haired youth in a black AC/DC T-shirt stood in the doorway.

"Man! Thank God you're in. I thought for a minute that only those deaf retards you share with were in, it took you so long to open the bloody door. Can you spot me a couple of grams of whizz?"

Danny saw Baggy hand over a couple of small packages, stuff some notes in his pocket and close the door without a word. They stood looking at each other for a few seconds.

No words were necessary. Both knew that the time had come to part ways.

A few days later, Danny, Declan and Molly met for a drink at the Lame Duck to talk about what they should do about the Baggy situation. They sat in one of the booths out of sight of the rest of the clientele. The fact that the pub was now a favourite for deaf students made it increasingly difficult to have a private conversation, as it just took a few minutes of observing to establish at least the gist of any sign conversations.

"*As much as I like him, we can't have people turning up at all hours to buy drugs. I say we should ask him to leave,*" signed Declan.

"*We can't do that. It's not really our place to kick him out, and least of all of us mine. I'm more of a guest,*" signed Molly. "*Maybe you should just try and talk to him, Danny.*"

"*I've tried several times and he always says that it's all under control and he assures me there'll be no more visits. But the next thing you know, there's another bang on the door at three in the morning. No, I think the best way to go about this is for us to move out. I've got plenty of money now, thanks to my grandmother, so we can find a decent place for the three of us, and the rent won't be a problem.*"

Molly shook her head in unison with her brother.

"*If we do find a place together, there's no way we'd let you pay the rent. I've got a job and our parents could also help.*"

"*Listen!*" started Danny. The twins, once again in unison, leaned their heads to the right with their faces showing exactly the same puzzled expression.

"*Oops, poor choice of sign. Just a figure of speech. I mean, you have to understand, my grandmother left me a lot of money, much more than I need, and I really want to do this.*"

"*So now you're bloody Danny Valentine-Rockefeller, are you?*" asked Declan.

Danny laughed. "*Not quite, but I promise I can do this. I want to do this.*"

"*Okay,*" signed Molly. "*On the condition you let me pay for all the shopping.*"

"*With what your brother here eats, I think I'd be getting the best end of the deal.*"

Declan gave him a friendly punch on the arm.

A few days later, they had an awkward meeting with Baggy to tell him of their intentions. Far from trying to persuade them to stay, he just sat in silence, scraping the label off a beer bottle with his thumb, his eyes firmly fixed on his handiwork while Danny diplomatically danced around why they had taken this decision.

"Fair enough," were his only words, before getting up from the table and going straight out.

It was only on the day that they moved out did he show any signs of being the old Baggy they had had such good times with. He saw them to the door as they trundled their suitcases out to the hallway.

"*Somebody should put wheels on these bloody things,*" signed Declan.

Baggy signed goodbye, and they all signed back and, just as they were all turning to leave, he grabbed Danny and hugged him, followed by Molly and Declan. He went to speak, but no words came.

It was the last time they were to see him alive. He died a year later of an overdose.

CHAPTER 18

The house they moved into in Withington was a typical Victorian terraced building, almost identical to the millions built during the Industrial Revolution that were a defining feature of most of Britain's towns and cities.

It was an unusually bright sunny morning the day they moved in. What would normally appear as a gloomy row of thirty anonymous dull-looking houses seemed to them like gleaming architectural masterpieces. Two storeys with identical square bay windows. Only the front doors differed according to the occupants' taste.

As Danny opened the door to let in his two McCrackens, he stood back to await their reactions. They were surely expecting a shoddy, nondescript student house with shoddy, nondescript furniture sourced from dumpsters. What Danny hadn't told them was that he had, in fact, bought the house, along with £100,000-worth of Microsoft shares at $2 each.

Better than having all his grandmother's money sitting around the bank, and Declan had him totally convinced that investing in Microsoft was an outstanding opportunity.

His criteria when searching for a property had been that it be renovated, and a quick trip to a furniture store had assured the patent absence of Formica or dusty birds' nest sofas.

The house was impeccable. Downstairs consisted of a large knocked-through living and dining room with a brown leather sofa and a matching armchair occupying half of the room.

A sturdy rustic wooden table with four chairs occupied the other half. The floorboards had been stripped and the walls painted a pale grey. A spectacular Shiraz Persian rug splashed the whole room with its vibrant reds and blues. One entire wall was bookshelves from floor to ceiling.

At the back was a small, well-equipped kitchen with white cupboards and dark wood worktops. A paned glass back door that opened out onto a small paved patio let the light flood the room.

Upstairs were two double bedrooms with the same stripped wooden floors and a simple clean white bathroom.

Molly and Declan stood for a few seconds at the door to the living room, contemplating their new home with eyes the size of plates, then simultaneously burst into a frenzy of signs to express joy, wonder and all-round appreciation. Danny observed, fascinated that the twins had chosen exactly the same signs in exactly the same order as if choreographed.

Practically the same scene was repeated as he led them from room to room.

"*Okay, Danny, how much are you paying for this?*" asked Molly.

"*Let's just say it's not something you have to worry about. I can handle it.*"

Molly just raised her eyebrows and gave him a look that he easily interpreted as meaning that her question would have to be answered sooner or later.

Declan seemed to have no qualms with such trivialities and expressed his delight at his new living conditions.

"*We are now officially yuppies, members of the bourgeoisie of Manchester.*"

"*I've got one more surprise for you, Declan. I've ordered a Mac and an internet connection.*"

"*I don't know what to say, Danny,*" signed Declan, his face showing the emotion that his hands couldn't.

"*Now you're on your way to being the world's top programmer, I figure you're going to need it. Besides, it'll be useful to all of us.*"

All three stood there smiling, each conscious that this was a new beginning.

It didn't take long for them all to settle in, the defining moment being when they had filled the bookshelves with all their books and had their first cup of tea at the table.

Soon they were all busy with their full schedules, and they rarely got the chance to sit down together, except for the odd Sunday lunch or a few minutes at breakfast.

Molly was becoming more and more involved with her charity work, spending all her time before and after her classes at the Deaf Centre, organising a team to train teachers to teach the deaf in a small town in the north of Kenya.

Danny still taught at the Deaf Centre on Fridays and, although his finances meant that it wasn't really necessary to subsidise the cost of his studies with his collaboration with the university, he continued to interpret lectures. He not only enjoyed and learned from most of them, but he was constantly approached by deaf students thanking him for his contribution to their education.

He had also started his ASL course and was finding it both fascinating and a real challenge. The fact that he already knew BSL was an advantage, but he soon appreciated why people said they were like two very different languages. Apart from the fact that the two languages only shared about thirty percent of signs, ASL used much less of the body to communicate. Most of the emphasis was focused on hand movements, and ASL used only one hand for finger-spelling, as opposed to both with BSL. He was pretty sure by now that his professional career lay in sign language interpreting.

Declan was excelling in his new field and was fast becoming an outstanding computer programmer, considered to be the best on his course. At home, he would be tapping away on the Mac into the small hours of the night.

It soon became apparent that not all these hours were dedicated to his technological advancement, as one day, out of the blue, he announced to Danny and Molly that he'd met the love of his life and his future wife.

Noticing that his sister and friend's faces were both expressing maximum scepticism at the logistical possibilities of Declan meeting anybody of the opposite sex, he explained that what had started as an exchange of emails with a young MIT student in Boston had bloomed into a full-blown cyber-love affair when they discovered that they were both deaf.

"*Can you believe it? We are both deaf. What are the odds? My tiny mind has been officially blown,*" signed Declan, finishing with miming shooting himself in the head.

"*I have to admit that God or whatever superior element that controls these things is definitely in your corner, my friend.*"

"*I know. I must be doing something right, right?*"

"*Declan, you certainly kept that quiet. What took you so long to tell us?*" asked Molly.

"*I was just waiting until I was sure. We've only known each other for five months and we've really only expressed our feelings in the last few weeks.*"

"*Five months? Now that's what I call a patient conquest,*" exclaimed Danny, smiling.

"*Don't take any notice of him, Declan. I'm so pleased for you. What's her name?*" inquired Molly.

"*Well, here's the kicker. Her name is pretty unusual. It's Kraken.*"

"*Cracken?*" Molly and Danny finger-spelled the name simultaneously, showing the same facial expressions.

Declan corrected them. "*With a K. No Cs.*"

"*With or without Cs, I've never heard of anyone with such a strange name,*" signed Danny.

"*Yes, I know. A strange name indeed. Her parents are from Norway and apparently she's named after some mythical giant octopus known as the Kraken.*"

"*Why on earth would her parents name her after an octopus?*" asked Molly.

"*She's been asking them since she found out the roots of the name, but they've yet to come up with any reasonable explanation. But the subject has helped her break the ice with plenty of people throughout her life. In fact, it was our first online conversation. Thanks to her parents' love of giant cephalopods, I have found the love of my life and future wife.*"

"*Fair enough,*" signed Danny.

"*But just think about it, guys. Thanks to her parents' love of giant cephalopods, I have found the love of my life and future wife.*"

Danny and Molly looked at each other. Declan's face clearly expressed frustration.

"*What?*" signed Danny and Molly simultaneously.

"*If we married, she'd be Kraken McCracken! Can you imagine how that sounds?*"

Danny repeated it to himself.

"*Destiny or what?*" signed Declan.

They all laughed.

"*I'm telling you, this relationship thing over the internet is the future. Internet dating! Someone should think about setting up a company to exploit it. The possibilities are massive.*"

"*I don't doubt it, Declan. I don't doubt it for a moment,*" signed Danny, patting his smiling friend on the back.

"*You'll have to teach me ASL, Danny. I can't spend the rest of my life writing to her.*"

"*Man, I should've known this relationship was going to complicate my life somehow.*"

CHAPTER 19

For the next three years, life in the Withington house was free of any drama or problems of any significance.

Molly and Danny's relationship had matured into a phase of mutual trust; trust in each other and, above all, trust in each other's feelings. They enjoyed being together when their busy schedules permitted; they nearly always had something to talk about, and even when they didn't, they were comfortable in their inexorable silences. They had never argued, nor did any faults they might have bother them or need to be dealt with by employing even the smallest dose of tolerance. These were just accepted, and neither could even contemplate their lives without the other.

With Declan's remarkable academic achievements and his strong cyber-relationship with Kraken came an ever-increasing self-confidence that made him less and less dependent on Molly and Danny's mentorship. His computer science degree practically assured, he was even contemplating a trip to Boston alone as soon as the term was over. It had already been decided that when Danny finished his degrees, Declan would probably start looking for his own flat and Molly and Danny would stay on in the house.

Suzie often came up from London to stay, quite happy to sleep on the sofa. She was genuinely loved by Molly and Declan, who enjoyed her chirpy energy and constant banter about celebrity gossip and humorous moaning about Johnny's shortcomings as a husband, provider and dog-walker.

Communication wasn't always easy when Danny wasn't around to help. Suzie's sign language hadn't improved much over the years, and she had picked up a tick of interjecting nearly all her sentences with the signs for 'shit', 'fuck' or 'bollocks', and usually totally out of context. Two swaying cupped hands was her favourite.

The more Danny tried to dissuade her, the more she did it.

It was in the spring of 1995 that the relative harmony that surrounded their lives began to experience its first bumps and nudges in the form of a series of events and circumstances.

Danny had just come out from interpreting a lecture on critical thinking to philosophy students. This had proved to be particularly challenging, as the subject was to enhance the students' ability to understand the structure of, and critically evaluate, other people's arguments and to formulate and clearly articulate arguments of their own. A man he judged to be in his thirties approached him in the hallway as he was strolling introspectively towards the exit doors.

It took him a few seconds to realise that the hand stretched out was directed at him.

"Hi, I'd just like to congratulate you on your wonderful sign interpretation in that lecture. Marvellous. Absolutely marvellous."

Danny, slightly taken aback, shook his hand and instinctively took in the man's facial expressions, showing him genuine friendliness and enthusiasm. Reading his lips didn't tell him what kind of accent the man had, but he was able to pick up a clear and precise pronunciation that told him he was well-spoken.

"Thanks. I do what I can."

"The name's Martin White. Have you got time to go for a quick coffee?" And before Danny could answer, he added, "I've got a proposition for you, Danny."

"How do you know my name?" asked Danny, now slightly on guard.

"I know just about everything there is to know about you, Danny Valentine-Rocker."

After a furtive look around them, and just using his lips, he mouthed, "It's a little delicate to explain, but I'm with Her Majesty's Government and I'm here to ask for your collaboration."

Danny was now feeling a little perplexed and confused. He looked the man in the eye, then contemplated his attire. He wore faded denim jeans, a black sweater and a faded brown leather bomber jacket. He certainly didn't look like a government official.

"Is this some kind of joke? Did Declan put you up to this?" he asked, looking all around him for any sign of his friend.

"No joke, Danny. This is totally above board. Now, can we go for that coffee and I'll explain everything?"

Still not entirely convinced, Danny nodded and indicated with his palm that his new acquaintance lead the way. They walked out of the university building in silence and were soon sat at a round wooden table in a small but cosy café on Oxford Road.

Only when a young and indifferent waitress had placed two cappuccinos in front of them did Danny speak.

"So, Mr White."

"Please, call me Martin," he said, after taking a sip of his coffee, which left him with a thin, frothy white moustache and momentarily made Danny wonder if he should point it out before continuing. He decided not to.

"So, Martin. How do I know you're who you say you are? And what do you mean when you say you're with Her Majesty's Government? Are you a tax inspector or something?"

Martin took out his wallet and presented a laminated identity card with a photo that he passed across the table.

Danny picked it up and examined it. 'Martin White. Senior Advisor to Military Intelligence'. A logo of a lion and a unicorn standing back to back, with the words, *Section Six*. Below this was a photo depicting a much more formal image of the man with the frothy white moustache sitting opposite him. He handed it back and leaned forward.

"Am I in some kind of trouble, then? What would MI6 want with me?"

"No, Danny. Far from it," Martin said, smiling and replacing the card in his wallet. "But first, please, lower your voice."

This was a tough request for Danny, as although he knew his spoken speech was considered as normal, he'd never fully been able to determine what volume he was speaking with. When it had been necessary to lower his voice, he had always made sure by whispering.

"Okay, but I repeat," he whispered, "what do you want from me?"

"I'll get right to the point. We're interested in employing your services when you finish your studies."

"Who's 'we' exactly, and what services?"

Once again, Martin took a furtive glance around before answering. "I'm with a special section of MI6 that's principally responsible for monitoring and surveillance, and we feel that your considerable lip-reading and sign language skills could be a very useful asset in contributing to national security."

Danny closed his eyes for a moment, hoping that when he opened them he'd be in bed and this whole scene had been a dream; but no, there sat Martin White, government agent, observing him carefully.

"Now I know this is some kind of joke. What are you? Some kind of James Bond or Smiley? Are you going to send me some kind of recording that destructs in thirty seconds?"

Martin wasn't smiling now. "Danny, I'm deadly serious."

Danny looked into his eyes and saw that he was indeed deadly serious.

"Okay, so how exactly do you think I could be of help?"

"We would use you to lip-read videos. Surveillance videos, videos of meetings, events, trials... you know, that sort of thing."

"That's all? I'd just sit in front of videos all day, telling you what's being said? Where does the sign language come into it? Are you spying on deaf people?"

"I prefer to use the word 'observing'; but no, not quite. The idea is we would get you into important international forums and meetings like the UN Security Council Meetings or G8 meetings, for example, under the cover of an SL interpreter. Your job would be to read as many conversations as possible between parties that we would indicate to you."

"But why me? You must have lip-readers on your books."

"You're right. In fact, this will be a new section, and we're building a team that can lip-read in nearly every relevant language in the world; but, as of yet, none are as good as you, and certainly none of them have the SL interpreter qualifications for both BSL and ASL."

"I haven't completed my ASL course yet, but something tells me I'm sure you're aware of that."

"We are, and we are confident that you'll qualify with flying colours."

"Thanks for the vote of confidence."

Danny sat there for a moment, thinking just how useful his skills could be to a government. He had to admit that it was perfectly plausible and made a lot of sense.

"There is one other skill you possess that could be of enormous help, given the way that the world balance of power is changing. Mandarin. You can lip-read Mandarin."

"I see you really have done your homework on me. I have to say that it's a little disconcerting. Just how much do you know about me?"

"Everything. Your parents are Suzie and Jonathan, you went deaf at around eight years old, taught yourself to lip-read, and became the youngest ever qualified BSL interpreter. You study English lit and political science here in Manchester and help by interpreting classes and lectures for the deaf students. You're expected to have completed both degrees this year.

"You've lived with Molly and Declan McCracken at 48 Maple Drive, Whittington, since 1992, the same year you inherited £200,000 from your grandmother, Mei Ling Higginbottom."

Danny suddenly began to tremble. He felt as if he'd just had all his clothes ripped off in public. He rubbed his palms over his face quite hard, as if when he removed them he would be a different person in a different world. He took a deep intake of breath and let it out slowly.

"I guess that's just about everything there is to know. But how did MI6 learn all this about me? How long have you been following my life?"

"Ahh. Now that, I'm afraid, is classified information."

Danny took another deep breath.

"So?" asked Martin, leaning forward.

"So what?"

"Would you consider joining us when you finish university?"

"Do I have to give you an answer right now?"

"No, of course not. Think about it. Take your time. I'll be back in touch in a couple of months. But, Danny, let me make it clear. You're not to tell anyone of our conversation, and before you ask me, no, not even Molly."

He instantly thought about Molly. He remembered her telling him when they first met that if he ever lied to her, it would be the end of their relationship. He hadn't taken that warning lightly then, and now, after living with her for the last three years, it was practically written in stone on his soul.

"If, and only if, I were to agree to join you, could I tell anybody what I was doing?"

"Nope."

"Not Molly, not my closest friends, not even my family?"

"Nobody. It would not only be a question of national security on the line, it would be your friends' and family's security at risk, too. You couldn't even tell your teddy bear. As far as everybody you know or come in contact with is concerned, you would be a sign interpreter contracted by the government."

Danny didn't need time to think about it. He had already made his mind up.

"Martin, I really appreciate your interest, and I have to admit that the offer sounds like a very interesting challenge, but I'm telling you now, I can't do it."

Martin closed his eyes and slowly shook his head as Danny spoke.

"I mean, I wouldn't be able to live with that level of deception, especially where Molly is concerned. She knows me, and sooner or later she would sense something. She'd see it in my eyes. Deaf people have an incredibly high sensibility to these things, and Molly more than most. I know that I'm incapable of lying to her."

Martin just sat back, picking up his teaspoon and spinning it around each of his fingers for what seemed an eternity. Both men sat in silence, contemplating the spoon's digital travels.

"Okay, I get where you're coming from," Martin abruptly announced, clasping the utensil in his fist. "But just promise me two things. One, you'll keep this conversation under your hat; and two, I'd like you to take my number."

He whipped out a gold pen and jotted the number down on a serviette.

"If you should change your mind at any time, please get in touch."

Danny laughed.

"What's so funny?"

"You guys in intelligence don't seem to be very intelligent."

Martin frowned, then lifted some interrogative eyebrows, inviting Danny to elaborate.

"I'm deaf, remember? How would I call you?"

"Just call. It'll be enough."

Danny shrugged, took the serviette and put it into his back pocket. "Sure, I promise."

At this, Martin stood and shook hands. "A pleasure meeting you. I hope this isn't the last time." He tapped his nose with his forefinger and glided out of the door.

Danny sat there for a good few minutes, shaking his head in bewilderment. Had he just had a conversation with a real-life government agent and been asked to join MI6?

He had to admit that he found the offer extraordinarily tempting. Who wouldn't?

His thoughts turned again to Molly, and he tried to imagine how feasible living a double-life with her would be. It didn't take even a minute to reaffirm his earlier evaluation of the scenario.

No, he couldn't do it. In a sense, just having had this conversation and not telling Molly compromised his honesty in his relationship. He then started wondering, though, not for the first time, if he would be with Molly all his life. They had been together for four years with not so much as an argument.

They were, he concluded, probably the happiest, most compatible couple the world had ever known.

While thinking about all this, he'd been watching a young couple across the café without really paying them any attention. His retrospective thoughts had been blocking his senses, and he was just staring. Their mouths were moving, but nothing was registering.

Abruptly, their words started to invade his consciousness and he was picking up threads of their conversation as if he'd been tuning into a radio station. Before he knew it, he was following every word. They were talking about OJ Simpson's murder trial, which had just begun in Los Angeles.

"Man, he's so guilty. They're going to fry him," said the young man, slamming his hand onto the table and making the cups rattle in their saucers.

"You watch," said the girl. "I bet he gets away with it. He's got that flashy lawyer. What's his name?" She was clicking her fingers in the air. "You know, the one who gets all those stars off?"

The man ummed and ahhed, and Danny felt like shouting 'Shapiro', the name she was looking for.

"Ah, it's on the tip of my tongue. Well, whatever his name is, he won't win this case."

Danny had had enough of the conversation and went to pay for the coffees. Her Majesty's government hadn't deemed it necessary to pay for them.

CHAPTER 20

Danny resumed his normal rhythm of life following his normal routines, but Martin White's proposal never strayed far from his mind. It would pop into his thoughts often while he was doing the most mundane things, like having a shower or washing the dishes. He would suddenly be aware that he had entered a dream-like trance, imagining reporting to Q or whoever ran the MI6 show in an office one kilometre below the streets of London.

As proof that Molly was highly sensitive to people's moods, and especially his, she had obviously picked up this subtle change in his demeanour, and one day, while he was ironing, she asked if anything was wrong. It caught him a little off-guard and, like most people who lie, he could feel the nose on his face triple in length while he casually convinced her that nothing was wrong, just a bit of work overload. Though the truth be known, he actually did have a work overload, which helped him a little.

Molly must have believed him as, the next day, she insisted he sat down with her to go over a spreadsheet that she had made of all his university and Deaf Centre commitments for the next three months, highlighting in red all those she felt he could dispense with or change.

The next few months went by with the only remarkable events being Danny getting his degrees and deciding to carry on collaborating with the university as an interpreter, but as an official, paid interpreter. He was back on track with his plans, and eventually his mind became free of day-dreaming about spying for HM's government.

What he hadn't expected as the Manchester summer changed into autumn, if only calendrically speaking, was that a particularly unremarkable event was to change everything. Forever.

He'd been walking home along his street, thinking about nothing in particular, when a football came flying out of nowhere and thumped him in the side of the head. It had hit him so hard it laid him flat out on his back on the pavement.

Two small faces looked down on him, framed by an unusually azure blue sky. It took him a moment to focus.

"Mister? Mister? You okay?" said the upside-down face on the left.

"Sorry, mister. We're practising goalie kicks. Didn't see ya."

Danny didn't move. Something he hadn't experienced for at least thirteen years was now reverberating in his head. Sound.

He closed his eyes tightly and concentrated for a few seconds on this familiar yet strange sensation. It was a kind of constant hum in his ears.

Danny had occasionally suffered a light buzzing noise of tinnitus over the years, especially at the beginning of his deafness, but this noise was different. He opened his eyes, hoping it would stop, but it was still there. In fact, it was getting louder. The two young faces were still there, but now he noticed a white line dissecting the deep blue canopy that framed their heads.

Danny remained still, observing its progress for a few moments, then realised there was a direct correlation between the hum he was hearing and the plane leaving its fluffy white smoke trail over the North Manchester suburbs.

He sat bolt upright.

"Easy, mister, you all right?"

Danny clasped each side of his head. He had heard the words. He brought his hands around to cover his face, his cold palms blocking out the world for an instant. He heard more words, and the humming was now more of a gentle roar. He slowly slid his hands down and placed them on the pavement on each side of him.

The boys continued to talk and though he could clearly hear their voices, the words made no sense. He was soon aware that one of them was grabbing one of his arms and lifting him in an attempt to help him stand.

He then found the rest of his body collaborating, and in an instant he was upright in front of them.

They couldn't have been more than ten years old. One was considerably fatter than the other. A mini Laurel and Hardy, Danny caught himself thinking.

156

"You all right, mister? You've gone as white as a ghost." This time Danny observed the fat one's lips, and he understood every word.

"I'm fine. Thanks," he responded, and, to his bewilderment, he was aware that his own words had sounded in his head. They seemed muffled, as though pronounced under water, but he had definitely heard them.

Without saying another word, his instincts told him to get home as soon as he could.

He needed to be alone. He walked off, leaving the two boys shrugging to each other, then turning to resume their game of football.

During the short walk to the house, Danny was noticing more and more sounds filling his head, most of them undistinguishable, but he definitely recognised birds tweeting and a car horn. Perhaps the most disconcerting of all were his steps on the pavement being accompanied by the sound of his own breathing that reminded him of the noise of a steam train chugging and hissing along the tracks.

As he approached the house, he now felt himself overcome by the rush of emotions overwhelming his whole being, and tears were beginning to blur his vision. He stopped at the garden path and tried to spot the birds that were now filling the air with their calls. He could now feel the hot tears trickling down his cheeks.

Opening the front door, he could actually hear the clickety click of Declan's keyboard coming from the living room, and he had to decide in an instant if he was going to announce his arrival or just go straight up to his room. Declan wouldn't have heard him arrive, and he needed to be alone and gather his thoughts and emotions.

Molly wasn't due home for a good two or three hours. He decided on the latter and headed for the stairs, pausing on the bottom step when the keyboard went silent for a few moments. Maybe Declan had sensed his arrival.

If he had or hadn't, he wouldn't know, as Declan quickly resumed his tapping and Danny continued on his way to seclusion.

He lay on their bed and concentrated on letting as much noise invade his senses as he could. His breathing continued to be the dominant sound at first; then, little by little, like the growing crescendo of Ravel's *Bolero*, more and more sounds were coming in waves and on multi-layers:

Declan's keyboard, cars, a motorbike, the ticking of their alarm clock, another plane.

Tears came again, but this time he was sobbing. His diaphragm shook with each sob. Just the sound of his own crying made him cry even more, and it took about a half an hour to extrude all the emotions he was experiencing through his tear ducts.

His breathing became calmer, and once again he became aware of the sounds that had set him off.

By now his thoughts were less focused on the sounds themselves and more on what repercussions and consequences these developments would have on his life or, more important, for the people he loved.

Molly popped into his head, and his first thought was that he couldn't wait to tell her.

He felt a wave of elation sweep over him, but then, almost immediately, as if a cloud had just passed in front of the sun, it occurred to him that fulfilling this scenario was perhaps not as straightforward and as simple as that.

Would he being a hearing person affect their relationship? It surely would, but to what extent? Why should it? he contemplated. I mean, we love each other, right? I'm sure Molly would be delighted for me. Or would she?

His own thoughts were now the only noise occupying his head. He loved his life, and Molly was largely responsible for this. Being deaf had no negative bearing or effect whatsoever. In fact, it was the opposite. Being deaf had given him practically everything he had in his life: his relationships with Molly and Declan, his mother, his father, his professional vocation, his work with the charity, the university.

The more he thought about it, the more he realised that him losing his hearing could only be considered a blessing. It had made him who he was.

He was thrust back thirteen years or so to when he had unconsciously made the decision not to reveal to anyone that he was losing his hearing. There were some ironic, almost paradoxical parallels about the two paradigms: if he now revealed his regaining his hearing, would his life change for the worse? Would everything change?

His head was spinning, and thoughts were spiralling up and down and around and around as if caught in a powerful tornado.

He sat bolt upright in an effort to make it all stop, and to a certain extent it proved effective as, after two or three seconds of dizziness, a degree of lucidity returned.

He needed to make some practical decisions, and his first was that before breaking the news to Molly, he would speak to his mother and perhaps even Declan. They could surely help him with his dilemma.

Of course, he had no idea if his regaining his hearing was permanent or temporary. He might wake up the next morning as deaf as he'd always been.

He looked at the alarm clock on the bedside table and saw that it was still only 4.30pm. It felt like he'd been laying there for hours. He got up off the bed and walked slowly to the bathroom to wash his face. Once he turned on the tap, he stood a full minute marvelling at the sound of the running water, before scooping it up to splash his face.

As there was no phone in the house, he headed out to the phone box at the end of the road, passing by the sounds of Declan still tapping away on his computer. He would speak to him a little later.

The small row of shops at the end of the road were made up of a newsagent, a pet food shop, a greengrocer, a ladies' hairdresser and a CD music shop.

He wasn't surprised to find nobody around, as all the shops would be about to close.

He was about to enter the red phone box on the corner when it occurred to him that he hadn't heard music for thirteen years.

The phone box was right outside the glass-fronted CD shop, and he excitedly pushed open the door and was greeted with a flat "Afternoon!" from a young man with a greasy ponytail, an acne-infested face, and wearing a black Metallica T-shirt stretched over his bowling-ball paunch. He didn't even look up from his *Daily Mirror*.

"Afternoon," Danny responded automatically. He fought to hide the shock at hearing the sound of his own voice. It had only been one word, but it seemed like a stranger had just pronounced it. It was deep and throaty; a man's voice. Apart from his muffled response to the two kids who had knocked him over with the football, he hadn't heard his own voice since he was a little boy. In all these years he hadn't really thought about what his voice sounded like, and now he knew.

He was alone in the shop and, as he contemplated the counters full of CDs by artists he'd never heard of, music started blasting out of the shop's speakers. The guy with the ponytail must have felt obliged to give him the full music shop experience.

"*I'm only happy when it rains,*" blasted a female voice accompanied by a heavy drum beat and a twangy electric guitar. Danny almost put his fingers into his ears. The cacophony of sound was almost hurting him.

"*Pour your misery down on me,*" continued the song.

Danny couldn't help wincing.

"What? You don't like it?" asked the man, as if he was taking Danny's reaction personally.

"Pardon," said Danny, thinking that that was a word he hadn't used for a long time.

"It's Garbage." said the man, holding two open palms up.

"It certainly is. Cheerful lyrics, as well." He was acutely aware that he was shouting above the music.

"No. The band is *called* Garbage. Don't you know them? They're in the charts and everything." He said in an imploring tone, his palms still up.

Danny listened for twenty seconds more out of politeness.

"Nope. Can't say I do," said Danny, and he walked out of the shop. Music could wait.

He opened the door of the phone box with the same caution as if it were Doctor Who's Tardis.

As far as he could recall, he'd never been in one in his life. Every available surface was covered in graffiti, mostly drawings of men's genitals, illegible signatures and references to oral sex; but one made him smile: someone had added to the phrase "Question everything" the word "Why?".

He followed the instructions, feeding a 50p coin into the slot, and went to push the buttons, hesitating only for a moment as he clawed at his memory for his home number.

Surprisingly, it came to him automatically after so many years, and after a few rings a chirpy voice answered. "One eight oh seven. Hello-oh."

He didn't respond. He couldn't respond. The sound of his mother's voice struck every chord in his body. Its familiarity overwhelmed him. He felt his throat constrict and could feel the tears welling up again.

"Hello-oh," once again. "Is anybody there?"

"Mum," he said with a croaky voice.

"Who is this?"

"Mum," he tried to say more clearly.

"Listen! Whoever you are, you pervert, you can go stick that phone up your ar…"

"Mum. It's me, Danny."

Silence. At the other end of the line, Suzie closed her eyes and waited. Her heart was leaping out of her chest. Suzie Wong came up to her, wagging her tail, and let out a little "woof", almost as if the dog knew something was going on.

"Mum. Are you still there? It's Danny."

"Danny?" Danny never called her. Why would he? This alone made her doubt. It was definitely him, but there was something about his voice that was different.

"Oh, my God, Danny! What's wrong?" she asked almost instinctively, although she knew he wouldn't be able to hear her. This call was obviously a cry for help. She was about to slam down the phone, get into her car and head up the M1, when he answered her question.

"Nothing's wrong, Mum. I can hear you."

"What? Hear me?" was all that Danny heard, followed by silence and then sobs, crying mixed with a strew of unintelligible words. A sort of cross between a Tarzan call and somebody gibbering on in Japanese.

"Mum, listen. I only had 50p for the phone. A few hours ago, I got hit on the head with a football and my hearing has come back."

"Oh, Danny!" followed by another slew of words from a Japanese Tarzan.

"Mum, the money's running out. I'll call you back reverse charge, okay? Pull yourself together!" The pips indicated that the money had indeed run out.

161

He waited a few minutes, contemplating the words on the receiver, "Jesus is coming" with the annex "in your mouth", then rang back.

"Yes. Yes. I'll accept the reverse call. Danny. Oh, my God, I can't believe it. I'm so happy for you. This is a miracle. I can't believe you can hear what I'm saying right now. I mean, what happened? Where? What? When? Oh, my God."

"Calm down, Mum. Calm down." He went on to explain all the events of that afternoon.

"That's just incredible. I still can't believe it. Oh, my darling, I'm so pleased for you!"

"Yeah, well, I can hardly believe it myself."

"How does it feel to be able to hear again? It must be crazy, right?"

"My head is spinning, Mum. I can't even begin to describe the sensation."

"I'd say I can imagine, but I really can't."

"No, Mum. You're right. You really can't."

Five seconds of silence passed.

"So, Danny, have you told Molly yet?"

"Not yet."

"Oh, my God. She's going to flip. She'll be so happy for you."

"Yeah, well. That's what I wanted to ask you, Mum. Do you think I'd be doing the right thing by telling her?"

"What do you mean by doing the right thing? Are you serious? Don't be so ridiculous. Of course you're going to tell her. Why on earth wouldn't you tell her?"

"I know this sounds silly, but I'm afraid our relationship would change. Both of us being deaf is what brought us together; perhaps it's what keeps us together."

"Nonsense. That's just not true. You love each other. You're probably the most solid couple in the world. Nothing would change that, and least of all, this. Anyway, how do you think you could keep something like that from her without her finding out? Even if you managed it at first, she's bound to find out sooner or later and then how are you going to explain it?"

"That's precisely my dilemma. If I tell her, I could lose her, and if I don't and she finds out, I would definitely lose her."

"Danny, just tell her, you'll see. That girl loves you. Deaf or not deaf."

"Yeah, I know she does. You're right, Mum. I will. I just have to find the right moment."

"Just don't leave it too long."

They chatted for another half an hour, agreeing that Danny and Molly would come down to London as soon as possible. He put the phone down and headed home.

He was a little relieved that there was still no sign of Molly as her coat wasn't on the peg, but he was met in the hallway by a very excited Declan. He was doing a little jig of a dance towards him.

"*Hey, Declan. What's up?*" Danny signed.

"*I've got some brilliant news,*" he signed, still dancing, a smile from ear to ear, his green eyes two sparkling emeralds.

"*Easy now, easy now.*" Danny gently placed his hands on Declan's shoulders to calm him down. "*I've also got some news, but you go first.*"

Declan didn't need an invitation. "*I've just got an internship at Microsoft's headquarters in Redmond, Seattle. Can you believe it? I've just now got the confirmation.*"

"*That's brilliant, Declan. I'm so proud of you. I didn't even know you had applied.*" He threw his arms around his friend and they jigged together. Declan broke off to continue signing. "*I've been doing a whole load of exams and tests over the internet. I didn't want to say anything until I had the results. But guess what? That's not all. Kraken has also managed to get an internship. We'll be together!*"

"*Wow! A double whammy!*"

"*Danny, just think. Declan McCracken in the good old US of A with the woman of his dreams and working in the best software company in the world. Molly is going to freak out when I tell her.*"

"*I'm sure she will.*"

"*So what's your news?*"

"*Declan, get ready for this. It's a big one.*"

"*Molly's pregnant? You're getting married?*"

"*Nope.*"

"*You've won the pools? You've bought a dog?*"

"*Declan, I can hear!*"

Declan's smile instantly disappeared, and his whole expression changed to one of shocked puzzlement. His eyes nearly popped out of his face and his bottom jaw hit the floor.

"I'm sorry. Did you just sign that you can hear?"

"I did."

Declan's arms started waving about doing windmills, making him look like a bird that had just been shot down, clearly struggling to form his signs into any kind of readable manner.

"Okay. Okay. Calm down, Declan. You're going to do yourself an injury. Stop flapping and take a deep breath."

Declan obeyed his friend. He put his arms to his sides and took in a long breath, then signed slowly, *"You can hear?"*

Danny nodded.

Declan interlocked his fingers on the top of his head as if trying to stop it from exploding and stood frozen for a few moments while looking into his friend's eyes.

He then machine-gunned a battery of signs: *"When? How? What? Where?"*

"Let's go to the living room." Danny ushered his flustered friend in through the door.

Standing in the middle of the room, Danny then told him all about his head's unfortunate encounter with a football that afternoon.

*"Wow. This is brilliant. Mind-blowingly fantastic and really weird at the same time. How do you feel? I mean, what's it like to hear after all this time? What's it like to **hear**?"*

"Fantastic and weird at the same time. I can't describe it. It's all so recent. The sensations and emotions are coming in waves. The truth is, I'm finding it a little overwhelming right now, but I can tell you that what most freaks me out is the sound of my own voice."

Declan watched him intensely with scrunched-up eyebrows. *"I'd like to say I can imagine, but..."*

"That's exactly what my Mum said."

"You've spoken to your Mum? She must've freaked out."

"You know what my Mum's like. She was babbling on like the crazy woman she is."

They stood in silence for a few seconds, then Declan threw his arms around Danny and they hugged for a few seconds more.

"Oh, Danny, I'm so pleased for you. This is massive. Just wait until Molly comes home. She's going to flip big-time. She's going to be so happy for you, not to mention how she's going to react to my news."

Declan noticed Danny's face wasn't reflecting the same elated emotions that he was experiencing.

"What's wrong?"

"Oh, I don't know. This is going to sound crazy, but I don't know if I should tell Molly yet, at least not for now."

"Are you crazy? You've got to be joking. Why on earth wouldn't you want to tell Molly?"

Danny explained, or at least tried to explain, what he'd talked about with his mother earlier, and was met with incredulity by his friend.

"That's ridiculous, and I hope that's what your Mum told you. We both know everybody knows how much you two love each other. You were put on this earth to be together. I'm telling you, I might be her biological twin, but you're her life twin. What Molly thinks, you think. What Molly feels, you feel. Danny, I can promise you Molly will be nothing but ecstatic. Believe me. Nothing will change."

"I know. I know, but…"

"But nothing. Look, I'll tell you what. I've just had a brilliant idea. You don't have to tell her straightaway. We don't have to tell her straightaway. When she gets home, we'll just tell her we've got some great news and that on Friday we can meet up at the Deaf Centre and go to the Lame Duck to celebrate, and we'll tell her together. What do you think?"

"Declan, my friend, you're not just a pretty face. You're a genius! That's a brilliant idea."

Danny was delighted with this proposal, as it would give him time to think things through and adapt to being with Molly as a hearing person.

***

When Molly eventually came home, she found Declan and Danny still standing in the middle of the living room, signing.

"Hey! What's up?" she signed, more as a question than a greeting. She had noticed how abruptly they had stopped when she came in. Something about their expressions, about the look they exchanged told her it was something important.

"What's wrong?"

Declan immediately started beaming one of his ear-to-ear smiles.

"Nothing is wrong, my dear sister. Quite the contrary. I have some brilliant news that is going to blow your mind."

Once again she noticed the exchange of glances. *"Well, spit it out. What is it?"*

If there was a sign for a hesitant 'errrm', Declan would have made it. Instead, he just expressed it with his face.

Molly looked at Danny. She had noticed something in his eyes. They had a sort of tinge of sadness. *"What's wrong, Danny? Are you sure this is good news?"*

Danny's eyes met Molly's. His emotions were all over the place. She'd been signing and speaking at the same time. He was hearing her voice for the first time. Her words were not well pronounced. In fact, it sounded like a mixture of mumbling and grunting.

He was immediately aware that something intangible, almost palpable, had come between them and was desperately trying to get to grips with it and to shake the feeling off.

"Nothing's wrong. It's just that Declan's news is going to change all our lives – perhaps even forever."

"Boys! The suspense is killing me. What is it?"

***

Declan sensed the tension in the air and decided that now was a good time to tell Molly all about his move to Seattle. Besides, he was absolutely bursting at the seams to tell her. Keeping it to himself until Friday was just not a viable option.

He animatedly signed the series of events that had led to him being offered the internship with Microsoft and, like when a magician produces the grand finale of his finest trick, he finished his speech with the news that Kraken had also got onto the same programme.

Molly rushed to her brother, crying and laughing. *"Oh, Declan! That's wonderful news. I'm so, so happy for you. You deserve it. You've worked so hard and you're obviously very talented."*

The next half an hour was spent at the dining room table going over all the practical details and logistics: dates, flights, accommodation, how long he'd be away, when he was going to tell their Mum and Dad, and finally agreeing to celebrate it on Friday at the Lame Duck after classes.

Molly couldn't help noticing that, although Danny was obviously proud and happy about Declan's plans, she still detected that something was wrong and, when Declan disappeared to the kitchen for a bottle of wine, she sat looking at him in silence for a few moments, before making an interrogative sign that didn't really say anything specific, but was unmistakably implicit.

"What?" responded Danny.

"Nothing. You just seem a bit distant."

"Really? I suppose it's just the emotion of the whole thing. I mean, this is incredible and kind of a surprise, albeit a fantastic one. It's just... I'm going to miss him."

She took her time before smiling, reaching out and stroking his hand affectionately and responding, *"Me, too."*

Declan returned with the bottle and glasses, and as he passed behind Molly, his eyes and nodding were urging Danny to tell Molly his news now. Danny just lowered his gaze as a clear signal that he was not going to do it.

***

The next four days leading up to the Friday were perhaps the strangest in Danny's life. Declan was plethoric and spent more time than ever on the computer, though he did make time to spend with Danny, who was now giving him an accelerated ASL class.

He had decided to keep the news as a surprise for his parents, planning to tell them all about it on the Sunday when all three of them had been invited for lunch. Not being able to call them on the phone helped contain his urge to tell them immediately.

Danny's day-to-day life at the university had now gone through a dramatic change as his senses were bombarded both in his own classes and those he interpreted. He was now listening, lip-reading and interpreting at the same time. He found that curiously he was still mostly lip-reading people even though he could now hear them.

A few hearing people he knew and dealt with on a daily basis had remarked that his voice sounded different, and he managed to satisfy them with a lame excuse, like having a sore throat or a cough.

His strangest sensations came when he was with strangers, people he hadn't known when deaf. He didn't feel like himself. He wasn't Danny Valentine-Rocker talking to them or even just being in the room with them. He was an imposter.

Everything he was proud of having achieved in life was now null and void. It meant nothing. He was Superman who had lost his power. For the first time since he could remember, he felt like an ordinary man doing ordinary things.

Of course, the most difficult time was that spent with Molly. As he had always feared, it was impossible that she would remain impervious to these subtle changes in his emotions and behaviour. She had to see it in his eyes, she had to feel it in her bones, and was continually asking him if anything was wrong.

There had been a couple of occasions when he was about to blurt it all out. Once, just after making love, when Molly had been, what seemed to Danny, extraordinarily noisy, and once when Declan had once again implored him to tell her before the Friday, as he was feeling his sister's unease.

The feeling that something indefinable and unfamiliar had come between them, that he felt almost estranged from her, made it all the more difficult to tell her. He longed for these feelings to disappear, but he was now not sure they ever would, whether he told her or not. He had made up his mind, however, that he had to know one way or the other how his regained hearing would affect their relationship, and on Friday night at the Lame Duck he would tell her.

The week dragged by. Each new day weighed heavily on his shoulders, pulling him down and grinding his every thought and movement into the ground. Friday finally came, and after his class, Declan came to the Deaf Centre to meet with him and Molly. He was a bag of anxiety and a small part of him felt relieved that he was finally going to tell Molly.

Walking behind the twins as they left the building, Danny read Declan's signing behind his back saying, *"Do it. Tell her tonight."*

As they went to cross the street, Danny heard a car horn accompanied by the loud screeching of brakes first coming from the right, before he saw a white van speeding into his vision. Declan and Molly, oblivious to the whole scene, were busy signing and had stepped out onto the crossing. Declan was on the right and Molly on the left.

Danny let out a futile scream of warning and at the same time threw himself forward.

In a split second he had to make a decision as to which of the twins to aim his dive at. It had to be Molly, not only because she was the furthest from the encroaching van, but because it had to be Molly.

At the same moment Danny pushed Molly, the van hit Declan and threw him into the air like a rag doll. Molly plunged forward and into the path of a motorbike that was coming from the left. Danny heard a barrage of sounds hit him simultaneously as he smashed face-first onto the black and white stripes of the crossing, a cacophony of crunching, mashing, screaming, thudding and tinkling.

These were sounds that would haunt him for the rest of his life. He instinctively tried to get to his knees. He could feel blood pouring down his face as he looked around for Molly and Declan.

People were now all around. He felt arms helping him up, some voices asking if he was all right, and others telling him to stay still and not move.

"Molly! Declan!" he shouted over and over. Ignoring everyone, he shook off the helping hands and he managed to get to his feet and, seeing first a mangled motorbike, then two crowds ten metres and twenty metres respectively to his left, he staggered over. He pushed through the first crowd to find a motorbike rider lying on the tarmac. His still wore his helmet, but was conscious and speaking.

Danny pushed through the next crowd to find Molly lying at its centre, her red hair matted with blood spread all over her face, screaming, "Declan!... Danny!" alternatively.

A young man in a suit held her left hand, and a young woman held her right hand. They were talking to her, trying to calm her down.

"She can't hear you, she's deaf," said Danny, kneeling down and coming into her line of vision. "She needs her hands to communicate." The strangers quickly released them, but they remained limp and lifeless at her sides.

"Danny. Danny. Declan!" she screamed, pronouncing their names with surprising clarity, her eyes scared and imploring through the curls covering her face.

Danny signed for her to stay calm, not to move, and he was going to find Declan. His tears were mixing with the blood streaming down his own face.

"Don't go," pleaded the man in the suit. "We need you here to sign."

Danny hesitated for a moment, then spotted one of his students from the Deaf Centre in the crowd.

"*Come over here and stay with Molly,*" he signed.

He pushed his way back through the crowd; he could hear the sirens of the ambulances getting nearer. About fifty metres down the road, he saw another small crowd and half ran and half staggered towards it.

"I'm his friend. I'm his friend," he shouted, pushing his way through. He found Declan lying like a marionette puppet that had been dropped to the ground, limbs strewn at impossible angles pointing in all directions.

"Oh, nooooooo. Declan!" he screamed, kneeling at his friend's side.

"He's still breathing," said someone out of Danny's vision.

Declan's body seemed lifeless, but Danny noticed that one of his eyes was open just enough to reveal a moving green pupil through a tiny slit. It stared at him.

"*Declan! Please don't die,*" he signed. "*I'm so sorry. I heard the van. I had to make a quick decision. You can't leave me.*"

His friend slowly moved his bloody right hand and, finding Danny's, turned it and placed three fingers on his palm.

"M…? Molly? She's okay."

The same hand travelled back up to his own face. He touched his bottom lip and then appeared to blow Danny a kiss, his outstretched hand instantly flopping down, hitting the road with a slap to become once again lifeless.

The slit disappeared, along with Declan's last breath.

Danny knew he hadn't just blown him a kiss. He had made the sign for 'thank you'.

It took the ambulance team quite a bit of coaxing and prying to get Danny away from the lifeless body of his friend. Still surrounded by a large crowd, he sat sobbing and rocking while he held Declan's head to his chest.

"Please don't leave me, Declan. Please don't leave me."

Stunned and trance-like, he was reluctantly but gently prised free, then guided into the back of the ambulance and was soon on the way to the Manchester Royal Infirmary Hospital.

"Molly? My girlfriend? Where is she?" he asked the medic dabbing at the open gash on his forehead with a swab.

"The girl? Don't worry. She's in the other ambulance on the way to hospital."

"But she's alive?"

"Badly banged up, but she's alive."

Danny passed out.

CHAPTER 21

Danny, with thirty-one stitches running diagonally across his forehead, was buzzed into ward 12 of the severe trauma unit on the third floor. His jeans and grey sweatshirt were caked with blood.

He was trembling from head to foot as he approached Room 5.

He had regained consciousness just fifteen minutes earlier on a bed in the corridor of the A&E unit dazed, totally disorientated, with his head feeling like someone had banged a ten-inch nail into it.

The first conscious thought was that he had just had the worst nightmare of his life, then flashes of the scenes and sounds of the accident exploded one by one behind his eyes. His hands quickly discovered an enormous bandage swaddling his head.

"Molly! Declan!" he shouted, swinging his legs off the bed.

A plump nurse appeared as if from nowhere and placed a gentle restraining hand on his shoulder.

"It's okay. It's okay, relax now. You've had a bang on de head and we've stitched up a nasty gash." Her Jamaican accent was soothing and friendly. "You've been unconscious since they brought you in, but the tests say you fine. Just need a little rest."

"My girlfriend, Molly. She was in the accident. Is she here? Is she okay? She's deaf and she'll need someone to sign."

"The girl with the red hair? She's being operated on right now."

"But she's going to be all right?"

"I really don't know, sir."

That image of Declan signing "Thank you" came back to him, and he felt his heart rip inside his chest and his lungs contract to leave him gasping for a breath. He started to cry and was soon sobbing and wailing uncontrollably while the nurse gently rubbed his shoulder in silence.

He knocked gently on the door of Room 5 and it was quickly opened by Maggie and Dennis McCracken, or at least two humans who vaguely resembled them.

"Oh, Danny!" Maggie whimpered, stepping forward to wrap him in her arms. They stood holding each other for a few moments in the doorway in silence. Dennis stood a few feet back, staring at the floor. The resemblance to Declan was more apparent than ever, and Danny felt what remained of his heart rip again.

"I'm so sorry... I'm so sorry," he repeated, while rocking Maggie in his arms.

"My poor babies," repeated Maggie between sobs.

They broke off, and all went into the room and sat on the three chairs that were distributed each side of an empty space where an absent bed should be, Danny on one side and the McCrackens on the other.

The room was charged with a sadness that seemed to swirl around them like sultry hot wind.

"Do we know anything?" asked Danny, struggling to get the words out.

"She's broken her back," said Dennis. "Something about her L1 vertebra shattering."

"Will she...?"

"Be able to walk? We still don't know. The consultant operating on her told us he'd be able to tell us more once he's opened her up." Maggie burst into tears again, and Dennis placed his hand on her arm.

"What happened, Danny?" asked Dennis.

Danny took a deep breath through his nose and blew it out noisily through his lips.

He started by telling them all about Declan's news, which made Dennis stare at the floor, slowly shaking his head from side to side as Danny told him what should have been the best news he'd ever heard in his life; his proudest moment as Declan's father.

He told them they were on the way to the pub to celebrate, and Declan had planned to tell them about it at Sunday lunch. Maggie's sobbing turned into wailing again, and Dennis squeezed her arm, which he hadn't let go of.

Danny paused.

"Go on, Danny, please."

Danny cupped his forehead with one hand and, kneading his temples in a small circular motion with his thumb and middle finger, he explained the events of the accident, including the part about him hearing the brakes of the white van, at which point Dennis expectedly interrupted.

"One minute, Danny. What do you mean, you heard the brakes? You're deaf. What the…?"

"I'll tell you all about that in a minute," said Danny, as he continued with his account, finding it more and more difficult to speak without his voice breaking into croaks. With a suffocating shortness of breath, he replayed every scene in his head leading up to his blacking out in the ambulance.

The three of them sat for a minute with their heads bowed, the only sound being sniffs and whimpers.

"I couldn't save them both, you see? I couldn't save them both," Danny bawled. "I'm so sorry. I'm so, so sorry. You know Declan was like a brother to me. I loved him so much."

Dennis got up and went to Danny. He squatted, placing a hand on each of Danny's knees.

It's okay, Danny. I'm sure you did all you could. Thanks to you, our Molly is still alive. Don't punish yourself with this. We know how much Declan meant to you, and I don't need to tell you that he, too, regarded you as a brother. You must also know you're like a son to us; part of the family. We'll get through this together."

The hours passed, and Danny was able to tell the McCrackens how he came to regain his hearing, recounting the story without embellishment.

"That's wonderful, Danny. A miracle even," said Maggie.

"I can tell you, I'm not feeling very blessed right now," said Danny.

"Just think, if you hadn't regained your hearing, we might have lost both our children," said Dennis.

"I bet Molly was both surprised and thrilled when you told her," said Maggie.

"That's the problem. You see, the thing is, I haven't told her yet. I was going to tell her at the pub..." Danny paused as it hurt just mentioning his friend's name. "Declan knew, and my Mum, of course."

Though obviously surprised, Dennis and Maggie didn't get a chance to ask why he hadn't told her, as, at that moment, the consultant, Mr Kapoor, came in, still dressed in his operating greens.

"Good morning."

Although Indian in appearance, his accent was pure Oxbridge. The light of dawn crept into the room, tingeing everything it touched in a greyish yellow hue, as he explained that Molly was fine and that she was being kept in Recovery. He had to move her lung and other organs to get access to her spine, so she was having some breathing difficulties. Maggie gasped.

He went on to say that this was to be expected and there was no reason to worry.

"So, what's the prognosis, Doctor? Will she...?" asked Dennis.

"Well, we've managed to clean all of the bone splinters from the spinal cord, and we've reconstructed the L1 using a carbon fibre cage and some bone grafts." He demonstrated by forming his long, elegant fingers into a box-like shape. "This should be sufficient to make sure there's no permanent paralysis in her limbs, and after approximately three or four months of recuperation with extensive physiotherapy, she should be on her feet and walking more or less normally. She will, of course, have to manage a degree of pain for the rest of her life."

When Mr Kapoor left, the three of them hugged in silence. Danny wanted to stay and wait for them to bring Molly up, but Dennis and Maggie convinced him to go home to get some sleep and to come back later with anything he thought Molly might need.

CHAPTER 22

After a twenty-minute bus ride surrounded by rowdy school kids, Danny alighted wishing he was still deaf.

On opening the front door of the house, the sight of all their coats and jackets hanging on the hooks and a bright red pair of wellingtons that Declan had been particularly fond of made Danny sway on his feet, and he had to steady himself by placing a hand on each wall of the narrow hallway. His Christmas boots, he called them.

He knew instantly that his time, that their time in this house had come to an end.

Declan's funeral was held on the Friday, exactly one week after the accident. After a brief and emotional service, at which Dennis spoke proudly of Declan's achievements and dreams, with Danny acting as an interpreter, friends and family, with the exception of Molly, gathered around the grave.

Under a heavy, dark sky, an undulating canopy of umbrellas fought against a blustery, swirling wind that whipped at black hats and sombre clothing.

Danny stood between Suzie and Johnny, his own thoughts billowing like the wind, ebbing and flowing as memories of his friend and their times together filled his head and then converged inevitably and entirely on Molly. His visit to the hospital with her the day before hadn't gone as he'd expected.

He swallowed hard to stop bursting into tears and fought not to drop to his knees right there and then. It was over, and so was everything. In the last ten days, his life had suffered an unexpected and diabolical paradigm shift.

Molly had awoken groggy and in obvious pain. She winced and groaned as she moved her head from side to side.

Danny had been patiently sitting for hours holding her hand, longing to see her eyes.

She still looked as stunning to him as the day he had first seen her at the Deaf Centre. Her unbridled red hair looked more exuberant than ever in contrast to the crisp white pillow.

What he least expected was, when her eyes finally opened and fixed on him, instead of warmth and love, they spat fire; two green angry orbs drilled him with unmistakable hate and loathing.

She shook her hand loose from his with vehemence and disgust, as if she had been holding a slimy slug.

"Molly, it's me, Danny," he signed.

"I know. Now please go." Her tubes moved with her hands.

"Molly. What's wrong? I don't understand." He took hold of her hand again and was once more repelled.

"Molly... I... I..." he started, but she reached for the button to give herself a dose of morphine.

The machine whirred and clicked as it administered the magic liquid into her arm. Her eyes fluttered for a moment and then closed. She was now oblivious to anything he wanted to sign.

He sat stunned for a few minutes, contemplating her face. His heart was beating fast, his stomach had tied itself into a knot. The silence was choking him, throttling him.

"Molly!" he called out loud, but he knew she couldn't hear him.

He leaned over to stroke her cheek gently with the tips of his fingers, urging her to open her eyes, only for her to turn her face away from his caress. He sat back in his chair and buried his face in his hands. The sound of her tubes moving made him look up and she was signing.

"Please, Danny, just go."

"I don't understand... What?... I..." He tried to sign all the questions he wanted to ask as quickly as possible before she closed her eyes again.

"You should have told me." The tubes moved again.

Danny didn't need her to elaborate. He had his answer, and she was right. He had no defence. He could only admit it.

"You're right, but please let me try to explain," he started to sign, but she quickly made the signs for 'stop' and 'quiet'.

He obeyed.

"You should've saved Declan. He had a lot more to live for."

Danny struggled to find the words. There was so much to say. So much to explain, but none came.

"*Just go, and don't come back,*" she signed, and, to make sure he got the gist completely, she finished with the sign 'forever', crossing her fingers as if wishing for luck.

"*Molly!*"

She closed her eyes again and turned her head. Danny remained at the side of the bed, staring at the back of her head and listening to her breathing for a few minutes, then turned and left. What was left of his heart now weighed a ton.

People were now moving away from the grave. Danny told his parents to wait for him at the car and solemnly approached Dennis and Maggie. He hugged them both and told them to tell Molly he loved her and if there was anything they needed, they could count on him.

As soon as he could, he moved out of the house in Whittington. Its silence had once hosted some of the happiest moments of his life, and now that very same silence tore his soul to shreds.

The hardest day had been when Maggie had come to pack up and take the twins' clothes, which Danny hadn't even been able to touch. It was a heart-wrenching and painful experience as they both folded the familiar garments with tears streaming down their faces. Danny asked if he could keep Declan's favourite T-shirt which depicted seven signs that finger-spelt 'FUCK YOU'.

Leaving all the furniture, he was able to rent the house out quite easily, and he found a small studio flat for himself closer to the university, where he was now officially employed as a full-time interpreter.

Apart from a bed, the only other things he bought were a desk and a hi-fi. He would spend all of his time at home at the desk. Declan's computer sat like an old friend in front of him, and he would sometimes find himself caressing the keys on the keyboard that his friend had given such a bashing. He also got a phone for the first time in his life, which seemed to please his mother, as she would call him every day to see how he was and ask him over and over again what he was going to do with his life now his studies were over.

The next year passed in a dispassionate limbo brought on by the despondent impotency he experienced every time he tried and failed to see Molly.

After spending nearly two months in hospital, she had moved back in with her parents to continue her difficult convalescence. Intense physiotherapy had gotten her back on her feet, but she still needed day-to-day help and someone to drive her to her regular visits to the hospital.

At the beginning, Danny called Maggie every few days to check up on Molly's progress and to ask if and when he could visit her, only to be told the same thing: Molly didn't want to see him, ever. Maggie was always glad to speak to him and sympathetically tried to encourage him by saying that she was sure that sooner or later Molly would change her mind, but as the months went by, it became increasingly clear that there was now an insurmountable abyss between them.

His calls eventually became monthly and he no longer asked if Molly would see him, just conforming with hearing about her progress.

The Deaf Centre was emotionally off limits to him, but he did keep in contact with the charity's boss, Jonathan Kenward. During one of his calls, Maggie had told him that Molly had started working with the charity from home, writing training manuals for teacher training in the field. Danny had contacted Jonathan to see if he could collaborate in any way, thinking that at least his life would maintain some connection with Molly's, albeit a tacit one through them sharing a common cause.

Jonathan gave him the solemn news that the charity was in danger of folding due to unsustainable financial commitments, and the most useful way to help would be to find at least half a million pounds within the next six months. He told him he just might be able to help out and, despite Jonathan's insistence as to how, he just said he'd be back in touch.

Danny hadn't needed to worry about money since his grandmother died. His expenses were minimal; just the rent of the studio and a diet basically consisting of Indian takeaways and fish and chips were his main outlays. The house in Whittington had cost him £30,000 and he had invested £100,000 in Microsoft, which left him £70,000 in the building society.

He more or less lived off the rent and the interest. He knew that Microsoft stock had been going up in value because every so often it would be on the news, and the ubiquitous Windows 95 was the standard operating system on a PC; but he had never sat down to work out how much his investment was worth.

Needless to say, he nearly fell off his chair when he finally made the calculation. He found his stock was now worth the staggering amount of £1.25 million.

This discovery left him a little overwhelmed, and for a few days he struggled to assimilate it. What should he do? He definitely needed some professional advice, and remembered that he had heard that James, their old flat mate, had started work in the city as a stockbroker.

It wasn't difficult to track him down, and he called him as soon as he found the number.

"James?"

"Speaking!"

"This is Danny."

"Danny?"

"Danny Valentine-Rocker."

"Bloody hell! Danny. How are you, old man? Been a long t... Wait a minute, aren't you deaf?"

"Is that a serious question to ask someone on the phone?"

They both laughed.

"It's a long story, but no, I'm not deaf. I got my hearing back about a year ago. I'll tell you all about it one day."

"Wow. That's amazing, brilliant, even. I'd love to hear it. So, what's up? Why the call out of the blue? It's been years."

"You're working in the stock market now, right?"

"Yeah, my old man got me the job. Pulled a few strings and all that."

"Can we meet up in London? I need some advice."

"Sure. It'll be great to see you and catch up. You still in Manchester with what's her name? Declan's sister?"

"Molly."

"Yeah, that's right. Molly."

Hearing her name still had the same effect as it had always done, and a wave of melancholy washed over him.

"No, we were together for four years, but we finished last year."

"Sorry to hear it; lovely girl. How's old Declan getting on?"

Danny swallowed before answering. "Declan died in an accident about a year ago."

"Bloody hell! What happened? Jesus! I mean, first Baggy, now Declan. Was that flat jinxed or something?"

"I'll tell you all about it when we see each other. I'll call you next week when I'm down in London."

"Okay, Danny. I'm so so sorry about Declan, he was a Rockstar. Looking forward to catching up."

Danny hung up the phone. Maybe James was right, he thought. Every single person who lived in that flat had suffered or was dead. He went to his 'important stuff' box to dig out the papers for his shares and came across the serviette that Martin White had given him in the coffee shop. He was surprised that he'd kept it. Only just over a year had gone by and so much had happened in that time. So much had changed. Perhaps it was time to consider leaving Manchester.

He dialed the number and felt his heart racing as it rang, and before anyone answered he hung up. Think, Danny. Think! Do you really want to do this? he thought, with the phone in his lap. Without any time to answer his own question, the phone rang and he literally jumped out of the chair and started batting a now airborne phone to keep it from hitting the ground, finally catching it after three bats and hitting the answer key before he'd got it to his ear.

"Danny?"

Just the one word was enough to tell it was Martin. He contemplated hanging up.

"Danny, I know it's you and I know you can hear me."

"I... I..." He was shocked. How did Martin know it was him, and, more important, how did he know he could hear?

"Yes, I know you're wondering how I know it's you and how I know you can hear."

"Bloody hell. Can you secret agents read minds?"

"Shhh! Please watch what you say. To tell you the truth, I was expecting this call sooner or later. Now I take it you've reconsidered my offer. I'm sure you haven't called just for a pleasant chat."

"This is all a bit weird. I found your number and just…"

"Shhh! I think we should meet in person for a talk. Can you make it down to London?"

Danny took a few seconds to think. Why not? It was time to open up a new chapter in his life.

"Sure. In fact, I'm coming down next week."

"That's just great. So call me when you're ready and I'll give you instructions."

CHAPTER 23

Every time Maggie tried to convince her to see Danny, Molly felt all her emotions intensify to the point of suffocation; her head span, her heart raced and her breathing became forced and laboured.

Life at her parents' house was grey and monotonous. Every room seemed dark and colourless. Nobody smiled, nobody joked, conversation had all but disappeared. Every ounce of humour had been sucked out of it, to be replaced by sorrowful desolation.

She was in constant physical pain and tried hard to give herself a reason to go on living.

Losing Declan had left an enormous vacuum in her soul; her very essence as a human being was now languishing without purpose or substance. Her parents' faces had aged, now yellowish grey and gaunt, a tangible reflection of a now defeated and nonsensical demeanour.

She could never forgive Danny, not only for saving her and letting Declan die, but for his deception, for not trusting in her love, for even contemplating not telling her he had recovered his hearing. She was adamant in her decision that this man belonged in her past, a past that no longer existed, that couldn't exist in her memory full of her beloved twin brother.

*****

The university term had come to an end, so it was a good time for Danny to make the trip down to London. He hadn't seen his parents for months and he had to admit that he was quite excited about spending some time with them. Johnny had convinced him to move in with them for the summer.

Sleeping in his old room and being surrounded by all the same furniture from his childhood gave him a sense of security and well-being that he hadn't felt since the accident.

Just the sound of the washing machine and his mother cluttering about in the kitchen triggered some kind of nostalgic memories of his life before he began to lose his hearing.

He spent the first few days of his return just sleeping, reading and eating. Suzie Wong, his grandmother's dog, quickly adopted him as her preferred human being in the house and followed him everywhere, hungry for his attention.

Johnny, who was more often than not either at the newspaper or at one of the UEFA European Championship games that the UK was hosting that June, gave Danny plenty of space and didn't ask him about his future or about Molly. Suzie, however, was constantly niggling at him with every chance she got. She often made him accompany her to take the dog for a walk in the park and made him read the lips of anybody within a hundred metres who was having a conversation.

Johnny took Danny along to the semi-final game at Wembley: England versus their old nemesis, Germany.

Miraculously, England had won a penalty shootout with Spain in the quarter-finals, and the whole country was sure that England's time had come for glory; that they would avenge Germany cruelly knocking them out of the 1990 World Cup semi-finals on penalties.

Alas, destiny had no sense of justice, and after a 1-1 full-time score, England once again was defeated on penalties. It was 5-5 when Southgate side-footed his weak shot, to be easily blocked by the German keeper.

Johnny begged Danny to watch the monitor and read the England players' lips as the cameras focused on their dismay. If Gareth Southgate had Danny's skills, he would've understood that words of solidarity were not exactly those chosen by his team-mates. When Muller converted his match-winning penalty a few minutes later, Danny picked up a slew of politically incorrect profanities that, if revealed, would surely cause Germany to break off all diplomatic relations with England immediately.

Danny loved going to the football with his Dad. As it was for many boys, football was the common denominator. It was what bonded their relationship. Danny picked up on this at an early age, conscious of the fact that if he wanted to have a conversation with Johnny, it was advisable that he chose football as a topic. At the very least, include some football analogy or he would surely either spend his time with him in silence or be the victim of what Suzie referred to as 'Mr Potato Head': the same big staring eyes, smiling mouth, and two sticky-out ears as the famous toy. He would nod and smile, stare at whoever was talking to him straight in the eyes, but not one word was actually registering in his one-dimensional brain.

Suzie would be chatting away to him at the kitchen table about this person or that, or perhaps something that needed to be done around the house, then she would suddenly stop. Her flow of words cut off mid-sentence, Johnny would notice that the humming noise accompanying his cup of tea had ceased.

"Sorry. What?"

"Oi! Somebody stick the ears back on Mr Potato Head."

"I'm listening. I'm listening."

She used to put him to the test by asking what she had been talking about, but as the years went by, she just carried on talking regardless, or she would just get up and leave him sitting there. Both were fine by Johnny.

It was at a football game when Danny was about sixteen that Johnny caught him by surprise by going completely off topic.

"Listen, son. There's something I've been meaning to talk to you about."

Danny scrunched his eyebrows, wondering what would be coming next.

"I suppose you've noticed the opposite sex by now."

Danny laughed.

"What's so funny?"

"Yeah, Dad. No need to have the birds and the bees talk. I know all about them." He noticed the look of sheer relief spread across his father's face, like he had just been pronounced not guilty by a jury.

"Thank God for that. Listen, I don't want to hassle you with all this. What do you think if we come up with some kind of code?"

Danny scrunched his eyebrows again.

"When you've put the ball in the net for the first time, you just ask me if I want milk and sugar in my tea."

Danny laughed, and they shook hands on it.

It was nearly two years later, at a football match, when Danny asked Johnny if he wanted a cup of tea at half-time. Johnny was busy scribbling away his report and nodded without looking up.

"Do you want milk and sugar in that, Dad?"

"Milk and sugar? You know I don't take sugar."

Danny stared his father in the eyes. "Dad. Do you want milk and sugar in your tea?"

"I just..." The penny dropped. He looked up to see his son nodding and smiling.

"Congratulations, son. Congratulations."

CHAPTER 24

They all sat at the kitchen table having their first Sunday lunch together for some years. Suzie Wong sat next to Suzie Valentine-Rocker, head to one side, waiting for a mouthful of roast chicken to be benevolently held out for her to gobble up. Johnny ate silently, reading the back pages of the Sunday paper.

"So, Danny. Have you thought about what you're going to do with your life?" asked Suzie, grabbing the paper, folding it and putting her glass on it. Johnny whimpered and made a face like a toddler who had just had his favourite toy whipped away from him.

Danny had already decided that, for now, he wasn't going to reveal the extent of his wealth to his parents. He had heard Johnny complaining that Suzie had blown nearly all her inheritance on shoes, holidays and garden furniture, so now didn't seem to be the time.

"You've finished your degrees. Are you going to stay up there working at Manchester University?"

Danny was about to answer, but Suzie carried on.

"Have you thought about doing anything else for a living, or are you going to carry on with the sign language thing?"

"Jesus, Suzie. Let the boy answer you before hitting him with another question."

Danny had no long-term plans other than to meet James and consequently help out the charity and to see what MI6 had to offer.

"Leave Manchester?"

It had crossed his mind, but leaving Manchester would mean giving up any real chance of getting Molly back.

"I really don't know, Mum."

Suzie had been a great help to him just after the accident, calling him every day and assuring him that sooner or later Molly would come around to seeing him.

Without letting Danny elaborate on his plans, she reached out, held his forearm, and grabbed Johnny's forearm with her other hand.

"Listen. Your father and I have been talking."

Johnny grinned, clearly feeling a bit embarrassed and uncomfortable with what his wife was about to say.

"Now it's only a thought, but how would you feel about becoming a journalist?"

"A journalist?" asked Danny, surprised.

"Not any kind of journalist. A gossip column journalist."

"Yeah, right. Why on earth would I want to do that?" He removed his arm from his mother's vice-like grip with a few twists and a jerk.

Johnny didn't or couldn't remove his as Suzie had grabbed it harder and was now shaking it as a signal for Johnny to intervene.

"Just think about it. With your lip-reading skills, you could go to clubs, parties, premieres and pick up all kinds of juicy celebrity gossip. Your father could pull some strings at his paper. Isn't that right, Johnny?"

Johnny duly nodded in rhythm with his wife's shaking.

Danny could see his mother was being very serious and had obviously put a lot of thought into this plan. He was sure she could already see herself going with him to all those big fashionable parties, rubbing shoulders with all those celebrities.

"Okay, Mum, I'll think about it." Though he had already decided not to dedicate a single second to the possibility.

That evening, he called Martin White. The now familiar voice seemed a little flustered and the conversation was brief and limited to giving him an address in St John's Street, EC1, and telling him to be there at 9am.

"Got to go. Dog's chasing a bitch. See you tomorrow."

The next day, standing armpit to armpit, jammed into a Northern Line tube train with half the working population of London and hordes of umbrella-wielding tourists, he was sure that Martin White had deliberately chosen this hour to meet to test his resolve.

At nine on the dot, he arrived at the address. He looked up at the narrow building which stood between similarly narrow buildings of which chic coffee shops, art galleries, a book shop and a pub occupied the ground floor. The building had four floors, three large square-panelled windows for each floor, the three biggest being on the first floor, and then gradually getting smaller the higher they were.

He hadn't expected a big sign saying 'HMG MI6', but he was surprised to find himself in the reception of a graphic design company called Cartilage-Adams.

A young girl of about twenty sat on a high stool behind a Mac computer. Her black hair, tied back tightly into a ponytail, revealed tiny ears, each punctured with half a dozen hooped earrings. Her black T-shirt with the slogan 'I wish these were brains' blazoned across her ample chest made Danny wonder if this was a perfunctory hope or a real desire.

Danny stood invisible for a full minute while she punched the keyboard with the index finger from each hand. He decided her T-shirt was, in fact, a declaration of stupidity.

At last she looked directly at him. Danny smiled. "Good morning. I have an appointment with Mr White."

He couldn't tell if the girl was smiling or if it was just that her hair was so tightly pulled back it just gave her that appearance.

Name?"

"Danny Valentine-Rocker."

"Eeeew, fancy name. Give us a sec," she said in a cockney accent, and pushed three buttons on her phone.

"Hi, Martin. There's a Danny Valentine-Rocker to see you."

Very informal, Danny thought. He was wondering if he had actually come for a job with the design studio.

"Okay, he'll be down in a minute." She went back to her single-digit typing.

Precisely a minute later, Martin White came bounding down the narrow wooden staircase to his left. He wore faded blue denim jeans and a navy V-neck jumper over a white T-shirt. He greeted Danny warmly with a big smile and a firm but friendly handshake.

"Danny! So nice to see you. Come on up. I'll show you around." He turned and climbed the stairs, taking four at a time, bounding like a gazelle.

The last thing Danny expected to see on the first floor was a real graphic design studio. High ceilings, hard wood floors covered with pine work benches. Several black T-shirted people went about their business drawing or staring at screens, surrounded by mugs of tea. Nobody acknowledged their transitory presence. A quick scan of conversations told Danny that they were actually talking about design.

Not stopping, Martin continued his record-breaking ascent of the narrow staircase, his red Converses flashing in front of Danny's face.

The second floor was identical to the first, but with slightly lower ceilings; however, it was occupied by four rows of desks, each with three large, surprisingly flat screens on them showing a variety of images. Danny had never seen such flat screens before. In front of each set of screens sat casually dressed men and women wearing headphones and operating a small console covered in buttons and dials.

"Nearly there," said Martin, taking the next flight of stairs with even more vigour and leaving Danny still contemplating the fascinating second floor on his own.

"Danny!"

"Coming. It's just I've never seen such flat TV screens before."

"Yes. Quite. All the mod cons here, you know. Come on!"

At the top of the stairs was a simple wooden door. Martin punched in a series of numbers on the panel just next to it and the door opened with a buzz.

The top floor held a large wooden desk. A rustic red and blue Persian rug covered a light hardwood floor and two worn brown leather Chesterfield armchairs in front of the desk.

"Here we are. Take a seat. Make yourself comfortable," said Martin, indicating one of the armchairs.

Danny sank into it and expected Martin to sit behind the desk, which was now at eye level. But he sat in the other.

"So? What do you think?"

"From what I was able to see in the ten seconds it took for us to get up here, the set-up looks very interesting. Not at all what I expected."

Martin laughed. "What did you expect?"

"Well, you know, what you see in Bond movies. Loads of corridors, sliding doors, large wood-panelled offices. Your receptionist doesn't exactly resemble Miss Moneypenny, does she?"

Martin laughed again. "Yeah, well, we're a secret branch of MI6, so we try to keep the operation reasonably discreet."

"Indeed. Is that a real design company on the first floor?"

"Yes, it is, but every worker is bound by the OSA and an NDA."

"My guess is you mean the Official Secrets Act and a Non-Disclosure Agreement."

"Absolutely right."

Danny nodded. "So, what do you do here?"

"Simple.We read lips. We're interested in anything being said by people who just might be saying something that could be of interest to our fellow MI6 colleagues."

Danny raised his eyebrows. "Fascinating. Ingenious, even."

"Yes, we think so. We monitor, observe and analyse. We only deal with visual monitoring. 'Audio' has another set-up not too far from here."

"What do you monitor?"

"We deal with issues mainly related to national security and government foreign policy."

Martin must have surreptitiously pushed a hidden button because, as he spoke, a big screen came down from the ceiling above the desk.

"We film and analyse any public or private meetings politicians and diplomats may have. Everything from a one-on-one sit-down between ministers to big foreign summits, whether political or economic, like the United Nations, UNICEF, the European Parliament, economic forums or international trade meetings."

"Interesting," said Danny, his eyes now fixed on the screen. "And is anything useful actually said at such events?"

"Oh, you'd be surprised at the sort of things we pick up in so-called private conversations."

"I'm intrigued."

"We're also asked to examine Secret Service videos or live feeds which MI6 deem to contain information sensitive enough to help them keep the nation safe."

"And you do all that from here?"

"Basically, yes."

"I counted four people downstairs. Are you telling me that the whole of your MI6's surveillance operation is in the hands of a handful of people in a graphic design studio in central London?"

"Well, it's a reasonably new division, but, more or less, yes. Again, what did you expect? The James Bond thing again?"

"Oh, I don't know. A huge underground bunker, fifty floors below ground, a bit like NASA's Mission Control."

Martin laughed and clicked another button. Images appeared on the screen.

"Don't underestimate the formidable team we have downstairs. What's more, the technology available to us is developing faster than you can imagine. The internet is going to change the way the world thinks and operates. Video is moving towards digital and images and information will be transmitted at speeds unimaginable only a few years ago."

Danny thought of his friend Declan's excited prophecies and blind faith in computer technology and smiled and nodded with a mixture of admiration and appreciation.

"Fair enough," he said.

"To give you a better idea, here's some footage of yesterday's UN Security Council meeting in New York to discuss Iraq chemical disarmament. The US are pushing for support and it seems the Chinese have initiated surface-to-surface missile tests. The Taiwanese are looking for unilateral condemnation. Cameras are not only focused on the key speakers. It's the private conversations that give us the most valuable information."

Danny sat transfixed as the camera panned the delegates around the hall. He was surprised at just how many were deep in conversations while a representative was addressing the attendees.

"I don't know how much you know about the UN, but apart from the five permanent members – the US, Russia, China, France and the UK – there are the fifteen seats each held by the UN regional groups like Africa, Latin America, Asia-Pacific and Eastern Europe."

"Apart from the subject on international affairs covered in my degree, I really can't say I'm an expert, but please go on," said Danny.

"Now there are plenty of conversations we're interested in, and obviously we're counting on your lip-reading skills for conversations in English and Mandarin."

"Just a minute," said Danny, quickly holding up his hand, almost thrusting his palm into Martin's face.

"English won't be a problem. But Mandarin? I told you back in Manchester that my spoken Mandarin was a bit rusty, but lip-reading it is about a hundred times more complicated."

"Well, if it's okay with you, let's take this as a practical test to see how you get on, and at the same time give me some information."

Almost on cue, the camera focused on the Chinese delegation busy talking among themselves while an American representative was speaking.

"Can you tell me what they're saying?"

Danny scrutinised the conversation with the maximum amount of concentration and immediately began to relay the conversation simultaneously of the two delegates sat in the middle of five.

"Girl last night very good. Suck very well."

"But she had a very big behind."

"Yes, very big. Very good to slap."

"What's the American talking about?"

"No idea, but I'm getting hungry…"

"Okay, Okay, stop there, Danny. Are you serious? You're not making that up?"

"Nope. That's what they're saying, I swear. I can't say that it's a word-for-word translation, but, more or less, that's what they're saying. Remember, I not only have to read their lips but almost guess the intonations, then translate it to English."

"Wow. I'm blown away. For being a hundred times more complicated, you really nailed that, Danny. Very impressive, though not exactly of any interest to Her Majesty's Government. May I ask, how on earth do you guess the intonation?"

"The eyebrows and the movement of the Adam's apple mostly. Much harder to read Chinese women."

"Undeniably. Well, content apart, I think you've demonstrated you can help us with Mandarin."

"As I said, I'm a bit rusty, but with a bit of practice, I could get up to scratch."

"That can be arranged. We can set up some training videos for you."

"Sounds good. When would you want me to start?"

He had surprised himself by asking that question. He had come to the meeting with an open mind; to observe, listen, then take his time to think about it.

"Don't you want to discuss money or the terms of your contract?"

"Okay. How much are you going to pay me?"

"Oh, I forgot. Danny Valentine-Rocker should change his name to Danny Valentine-Rockefeller. We know about your stock investments."

Danny remembered that Molly had already made that joke what now seemed a life time ago.

"Why am I not surprised?"

"Okay. You'll be paid £80,000 a year. You'll be based here, where you'll be expected to report at 9am sharp every morning. However, when we have a live feed coming in from different time zones that we need you to relay, you'll have to adapt to some very odd hours."

"Fine, and the start date?"

"Whenever you're ready, but the sooner the better. There's a lot going on in the world right now, what with Bosnia, Taiwan, Sudan, Iraq and chemical weapons."

"Okay. I have quite a bit of personal stuff to sort out first; finding a flat in London, closing up everything in Manchester and moving down."

"Of course. My condolences, by the way. We know all about the accident."

Danny just nodded, and a few seconds of awkward silence followed.

"You'll have to sign all of our confidentiality documents. Non-disclosures and all that. And remember that nobody, absolutely nobody, must know what you're doing for us. As far as the rest of the world is concerned, you're contracted by the government as a sign language interpreter."

"But why does it have to be a secret?"

"It's not all just sitting in front of the screens lip-reading. There is some field work. As you can imagine, there aren't always cameras around to film. Especially when there are the private, behind-closed-doors meetings and summits that members of our government attend, here and abroad."

Danny raised his eyebrows even higher this time.

"We'll be asking you to travel to some of these events or meetings undercover, perhaps as an interpreter for Chinese or an ASL or BSL interpreter."

"Now we're talking. Spy stuff. Do I get to carry a gun?"

"Quite," said White.

All this time Danny had tuned in and out of the Chinese conversation on the screen.

"By the way. They are going to veto."

"What?"

Danny pointed to the screen. "The Chinese. They've just said that whatever resolutions the Americans propose today, they're going to veto."

"Now that's what I'm talking about," said Martin with a big smile, getting up to pat Danny on the back and shake his hand. "Welcome to MI6. At last, we finally have you with us. I'm just sorry about the circumstances that perhaps made you change your mind."

"Yeah, well," he said, lifting his shoulders and letting out a sad and resigned sigh.

"I think you're going to be a great asset to the team. Now just give me a minute and, if you have time, I'll take you down and introduce you to them."

"Sure."

Martin picked up the phone and dialled.

"Our oriental friends are going to veto" and "Yes" was all Danny heard of the conversation.

"Right. Ready, then?"

"After you?"

They descended the narrow stairway to the second floor. The four people sat in front of their screens showed no signs of recognising their presence. Danny felt like the new boy at school who had started classes late, as David led him to each one.

"This is Victor, our Russian interpreter and lip-reader." A thin man with a shaved head and big, bulging, disconcerting dark orange eyes swivelled around to shake Danny's hand quickly and curtly, then swivelled back to his screen and typed frenetically on his keyboard.

"He doesn't speak much. We found him at the LSE doing a doctorate in economics. He's actually from eastern Ukraine. Our contacts brought him to our attention as they're instructed to do when he revealed on his application papers that he could lip-read. A bit of an unsociable bugger, though. I think in the five years he's been with us, the only words he's mustered outside of what he's been asked to interpret or relay have been 'hello, goodbye, good, not good, yes and no'."

"Is he deaf?"

The fact White's candid observation had been made behind Victor's bony head without even the slightest hint of a reaction, made Danny jump to this obvious conclusion.

"Nope. Just a weirdo. But bloody good at what he does."

The Russian held up his right hand in a fist, middle finger extended. Martin just smiled.

At the next set of screens was a man in his forties with a dark, swarthy complexion. He wore an impeccably ironed light blue shirt and jeans.

"Danny, this is Sammy, probably one of our most valuable operators. He's originally from Lebanon, but grew up and was educated in the Arab quarter in Jerusalem. He speaks and lip-reads both Arabic and Hebrew."

Unlike his Russian neighbour, Sammy had turned to Danny and smiled an immaculate white-toothed grin and shook his hand like a long lost friend.

"Delighted to make your acquaintance," he said in a surprisingly Oxbridge English.

"We found Sammy at Cambridge reading political science. He often accompanies the State Department or even the Prime Minister on visits to the Middle East as an interpreter. He's provided us with some invaluable information over the last couple of years."

"Where did you learn your lip-reading skills?" asked Danny.

"When I was a boy, my neighbour was a journalist for the *Jerusalem Post* who had lost his hearing in a bus bombing when he was twelve and could read lips. I was so impressed that I begged him to teach me and, with his guidance and many years sitting with him on the street in front of the apartment block practising, I was able to learn."

"Impressive."

"Thank you. I understand you can lip-read Mandarin. Now that's impressive."

Danny felt a little embarrassed. "Oh, I'm working on it."

"I look forward to seeing you in action. Nice meeting you." Sammy turned back to his screens with images of what looked like an important Arab summit. Unlike Victor, Sammy relayed into a small microphone which jutted out from his headphones, which he hadn't removed to talk to Danny.

At the third table sat a skinny man with skin the colour of dark chocolate. He turned and placed his headphones around a scrawny long neck as they approached. A yellow toothy grin dominated his drawn, narrow face. A yellow shirt stamped with pink flowers hung off his tiny frame like it was several sizes too large.

"This is Jean-Michelle. Our African languages specialist, though we also use him for French."

"*Enchanté.*" He held out a bony hand. Danny shook it gently as it looked like it might break.

"The pleasure is mine."

"Jean-Michelle is the son of a diplomat of the Democratic Republic of Congo. We found him studying Fine Arts at the Sorbonne in Paris. Speaks and lip-reads French, Swahili and Arabic, which basically covers most of the important languages in Africa. At the age of fifteen he got some sort of ear infection from swimming in a contaminated river, which left him ninety percent deaf. His parents, not seeing themselves capable of learning sign language, brought in a private teacher to teach him to lip-read in French, who just happened to be half-Algerian. A year later, he unexpectedly recovered his hearing, but not before he discovered his extraordinary talent to read people's lips. He continued to perfect it until he could relay even the most remote dialects of Swahili."

"Wow. That's some talent," said Danny.

Jean-Michelle had kept his toothy grin throughout Martin's mini-biography.

"*Mais oui!* Bananas, apples and oranges all in one basket," he said slowly and still grinning.

Danny looked at Martin with raised eyebrows, appealing for any kind of correlation between this fruity statement and Jean-Michelle's talent.

"He does that," said Martin. "Just says something about fruit completely out of context. He's never told us why. If you ask him, he'll just reply with something like…"

"Pineapple and mango, always good for breakfast," said Jean-Michelle, before turning back to his screen.

"Indeed," said Danny, with a baffled shake of his head.

Martin shrugged, holding out up-turned palms, and moved him on to the next desk.

"Last but not least, this is Shane, our American in-house editing genius. His job is to make sure our specialists don't have to wade through hours of useless video footage. When something of interest is detected, he isolates it and records it on a separate disk."

A muscular man about the same age as Danny, with lanky shoulder-length blond hair, who wouldn't look out of place on a Hollywood movie poster, sat in front of a bank of buttons, lights and dials. He suddenly made a complete three hundred and sixty-degree swivel before coming to a stop to face them. Bulging biceps bursting out of his black T-shirt sleeves, he held out his hand.

"Hey, man. How're you doin'?" His voice was a high falsetto which resembled Mickey Mouse.

Such was Danny's surprise, that his outstretched hand paused for a nanosecond midway to meet with Shane's.

"Good. I'm good," said Danny, hoping his reaction had gone unnoticed.

"Looking forward to working with you. Should be fun." He did another three hundred and sixty, before arriving back around to face his editing suite. One look at Martin's smiling face told him that his reaction had not only been noticed, but had been expected.

"So, that's the whole team," he said, accompanying Danny downstairs to reception. "What do you think?"

"Strawberries, blackcurrants and pears," said Danny.

Martin gave a hearty laugh and slapped him on the back. "You'll fit in just fine here."

Once back on the street, Danny felt as if something had shifted deep inside of him. His life was changing fast, and he was making decisions as if driven by some kind of invisible force with no definitive premeditated plan. He was now, for all intents and purposes, a government secret agent belonging to an entirely different world to all of those around him, including his family.

On the tube home, he found a seat and thought about his next moves. As he wouldn't be able to tell his parents all the details about his new job, he surprisingly found himself contemplating his mother's crazy idea to be a gossip journalist. The more he thought about it, the more it made sense. Although his official cover was that he was a Government interpreter, it might act as an extra distraction from what he was really doing and, at the same time, make his mother a happy woman. By the time he had arrived at the familiar front door, he had made his mind up to put it into motion.

A few days later, leaving a delighted and exceedingly excited Suzie to co-ordinate Johnny's string pulling, Danny met James at a wine bar in Covent Garden. He hardly recognised him in his pinstriped suit, though he hadn't quite pulled off looking like a city slicker. He looked more like a rugby player at a wedding.

They shook hands and man-slapped each other's backs with genuine affection.

"So, Danny. A lot of water under the bridge and all that since we last met, and from what I hear, a whole ocean has passed under yours."

"Man, you can say that again. That Owens Park flat we all shared seems to be a distant dream from another life," said Danny, swirling his wine around in his glass. James did the same, and a comfortable silence followed as they both gave themselves a few moments of contemplation.

"Baggy was shocking news," said James. "You know, I often think about him, especially his story about going down for robbing Disney videos."

They both laughed.

"Quite a character, that's for sure," said Danny. "I can't help thinking that if we hadn't left that flat, it all might have been different. That Baggy would be here today."

"Nah. Don't even think about it. That guy just had a self-destructive nature. You just knew that sooner or later..." James didn't finish his sentence. He didn't need to.

"To Baggy," said Danny.

"To Baggy," said James, and they clinked glasses and drank.

"So, what happened, Danny? If you don't want to talk about it, I understand perfectly."

Danny took a deep breath and blew it out slowly through his lips. He recounted the events leading up to the accident and a blow-by-blow account of what happened on that zebra crossing, the words getting stuck in his throat as if they didn't want to come out. Images that regularly haunted his dreams ever since.

James just shook his head slowly. "I'm truly sorry, Danny," he said, rubbing Danny's shoulder. "That really is so fucked up."

"Yeah, well, Molly hasn't forgiven me for saving her instead of Declan, among other things. She refuses to even speak to me. Let's just say that in a split second I lost the two people I loved most in the world, apart from my Mum and Dad, and all because I got my hearing back."

Another silence passed between them, which they spent swirling and drinking their wine.

"What's it like to get your hearing back?"

"Noisy."

They both laughed.

"You know, it's kind of weird. The more time that goes by, the less I remember what it's like to be deaf."

"How are your lip-reading skills? Have you lost them now you can hear?"

"Nah. I'll be lip-reading all my life. I find myself constantly tuning into conversations without really wanting to."

"Really? I always found it impressive. One of the coolest things I've ever known. I always tell people about you. Hey! You see those two suits over there? What are they saying?"

He pointed to two young men in their twenties, chatting at a table about thirty feet away. Both wore the same grey pinstriped suits and would have been hard to tell apart if it were not for the fact that one had a purple tie and the other a bright yellow one.

Danny began to relay their conversation. They were talking about how they were going to take advantage of some very interesting news that had come from inside a small component maker in California. This small company had apparently patented and was producing a key element that would make chips smaller, faster and cheaper.

The purple tie was scrunching his eyebrows as he tried to follow his companion's technical explanation of the virtues of this technology. This company was currently on the penny market and was about to be bought by the world's biggest chip maker which, by all accounts, should send the price through the roof.

Danny stopped relaying to ask James if he'd heard enough.

"Jesus! Don't stop. Don't stop. This is gold."

James was almost jumping up and down with excitement, so Danny continued.

"So what do you think the upside is on this?" asked the yellow tie.

"Robert reckons we're talking about times ten at least."

Yellow tie whistled.

As did James, who was now fanning himself with both hands.

"That enough, James?"

"Bloody hell, Danny. That's pure gold."

"Why? You think you could do something with that information?"

"I need to do a bit of research, but if what they say is true and we're talking about an upside of times ten, I could make an absolute killing."

"You'd know what to do, then?"

"This is what I do for a living, man. I should bring you down here more often."

"Pleased to be of service. Listen, that reminds me why I wanted to talk to you. I need your advice."

"Shoot," said James, his mind clearly somewhere else.

"James. This is important. Listen."

"I'm listening. I'm listening."

"Do you remember all those years ago how Declan was so sure that Microsoft was going to be massive?"

"Do I remember? I've never bloody forgotten it. That bloody stock goes up every day. How I wish I had taken it a bit more seriously."

"Well, here's the thing. I did. I invested 100,000 of what my grandmother left me in Microsoft shares, and the last time I looked it was worth 1.2 million and rising."

James whistled. "Jee-sus, Danny. Declan did you proud. You're a bloody millionaire."

"I suppose I am, but somehow I don't feel like one. What do you think I should do? Cash it in? And if I do, what do I do with it?"

James stood, chewing on his bottom lip. Danny could almost hear the cogs turning in his head while he waited for a response.

"Are you ready to take a risk?"

"You're not thinking about using that information about that stock?"

"Why not? I'm telling you, if this works out, I could make you so much money you wouldn't be able to spend it in three life-times."

Danny looked at his friend's face, then over to the suits who were now clinking glasses. He didn't have to think about it. Snap decisions were his thing these days.

"Let's do it. But if it does work out, I insist you make money out of it as well. In fact, I'll tell you what. Why don't you take over my portfolio and do with it what you need to?"

"Are you serious? Of course I'd love to, Danny. My goodness. Am I glad you called me. But one thing we need to have clear: although I'm going to do some serious digging regarding what those guys have talked about before making any decision, it's still a risky move. You understand that?"

"Totally."

They shook hands and spent the next hour talking about how James was going to go about managing Danny's affairs and what the details of their arrangement would be. James mentioned that he'd heard that Steve Jobs was now back at Apple and the market buzz was that it would be a good time to buy stock. Danny remembered Declan's love affair with his Apple Macintosh and agreed immediately. Declan had been right about Microsoft and Danny was a hundred percent sure he had also been right about Apple.

It was about 11pm when they parted company with another affectionate man-hug.

Danny took a taxi back to his parents', feeling that his renewed relationship with James was one of the most positive things that had happened to him for a while. Not only for business reasons, but also because it gave him a nostalgic, albeit abstract, re-connection with his time with Molly.

The meeting with Johnny's contact at the glossy gossip magazine went as well as could be expected. The managing editor, Roger Abbott, sat with a sceptical frown, in a suit definitely made for a much thinner man, as his assistant popped a VHS tape into the machine.

"This is footage of this year's Golden Globes awards. Let's see what you've got."

Suzie couldn't help giving a little clap of enthusiasm as the camera panned over all those familiar Hollywood faces.

His face slowly changed as Danny relayed the snippets of conversations he picked up. Most of the conversations were more than a little banal; the shiny celebrities exchanging compliments about each other's work or clothing, with the occasional enquiry about children or mutual friends; but Roger couldn't contain his excitement when Danny relayed a conversation between two well-known actors. Their heads were close together when one asked his neighbour if he had any coke and was told to meet him in the men's room in five minutes.

"Now that's what I'm talking about," said Roger, pointing to the screen as if his finger was a gun.

Two minutes later, Roger jumped out of his chair, danced a little jig, and punched the air as if he had scored the winning goal in a cup final, when the camera panned the crowd to pick up the reactions to the announcement of the winner of the Best Leading Actress in a Comedy. Two smiling, glamorous women clapped and bitched at the same time.

"That's what you get if you suck the right cocks."

"And have the best tit job in town."

Roger's considerable belly was flopping up and down so vigorously that a shirt button, already taking more strain than a sumo wrestler's jock strap, could take no more and popped off, flying across the room and hitting the wall with a ping.

Roger stopped dancing, cleared his throat, and sat down with a flushed face.

"Right, I think we've seen enough. So, Danny, let's start you right away. There's a big new club opening on Saturday night in Leicester Square and I can get you into the inauguration party. We'd give you five hundred quid for every event we send you to and we'll double it if you come up with anything juicy enough to print."

"I'd need my mother with me to point out who most of these people are."

"You wouldn't have to pay me," jumped in Suzie.

Twenty minutes later, Suzie skipped at her son's side, clapping her hands with boundless glee as they walked away from the front entrance of the building. She assaulted him with a barrage of celebrity names, most of whom he'd never heard of, that she'd hope to encounter at the assignment. She reeled off all kinds of gossip and conjecture. It was at times like these that Danny wished he was still deaf.

In the next few months, Danny managed to complete his move from Manchester, start his two new jobs and move into a flat on the forty-second floor of the Shakespeare Barbican Tower. In a short time, James had become his closest friend and the only person who knew the full extent of his ever-increasing wealth. The information gained in the wine bar had proved to be correct. James had been able to juggle Danny's shares and make an exorbitant amount of money out of the operation. On paper, Danny was now worth tens of millions of pounds. James was able to quit his firm and move into his own very smart offices in Old Street, Central London.

Danny had insisted that he wanted to remain anonymous and that James kept his name as confidential as possible. He had decided to tell his parents that he had earned a bit of money out of the shares he had bought with his inheritance, but not just how much money.

He had to somehow justify how he could afford a luxury flat overlooking the Thames. What his parents didn't know, as they stood at the living room window admiring the twinkling lights of the city and the moonlight shimmering on the river, was that, through James, he had bought another ten flats in the same building.

He also had James set up a trust fund that would finance projects related to helping the deaf and, with a hefty contribution, became the controlling director of Molly's charity.

John Kenward was understandably delighted to get a call from James and accepted that the new benefactor wished to remain anonymous.

Kraken, now working at Microsoft in Seattle, received a cheque for $300,000, made out by a trust called DDM Holdings. No amount of investigation revealed the real origin of the money, nor why it had been given to her.

CHAPTER 25

Molly sat in her eternal silence staring out of the living room window at the front garden. A low spring morning sun sprayed the bayleaf plants and rose bushes with gentle rays, making the tiny dew-drops sparkle like fairy lights, but Molly saw none of it. She may as well have been staring at a whitewashed wall. Her back was sore, and she shifted her angle a little to find a more pain-free position.

Every morning her first waking thought was Declan, then constantly throughout the day, every day, whenever she wasn't distracted, which was almost always. Staring out of the window, his face, his eyes, his over-passionate signing, and memories of their lives together invaded her thoughts, spinning in circles like debris in a tornado. Inevitably, Danny made his usual appearance in among these recollections, the three of them together, laughing and signing.

She shifted again in her chair, wincing as a sharp pain stabbed at her lower back. She shook her head and the images began to swirl as if they were water in an emptying sink, the swirls getting faster and faster until they disappeared.

She missed them both so much it hurt. She could physically feel their absence in the pit of her stomach as if she had a large pulsating ball sitting just below her sternum.

Danny no longer called, and that was fine; that part of her life was over. She could never forgive him. She had asked herself a thousand times how could he not have told her that his hearing had returned as soon as it had happened? Why couldn't he have trusted in the love that they had had? She would seethe every time she found no answers. Why did he save her and not Declan? She knew the accident hadn't been Danny's fault, but who was he to play God and decide who should die and who should live?

Declan had at last become everything he thought he would never be, achieved things he'd thought he would never achieve, and his life was just beginning. Danny, who had been greatly responsible for all of it, had then been in some way responsible for taking it all away.

She knew the moment she saw his face in the hospital that his very presence hurt her. Hurt her on every conscious or subconscious level. Physically and emotionally. He couldn't be part of a life she wasn't even sure she had the will to live.

For two months she had lain in the hospital bed, the morphine dulling her capacity to rationalise, to think about the future. She slept and wept day and night. A constant stream of nurses tenderly bathed her, turned her and pumped her full of drugs. Their kind words were lost above her bed as she cried in her silent world.

Her parents spent as much time as the hospital would permit at her bedside. Her mother would even spend some nights in the chair next to her bed, sleeping in short spurts, but wide awake to interpret the nurses' or doctors' questions or instructions. In time, with Molly's gradual improvement, her parents could wheel her around the hospital and, when the weather permitted, out through the hospital entrance to the street. She would sit among the smokers who were chugging away as fast as they could on their cigarettes while the damp air whipped at her hospital gown, and she began to feel part of the real world again.

Physiotherapists appeared at irregular intervals to help her shuffle up and down the corridor with her Zimmer frame. Their simple instructions were relayed with graphically mimed demonstrations, and a defining moment came with Molly being able to get to the bathroom and finally liberate her from the ever dehumanising bedpan.

Once home, her parents used her recuperation to avoid the pain of their loss and palliate their grieving. If they ever cried, she never saw them, and she certainly never heard them.

Still staring out at the unseen garden, her thoughts turned to her plans for the future. In the seven months that had passed since the accident, her thoughts had only dwelt on her past and present. Pain and grief were two overwhelming ingredients that weren't conducive to contemplating what to do next.

John Kenward's recent visit had been the catalyst of this change. With the help of her mother as an interpreter, he had brought her up to date with all the events at the charity. He excitedly told her about the appearance of an anonymous benefactor who, through a trust called DDM Holdings, had injected twenty million pounds, effectively making them Britain's biggest charity for the deaf. As a consequence, their plans for setting up teacher training for the deaf in Kenya were now fully operational, and they were now in talks with the local governments to obtain authorisation to extend their activities to other African countries.

He told Molly that he hoped that as soon as she was well enough, she would resume her contributions to their projects.

A steady stream of get well cards and best wishes had arrived from her students at the Deaf Centre, but she knew that she could never return. The idea of getting involved with African projects started as small seeds buried among the debris in her thoughts and had slowly sprouted tiny green shoots. They were now fresh vines disseminating throughout her body. Kenya was calling her, alluring her, beguiling her to take her as far away from her past as possible.

CHAPTER 26

Danny's first weeks at the St John's Street office were spent watching Chinese videos.

Martin had managed to find an unending supply of Chinese movies for Danny on which to hone his Mandarin skills. Most were poorly made martial arts epics full of somersaulting and flying gowned heroes set in indeterminable times, but some were veritable masterpieces like *Raise the Red Lantern* by Zhang Yimou or *Farewell My Concubine* by Kaige Chen.

He could have watched most of this material from home, but Martin thought it would be more useful if Danny could get used to using the equipment and technology in the studio and get a feel of what went on every day.

He was given a new desk next to Shane, with his own three screens and, with the American's help, was soon able to manage the dials and buttons needed to manipulate the images.

From time to time, one of his colleagues would disappear from the studio for a few days, off on a mission that required his presence.

Eventually, Danny was fed his first official projects and within three months he was relaying live feeds and video from international summits and forums like the G7, UN, UNICEF and, ever increasingly, from the Security Council meetings.

President Clinton, recently re-elected, was under pressure from the Republicans to insist on disarming Saddam Hussein with a particular onus on the possibility of him possessing WMDs, mostly chemical weapons. With the help of the team, everything that was said in English, Russian, French, Arabic or Chinese was recorded and passed to the MI6 analysts.

The information the team had relayed had proved so impressive that the American CIA sent a team to observe how they operated.

Danny struck up a good working relationship with Sammy when they travelled together with the British Prime Minister John Major's party for some high-level talks with the Israelis and Palestinians. Sammy's role was to be the interpreter, and Danny went along as part of his training. Sammy showed him the sites in Jerusalem and where he'd grown up, and invited him to have dinner with his family in a humble flat in the eastern part of the city.

Like his own family, they had no idea that Sammy was working with MI6. As far as they knew, he was an interpreter assigned to the British Foreign Office, but they were proud of his achievements. Danny blushed when his friend proudly boasted about Danny's ability to lip-read Chinese.

As the Iraq issue became more and more critical, they were both dispatched to the UN Security Council in New York on a regular basis to discussions on weapons inspectors.

Sammy indoctrinated him on the ways and workings of the Council and, above all, where the really interesting information was to be acquired: in the halls, lounges and dining rooms that were periphery to the main chambers. This was one of the main reasons for him being dispatched in person to the UN rather than relaying video coverage back to his London desk.

Danny quickly became accepted by delegates, organisers and journalists at the UN building as a BSL and ASL Sign interpreter and was, from time to time, also used by anyone with the British delegation who needed a Mandarin-to-English interpreter for private meetings.

He also had a good relationship with Jean-Michelle, the African operator, who was always pleased to see him when he arrived and would make him laugh with his non-correlated outbursts about fruit and what seemed like an unlimited amount of bright floral shirts. He had never worn the same one twice.

In the office, Victor restricted his communication to monosyllables, so when he accompanied them on a UN Security Council trip, Danny was astounded by just how loquacious he could be when interpreting. White was right. He was very good at what he did.

Shane, the American, mostly talked about his sexual conquests, which Danny responded to with the admiration that Shane obviously craved, but in the most part, social chit-chat was kept to a minimum when working in front of their screens.

Martin White spent most of his time ensconced in his office on the top floor and from time to time invited Danny to join him for briefings on field assignments that required him to travel with a governmental delegation. Danny's reputation as both a sign language interpreter and Mandarin interpreter was growing, and the Foreign Office and even the Prime Minister's office were specifically asking for him for some of their meetings. This complicated White's life considerably, as he had to constantly remind both offices that Danny was an MI6 operative under cover, placed to surreptitiously obtain specific information.

Tony Blair was elected in 1997 and would often insist on Danny accompanying him in meetings with the Chinese. He was adamant that he be his official interpreter in Hong Kong for the hand-over ceremony when Britain gave the region back to China after one hundred and fifty-six years.

In the intelligence field, Danny's skills and the information he had obtained were making him not only a valuable MI6 asset, but an international one.

The CIA asked expressly for Danny to go undercover as an interpreter when Bill Clinton visited China on the first US State visit since the 1989 Tiananmen Square massacre.

The US President was so impressed by Danny's lip-reading skills, which he had made full use of during the visit, that he asked for his services to help him avoid impeachment after accusations of an affair with one of his political aides. A request that MI6 diplomatically rejected.

By the end of his first year, Danny was struggling to find minutes in the day to fit all his activities in. Juggling his agenda was becoming an art in itself. Combining foreign and journalistic assignments was becoming a nightmare, and with each excuse he had to give Roger Abbott or his mother, he knew it was soon to be unsustainable. Suzie knew he was working as a sign interpreter for the government and was proud of him, but when he had mentioned that he wouldn't be able to do both jobs for much longer, she begged him not to abandon her. Danny was more than aware that his mother was having the time of her life, and she wasn't even being paid a penny for accompanying him. She was like a person reborn and revelling in her regular doses of glamour. At least one night a week he would be asked by the gossip magazine to attend some event or other.

As he still hadn't found the time to learn to drive, he'd pick her up in a taxi and take her to the assigned venue. She would excitedly fill him in on all the expected celebrities that would be attending and what he should be looking out for. Suzie was a walking glossary on celebrities' lives and careers. The worst nights for Danny were night club openings. Perhaps it was a direct result of living in silence all those years, but the loud music seemed to enter his head through his ears and force itself out through his eyes.

Roger and Suzie were pleased with how the arrangement was working out. He hadn't come up with any massive scoops, but the array of gossip he had managed to pick up seemed to keep everybody happy: up and coming weddings, new film or TV projects, pregnancies, and the odd bit of adultery scandal.

Whenever he could, he would go to a game with Johnny, but not to pick up gossip.

Unlike the celebrities, footballers had caught on that their lips could be read and had started covering their mouths when they spoke.

Danny was also spending quite a bit of time at James' office. There was increasing amounts of paperwork and red tape to attend to related to the Deaf Charity. The fact that he had instructed James to set up a new charity to supply and carry out cochlear implants for children in South-East Asia, Africa and Central and South America added to the already heavy workload that managing Danny's affairs entailed. It was beginning to put a huge strain on their working relationship. It took an increased fee and an unlimited budget to employ and get in place the very best charity managers to make his friend happy.

James, thanks to his operations involving Danny's investments, was by then already independently successful, and didn't need Danny's business to make a decent living; but their friendship and the fact that, if it hadn't been for Danny, he wouldn't be in such a privileged position, kept him loyal.

His nights out with Suzie gave Danny plenty of opportunities to meet women, but none really interested him. His heart had a stone wall around it, and only one woman on earth could bring it down. He would always be comparing them to Molly and would only be mildly attracted to those who had some physical resemblance to her, mostly women with dark red hair.

It was at quite a low-key fashion party thrown by one of London's hottest designers that one such woman managed to briefly get a foothold on that wall.

Suzie had broken away from him to do one of her habitual scouting missions, on the look-out for any private conversations between people that might interest the magazine's readers. From across the room he spotted at the bar the dark red hair that fell in waves down the owner's back, then felt something jolt in his chest when he saw that she was signing with a plump blonde girl next to her. They were signing about what kind of shoes they were looking for.

Such was the effect her appearance had on him, Danny could feel his heartbeat quicken as he approached them, his pulse banging like symbols in his ears accompanying each beat.

As she was facing him, the blonde girl spotted him.

"Here comes another asshole who's going to ask us if we're both deaf and all that. I have to admit that this one's pretty cute, though. Shall we play with him a little?" she signed.

At which the redhead turned to look. *"Oh, yes, he is cute. Okay, let's play."*

Danny stopped between them, the redhead on his left and the blonde on his right.

They both picked up their drinks and sucked on their straws. The redhead smiled a big white smile that had him reeling and caught him off-guard for a split second.

"Er. Um. Er. Hi. Can either of you hear me or are you both deaf?" he asked out loud, while pointing to his ear. He had already decided to play a little himself.

They exchanged looks and burst out laughing. Danny immediately knew just from hearing their laughs that the blonde one was deaf. Deaf people to Danny had distinctly different laughs to hearing people.

Sometimes the difference was only subtle and sometimes it was quite obvious. Danny remembered being particularly aware and self-conscious about his own laugh when he was deaf. Apparently, according to his parents, his laugh sounded pretty normal, as did his sneezes, but he was fairly sure that he would have been able to detect the differences if he'd been able to hear himself.

It had been Molly's laugh that had stood out most to him during that strange period between recovering his hearing and the accident. He had always adored her laughing face. Her eyes lit up, she'd throw her head back and expose her perfect white teeth. Her laugh had always brought on a rush of affection that made him almost giddy with love, but it had been during that fatal period that he found that she actually laughed like a donkey and he often wanted to put his fingers into his ears.

"What's so funny?" Danny asked the two girls when they had calmed down.

"Nothing," said the redhead. "Just a private joke. No. I'm not deaf, but Jenny, my friend, is."

"Nice to meet you both. I'm Danny," he said, patting his chest as people do when telling deaf people, toddlers or foreigners their name. The symbols stopped clashing, and his heart had gone back to being just a heart. Although ridiculous, he had hoped that the redhead was deaf.

"*This is Dickhead*," signed the redhead to her friend.

Danny recriminated himself on thinking he'd found another Molly.

Jenny laughed and shook Danny's hand.

The redhead introduced herself as Mabel, and Danny shook her hand.

"Can I get you a drink?" He lifted an imaginary glass to his lips.

The girls looked at each other.

"*Let's ask him for a couple of glasses of champagne. See what he's made of*," signed the blonde.

"Champagne would be nice," said Mabel.

"Champagne it is then," said Danny, and called the barman.

"*He must be loaded. We should have ordered a bottle*," signed the blonde. "*Maybe we could have a good night with this one*."

"So what brings you two here?" he asked.

Mabel signed to her friend. "*He asked what we're doing here*."

"*Tell him we're high-class prostitutes, and if he wants to shag us both, it'll cost him three grand.*"

"We're fashion buyers," said Mabel, giggling. "And you?"

"I'm a journalist." He paused so Mabel could sign his answer.

"*He's a professional cock-sucker.*"

Jenny nodded and smiled. "*Ask him if he's got a big one,*" she signed.

"Jenny asked if you're here to report on the fashion show."

Danny kept a friendly smile on his face.

"Yeah, not a bad way to make a living. How come you know sign language?"

Danny noticed her slight roll of the eyes before answering.

"My mother is deaf, and it was kind of a no choice situation from an early age."

"Of course. Makes sense. I imagine you get asked that all the time."

Mabel smiled and signed to her friend as if relaying the conversation.

"*Let's get another glass of champers out of him and then blow him out before he bores us to death.*"

"*Yes. Next will come the 'Have you been deaf from birth' question,*" signed Jenny.

Danny pointed to Jenny.

"Ask her if…," he said, pausing. "Ask her..."

"*Here it comes,*" signed Mabel. "If she was born deaf?" she said.

"*If she's always been such a stupid, rude bitch,*" signed Danny.

He stood there smiling and revelling in the reaction on their faces as they both simultaneously put their hands up to cover their mouths.

"*I wouldn't pay 3p for the both of you, and yes, I have an enormous cock. Have a nice day,*" he signed, tipping an imaginary hat and walking off.

CHAPTER 27

Molly had been excited about the charity benefit dinner at the Grosvenor House Hotel in Park Lane. There had been rumours that the charity's benefactor, who had funded the event, was actually going to make an appearance, though nobody knew who he was or what he looked like. Not even John Kenward. She was also in the same city as Danny and knew that he'd been sent an invite as he was on the list of contributors. She hadn't seen or heard from him for two years. Her mother had told her that he was now working as a journalist for the pink press.

As she sat alone at a table full of sparkling glasses and silver cutlery, she shifted her position a little to relieve the dull pain in her lower back and observed her fiancé across the room, in among the throngs of the other guests. He was talking animatedly with three other men, who looked like they were hanging on his every word.

She thought he looked so elegant in his black-tie suit with his perfectly groomed mop of silver-streaked black hair as his audience cracked up laughing at his every sentence and gesture.

Simon Smith-Jameson was a TV producer she had met at a previous charity dinner the year before. In fact, it had been her first outing since the accident, and she was immediately drawn to Simon's good looks and easy conversation. He could sign, as his little brother had been born deaf, hence his family's involvement in the charity. He'd stuck by her side the whole evening and, for the first time in a long time, Molly actually found herself laughing.

A whirlwind romance proceeded, and six or seven months later he proposed to her on the deck of a luxury yacht in the Bahamas. They had spent the day swimming with wild dolphins. Standing on the deck as a huge red sun sank below the horizon, splashing the sky and a mirror-like sea with an array of pinks and violets, Molly felt euphoric. The dolphins that had swum and danced around them that day had charged her mind and body to an extent that she probably would have agreed to marry anyone at that moment. Simon's suntanned face looking up at her from his kneeling position as he signed, *"Will you marry me?"* made it impossible to say no. She had come a long way from staring out of her parents' living room window.

She moved into his house in Didsbury just three months later.

Simon supported her work with the charity, and she felt happy in her new domestic situation. She got on well with his family and especially with his brother, who was delighted to have a sister-in-law with whom he could confide in and understood the difficulties that life for a deaf person presented.

Simon converted one of the spare rooms into an office for her, and she spent most of her time planning and organising teacher training courses for the teams that would be setting up the schools to teach the deaf in Tanzania, Kenya and Uganda. The project was coming along nicely; the charity was just waiting for the corresponding African governments to give the green light.

There were moments, though, that small clouds appeared to dot the blue sky of her new life with Simon. These mostly appeared in social situations with his friends or business associates. She couldn't help that isolated feeling that deaf people suffer when in the company of the hearing. All of her life she had been almost exclusively among the deaf or with people who could sign. Now, for the first time, she felt like she could only relate to people through Simon, always through Simon. She had the sensation that nobody knew her and she knew nobody. It was like being in a foreign country and relying exclusively on an interpreter to communicate.

As she now sat alone at the table, watching him from across the room, she had the feeling that those clouds were getting bigger and darker.

A few people she knew approached her and stayed briefly to sign 'hello' and ask how she was feeling. Some congratulated her on her engagement.

She spotted Danny. She was surprised when she felt the flutter of butterflies in her stomach and that her pulse rate had increased. He hadn't changed a bit and looked dashing in his black tie. He was smiling and heading directly to her.

He signed, *"Hi. How are you?"* from twenty metres away. She smiled. His signing was so familiar to her, she felt like she'd just put on her most comfortable shoes.

"I'm fine," she signed.

She noticed her mood, which had been already quite solemn, had suddenly swung to being irritable, bordering on vehement. Not only did the memories and feelings come sweeping back like a returning tide, but she was also aware that she was incoherently blaming Danny for the dark clouds appearing in her future marriage.

***

Danny had been excited and a little jittery in the taxi on the way to the Grosvenor House. He had been invited to these dinners before, but this one was different.

He had gotten James to organise it and to make sure that Molly was going to be there. The catalyst being that he had heard that she had got engaged. He had to see her, and he had to meet this fiancé. Perhaps a little naively and egotistically, he had never imagined that his Molly would ever find another man.

He had thought of her every day for the last two years, but not once had he contemplated that she would be with somebody else. He'd been one hundred percent sure there would never be anybody else, given the circumstances and her previous nonexistent experience with men prior to them meeting.

Ever since he had found out about her engagement, he felt out of sorts with himself and everything around him, as if he had been locked out of his house and was standing at the window looking in.

He'd always felt her absence and longed to recapture all he had lost with her. They were no longer Danny and Molly, but he had always felt deep down that one day they would be. It was just a question of time; time was a great healer. Sooner or later, Molly would be healed. Two years had passed and, for him, she was still his Molly. The thought of another man holding her, kissing her, making love to her, made him feel physically sick, and he struggled to keep images of such a scenario from his spiralling imagination, shaking his head violently to expel them from his mind to make them disappear.

Now, as the taxi drew up to the ornate canopied entrance of the Grosvenor, he was going to come face to face with someone else's Molly.

His invitation was scrutinised at the door to the Great Ballroom by a burly security guard who had no idea he'd paid for the whole event, and he was told to go through. There were at least a hundred elegantly dressed people milling around with glasses of champagne, chatting and nibbling on the canapés, but he had no trouble spotting Molly sat on her own at one of the far tables. She wore a simple black dress with thin straps that contrasted with her pale white skin. Her wild red coils were pushed back and tamed into a bun and, for Danny, she stood out among a mass of blurred, colourless shapes like a radiant red rose standing tall in a misty grey field of curling weeds. He felt his skin break out in goosebumps and a shiver rise up his spine.

From across the room he could see that her green eyes had met his and he signed, "*Hi. How are you?*"

"*I'm fine,*" she signed. Just a simple tap to her chest and then two outpointed thumbs, and Danny was back to the very first moment he had seen her in that classroom at the Deaf Centre all those years ago.

He quickly covered the space between them, oblivious to all around him.

"*Hi again,*" he signed when he reached the large round table. "*May I sit?*"

"*Of course.*"

He didn't sit next to her. He left a seat between them, giving him space and a slight angle to sign. He felt awkward and nervous. The last time he'd felt the same was waiting for Molly to wake up in the hospital. He had wondered what he would say to her for two years, and all he could come up with was, "*So, how are you doing?*"

Molly smiled and Danny melted.

"*Fine.*"

"*You look beautiful.*"

"*Thank you.*"

He noticed a slight tremble as she signed.

"*Nice turn out,*" signed Danny.

Molly just nodded.

"I know these events are necessary to raise funds for the charity, but I can't help thinking just how far removed all this opulence is from the world we're trying to help."

***

Molly nodded again. She had been thinking exactly the same thing, but had no intention of showing Danny anything but resentment.

***

"I hear you're a journalist," she signed.

"Yes." He lowered his head. If she knew that, then she surely knew what type of journalist, and he felt an instant sense of shame. *"You could call it that."*

"For a gossip magazine?" she signed, making a face of disgust, her hands chatting to each other to express 'gossip'.

"Yeah, well, I do that for my Mum. You know how she is with all that? I also work as an interpreter for the government," he signed, but it was as if she hadn't been watching him as she angrily went on to reprimand him. He hadn't been facing her when he'd answered her.

"I can't believe you're wasting your incredible talent on such frivolous rubbish. You're not deaf, you could do whatever you want. I mean, really, Danny. I always thought you were going to do great things in life."

"You're right about the gossip stuff, but…"

She didn't give him time to finish. Which was a good thing. He had felt the need to tell her everything: about his work with MI6, how Declan's vision had instigated him amassing a fortune, that he was the charity's anonymous benefactor; but there were plenty of signers in the room. Now was not the time.

"But what, Danny? And your charity work? I suppose you've given that up, too. Do you think that contributing a few pounds and turning up to these fancy events is enough?"

Danny was surprised by the spitefulness of her signing. She was clearly angry. He let her finish her tirade, resisting the temptation to defend himself, despite the risks of being read by half the room, and changed the subject.

"*And your back?*" he signed, keeping a smile on his face.

"*Broken,*" she signed violently, snapping an imaginary twig.

The conversation wasn't going how Danny had always imagined it would. They sat for a minute avoiding each other's eyes and staring out at the party.

Molly then looked at Danny.

"*I hear congratulations are in order,*" he signed.

"*You heard right,*" she replied, emphasising her sign for 'hear'.

"*No need to be facetious. I'm happy for you, really.*"

Molly rolled her eyes.

Danny knew she had detected his lie. A deaf person was an expert on body language, and not even a micro-twitch escaped them. They were also together for four years.

"*Okay, you're right. I'm not at all happy. I mean, I'm happy for you, but not for me. I really never thought you would find someone else.*"

"*Really, Danny? And why is that?*"

One look at her eyes and Danny knew he had just tapped a fire-spitting dragon on the back. He quickly realised he had dug himself into a deep hole and desperately tried to scrape his way out of it.

He'd recently been reading research on whether people stuttered in Sign. Now he had irrefutable proof that it did indeed exist, as he tried to sign, "*That's not what I meant to say.*"

His arms and hands were all over the place. "*I meant...*"

Molly made the sign to be quiet. Her thumbs and index fingers grabbed the two ends of an imaginary bow in front of her and pulled outwards horizontally to untie it.

They turned their attention to observing the guests again, both of their hearts beating fast. A few minutes passed. Molly continued to scan the room, while Danny drank in the opportunity to observe her beautiful profile. He felt hurt and ached to embrace her, to start the conversation all over again.

"*I wonder if the benefactor is here yet,*" signed Molly. "*Nobody even knows his name, let alone what he looks like.*"

Danny shrugged. "*I'm sure he's around somewhere.*"

"*Just think. He could be sitting right next to you and you wouldn't know it.*"

Danny didn't respond.

A few more minutes passed.

"*So, where is he?*" signed Danny.

"*Who knows?*"

"*No, I mean your fiancé.*"

Molly saw Simon still surrounded by his fan club in the same place and indicated with her head.

As they watched Simon entertain his audience, Molly was dying to ask Danny if he could relay the conversation. He was definitely lip-reading them; she had always been able to tell when Danny was lip-reading. His eyes grew larger and he stopped blinking. Simon's audience was splitting their sides; then, when they all leant in close to Simon to listen to him whispering something obviously for their ears only, the temptation was unbearable.

When Simon's little huddle broke up with more belly-laughs, Danny turned to Molly.

"*What?*" she signed.

She had seen the expression on his face before. It normally meant bad news.

Danny sat biting his bottom lip and was clearly pondering on something, then he took a deep breath. "*Are you guys happy?*"

"*Why? Why do you ask? What's that got to do with anything?*"

"*Do you love him?*"

Molly's eyebrows were fully scrunched up. "*I don't think that's any of your business.*"

"*Okay, okay, forget I asked.*"

Molly had turned towards him. Danny could feel those green eyes trying to read his thoughts as they scanned every inch of his face and settled on his eyes, two green, piercing laser beams.

"*Oh, come on, Danny, just tell me what he was telling his friends. I know you were lip-reading him and I know you.*" Her face expressed anger, impatience and worry simultaneously.

"*Are you sure you want to know?*"

She continued to fix her eyes on his while she contemplated her answer. "*Forget it, Danny, forget I asked. I don't care,*" she signed, and went to get up.

Danny put his hand on her bare arm to stop her. "*He was telling them about an adventure with two prostitutes on a recent business trip to New York and in graphic detail.*"

Molly took a deep breath.

Danny watched her face. His mind was now racing. Should he have told her? Why did he tell her? He could have just made something up. What did he think? That by telling her she would run back into his arms? He felt his chest tighten, making it hard for him to breathe. This revelation was only going to hurt her and, once again, he'd already played a major part in turning her life upside down.

He gave her arm, on which he still had his hand, a loving, consoling caress and was thrown off his guard when she violently shook it off as if it were a kind of disgusting bug.

"*Liar,*" she signed. "*I can't believe you could come up with something so...*" She paused as she struggled to find a suitable adjective. "*Cruel.*" She drilled a hole in her neck with her index finger. She felt nauseous as she took her eyes off Danny's, which were showing all sorts of emotions: alarm, surprise and, what annoyed her most, pity. She focused again on her fiancé, who had now finished his private show and was signing for her to come join him.

"*Molly,*" signed Danny, but she had stood up and was facing him with her back to the rest of the room.

"*After everything that has happened, after all the pain and the heartache we've shared, you want to destroy any happiness I've got just out of...*" She paused again. "*Jealousy? Spite? I thought I knew you, Danny. I was actually genuinely happy to see you again, but after this, I can honestly say that I hope this will be the last time.*" She turned and went off to join a smiling Simon Smith-Jameson.

***

She felt her blood boiling and her guts churning as she crossed the room. 'New York,' she thought, 'how would Danny have known that Simon had recently been to New York?'

***

Danny sat in a semi-state of shock. He saw her fiancé greet her with a peck on the cheek and ask who he was. *"Nobody, just a guy who thought he could impress me just because he could sign."*

His last thread of hope that he'd been holding onto for two years had just been snipped and he could feel himself free-falling into a dark, bottomless pit. He toyed with the idea of following her over and confronting Simon face-to-face, but it was a fleeting thought.

He couldn't do that to her. It was time to make his exit.

CHAPTER 28

Molly sat as far away from Simon as possible in the back seat of the black cab that took them to their hotel in Kensington. She leant her forehead against the cold window in an attempt to calm herself down. The cab was dark, making communication almost impossible, which suited both of them. They had had a very angry confrontation under the awning of the Grosvenor on Park Lane. A cold, damp wind whipped their coats as they signed aggressively in front of a stoic doorman.

"So, Simon. Do you have anything to tell me about what you did on your trip to New York?"

She hadn't been able to refrain from confronting him on the issue until they were back in their hotel, as she had wanted. The charity evening had become an interminable torture for her. She had looked around for Danny, but he had left, and she was surprised how much this affected her. The speeches were relayed by a very dull signer, and she couldn't even look at her dinner. Simon hadn't even noticed the change in her mood, so when he was laughing and signing about how much he had enjoyed the evening while they waited for a taxi, she could hold it in no longer.

"New York?" He signed, as if she had just mentioned an unknown place in Tasmania.

"Yes. New York. You were telling your friends all about it tonight."

"I'm sorry, I don't follow you."

"A threesome, Simon. With prostitutes. Do you follow me now?"

"What on earth are you talking about?"

"You've no idea?"

"I'm sorry, Molly, but I haven't got a clue."

"Your hands are saying you haven't, but your eyes are telling me you know perfectly well what I'm talking about."

"Molly, sweetheart, I really don't know what you're on about. What's all this about a threesome? What bloody threesome?"

She noticed that he had signed averting his eyes. *"Simon. My friend is a lip-reader. Probably the best lip-reader in the entire world. He followed your whole conversation with your little band of admirers."*

She watched his face show several different expressions in a fraction of time.

"We're talking about Danny, right? He was here tonight? That was him you were sitting with?"

"It doesn't matter. That's not the point. This isn't about Danny. It's about us."

"Well, I bloody well think it is."

The cab pulled up in front of them, and the doorman opened the door for them. Simon was quick to jump in first, as if the cab was a safe haven where its darkness would give him time to think.

Back in the hotel, he vehemently denied everything and accused Danny of blatant lying and trying to sabotage their marriage. Simon was signing like a mad man and wasn't going to back down and admit anything.

Watching her fiancé standing there in just his black socks and red and white-striped boxers, attacking Danny with his eyes popping out of his head, Molly quickly realised three things. The first, he was going to deny it until he was blue in the face. The second, it was true. Danny had relayed the truth; and last, this was the beginning of the end of her engagement.

As she lay in bed that night, she made up her mind that as soon as the charity had the green light, she was off to Kenya.

CHAPTER 29

Danny spent the next three days in hibernation. He locked himself away in his flat overlooking the Thames and gorged himself on ordered-in junk food and TV, both made consumable by washing them down with gallons of red wine. The Christmas before, James had sent him a crate of the apparently highly regarded Chateauneuf-du-Pape Chateau Rayas 1990. It had remained forgotten at the back of his shoe cupboard until his search for alcohol – any alcohol at all in his flat – unearthed it.

For three days, he switched on his answerphone and switched off his brain, sharing his drunken solitude with only ghosts and memories.

On the fourth day, he'd been dreaming that he was underwater and gasping for air, his lungs screaming out for oxygen as he desperately scampered for the surface that he could see above his head, but didn't seem to get any closer no matter how much water he pushed behind him. The phone ringing woke him and left him sitting up on the sofa, covered in sweat, sucking up big gulps of air into his needy lungs.

He was aware that an unfamiliar voice with an aggressive tone was now leaving a message on his machine. He let it finish without really listening to it as he coughed, then vigorously rubbed his face with his palms. He winced at the morning sunlight now invading his living room and lighting up the empty green bottles on the coffee table. It had been the mention of Molly's name that made him jump up and, with a pounding head, hit the replay button.

"You fucking little shit," was how the message began. "Pick up the fucking phone."

Danny heard the sound of someone lighting a cigarette and blowing into the mouthpiece.

"Right. Now listen to me. I don't know what exactly you told Molly or what your game is, but, thanks to you, my relationship is in deep shit. According to Molly, you are a fucking master at lip-reading and you read a supposed conversation I had with some people at the charity do. First,

227

nobody can fucking lip-read from that far away and second, you should learn to keep out of other people's business."

Another loud drag on the cigarette interrupted his tirade.

"This is just to let you know that this is not over. No matter what happens, I'm going to take you down, you fucker. I've got some pretty powerful friends, and you can rest assured that you're going to rot in hell."

The only information that stayed with Danny was that their relationship was in deep shit. He played it three times just to make sure. Each time made him feel more elated than the last, pumping a little more life into him as he punched the air with joy.

"My relationship is in deep shit."

"Yeeeeeeeess!" he screamed at the ceiling.

He showered and shaved for the first time since he'd locked himself in and drank three large cups of coffee. It was time to rejoin the world and pick up on his hectic routine.

He left the building humming the tune of *What a Wonderful World*.

CHAPTER 30

A week later, Danny was pleased to be invited up to David's office to be briefed on a new assignment that would take him to Nairobi with Jean-Michelle. The American embassies in Nairobi and Dar es Salaam, Tanzania, had been bombed. Hundreds were dead and thousands more injured. Clinton's team had made a specific request to the section for English and African interpreters with lip-reading skills to accompany intelligence, military and diplomatic teams to some high-level talks.

The timing and destination of this mission for Danny was as if some divine intervention had taken place. He had received a call from James that John Kenward had been in touch, asking how the procedures were going to obtain permission to open the teacher training camps in Kenya.

He hadn't heard any more from either Molly or her enraged, hopefully soon to be ex-fiancé. He had decided to bide his time and not make any potentially counterproductive approaches to Molly.

The team found Nairobi in a state of lock-down, and Danny and Jean-Michelle were whisked from the airport in a heavily guarded convoy of diplomatic cars directly to their hotel. The roads were a mixture of dirt, bitumen and pot-holed lanes. At every mile or so the convoy had to navigate between large spiked metal plates with a dozen rifle-carrying soldiers to scrutinise every form of transport that passed through them. Every time they had to wind down the windows of their large 4x4 vehicles to show their credentials, a waft of putrid smells attacked their nostrils.

"Nairobi, a big bowl of rotten fruit," said Jean-Michelle. They had been his first words the whole trip.

The traffic was chaotic, and there seemed to be no rules regarding respecting which side of the road to drive on or even to drive on the road at all. Everybody seemed to treat their trajectory like a rally race, often missing by a whisker the people who sat on rubbish-strewn banks that lined the road.

There was no uniform architecture to speak of. In a short span of five minutes, Danny saw modern embassy buildings interspersed with shops in the form of shabby huts selling either secondhand clothes, dusty shoes or unidentifiable fruit and vegetables. Then wooden shacks would appear, covered in plastic sheeting or tin that masked gaps in the walls and roof. Any building of any size and importance had a fence lined with barbed wire and massive gates with armed security guards. They weren't driven past what had remained of the US embassy.

Their brief was to accompany a small group made up of FBI and CIA analysts, along with two high officials belonging to the American foreign secretary of state, Madeleine Albright. They were to attend a set of meetings with Kenyan intelligence and the President, Daniel Arap Moi.

The next morning, their twenty-strong party was driven about ten minutes from their hotel to the State House, the President's official residency. It was a large, white, palatial building set back in about three acres of lush, green palm trees and vibrant tropical flowers.

Most of the interpreting was done by Jean-Michelle. Danny's presence was surprisingly unchallenged. He just sat alongside the rest of the US party, all wearing anonymous khaki trousers and variations of the same plaid shirt. Jean-Michelle stood out in one of his array of coloured tops, eerily replicating the land that surrounded the building.

Most of the conversations dealt with Kenya's claim for compensation, but Danny was present at more than one meeting that had clearly identified a certain Saudi national called Bin Laden and his organisation, Al-Qaida, as the culprits.

The team spent three weeks travelling back and forth to these meetings, and every time they arrived back at the hotel, they were debriefed by the American intelligence group to report on any conversations they had picked up. Jean-Michelle was only able to relay insults and anti-American comments. Danny, who was only able to relay English conversations, had nothing to report and questioned why he was brought on board in the first place. With only a couple of days of down time, he did, however, take advantage of his trip. With Jean-Michelle's help and a little palm-greasing, he could contact top Kenyan officials to obtain permission for his charity to establish the teacher training centres in Kenya.

CHAPTER 31

It was with reluctance that Danny accepted another assignment from Roger Abbott the first week he'd been back from Nairobi. He had already told Suzie when he was at home for a Sunday lunch that the next one would be the last and the end of his journalistic career.

Molly's comments about wasting his skills on such activities had had an effect. It was a low blow, but she was right.

"Come on, Danny," said Suzie. "You know you enjoy it."

"That's just the point, Mum, I don't. I do it for you. It's you who enjoys it."

"Johnny. Tell him. Tell him how much this means to the paper. How important this work is."

"Oi!" said Johnny, who had been hidden from the conversation behind the newspaper until Suzie had taken a swipe at it to get his attention. She repeated her request for support.

"If he wants to give it up, let him. It's not as if he needs the money."

"Thanks, Johnny. Thanks a lot for your usual unconditional support. Go back to reading about your bloody football."

Johnny shrugged, rolled his eyes at Danny, and lifted his newspaper shield again.

***

The assignment was the 1999 Bafta awards after-party at, of all places, the Grosvenor House Hotel. The same venue as the Deaf Charity Ball.

A few days later, Danny and his mother sat at an empty table, watching celebrities mingle, Danny in black tie and Suzie looking like she was about to walk the Oscars' red carpet. The stars of *Shakespeare in Love*, which had received the prize for best film, were getting most of the attention.

Although they were mother and son, to the rest of the party they made an attractive couple who didn't look out of place among the glitzy and glamorous crowds. At forty-nine, Suzie didn't look twenty-two years older than her son.

As usual, she was constantly asking Danny to relay any conversations she felt might be interesting. She knew that he could read multi-party conversations within a radius of twenty to thirty yards, so she would pick out people right across the room.

Danny was leaning back in his chair, relaying snippets of these conversations with his usual bored demeanour, when a conversation being held by two women on the next table, their body language indicating they were having a confidential chat, made Danny sit up.

They were talking about a well-known and respected British actor that even Danny had heard of. Their heads were close together, and the conversation had started with the one in the pink dress telling her confidant in the red dress that what she was about to tell her was so mind blowing and shocking that she should swear to never mention it to anybody. Not even her most trusted friends and family.

Suzie's already vice-like grip on Danny's forearm was getting stronger and stronger the more of the conversation he relayed, practically cutting the flow of blood to his hand.

"Danny. Danny. This is the big one," she said, when the two women paused to take a gulp of their champagne.

"Okay, Mum, but could you stop trying to amputate half my arm?"

"Just keep lip-reading," she said without moving her lips, like a ventriloquist.

"So, anyway, as I was saying, not only does he have a penchant for cross-dressing as a princess behind closed doors, he's..." The red dress paused and looked around. Danny wasn't sure if she hadn't looked right at him before continuing. "He's also got two little Arab boys who work for him in the house. Apparently found them in Marrakesh; paid for the whole family to travel to London, and has set them up in a small flat in Balham. I heard he pays the two boys' wages directly to their father."

"You *are* kidding? And these two Arab boys, *does he*? Does he, well, you know?"

"Shhh!" said red dress, with another stealthy scanning of the room. "Yep."

"How old are they?"

"About ten or eleven."

"Oh, my God! Bloody hell. That's disgusting! The man's a sexual deviant. Who'd of thought it? I mean, he was on the telly only last week talking about his visit to Buckingham Palace next month to get his bloody knighthood. And what about the mother and father? Do they know what's going on?"

"What do you think?"

"Bloody hell."

"I know. It's unbelievable. In fact, I didn't believe a word of it when I was told, but I'm telling you, this is hundred percent true."

"Who told you, anyway?"

"That I can't tell you. But take it from me, I swear on my kids' lives, this is the God's honest truth."

Almost on cue, at that moment another couple sat at the table, blocking Danny's vision, making the two women pick up their drinks and saunter off into the crowds.

"Jesus!" said Suzie. "Jesus, Jesus, bloody Jesus H. Christ. You've got to be kidding me. You're now going to tell me that everything you just relayed was one of your twisted jokes and that they were actually talking about shoes or how to slow-roast a lamb, aren't you?"

"Nope."

"Wow. I'm speechless. I just don't know what to say."

"I'm sure you can think of something, Mum. But what we have to do now is decide if we're going to call the police."

"Let me think a minute."

"What's there to think about? That man can't be allowed to carry on like that. I really think the right thing to do is go to the police. Mum, I hope you're not thinking of passing this on to Roger Abbott." One look at his mother's face confirmed his suspicions.

"No way!" he said. "Besides, how do we know it's true, for a start? This is not like passing on a bit of gossip about celebrity couples or impending weddings and babies."

"But she swore on her kids' lives and everybody knows you don't do that unless you're telling the truth."

"Oh, well then. If she swore on her kids' lives."

"Come on, Danny. This is big. Think about it like you're going to do a favour to society and saving the two boys at the same time. If this is our last assignment, as you said it was, this is our chance to go out with a bang."

The bang turned out to be a big bang indeed. An atomic fall-out followed. Roger Abbott kicked the paper's legal team out of the office, defiant and determined to publish against their advice not to do so. His argument was that the source of the information was credible enough for it to be true and to be able to back up the story with concrete proof. He was that confident in Danny's scoop. Suzie had offered to put her name to the story given Danny's reluctance and his government job.

The day after the story was published, the named actor started legal proceedings to sue Roger Abbott, the paper and Suzie, as the named journalist, for defamation. Their lawyers told them they didn't stand a chance of fighting the suit. Primarily because the law states that it is up to the defendant to prove that the claimant's information published is true and the fact that the actor hadn't even set foot in Britain for two years made this an impossible task.

The actor's lawyers were talking about suing for millions of pounds and, given the facts, if it went to court they would easily win, so it was increasingly clear that an out-of-court settlement would have to be arranged. It was in their favour that the actor was keen to put it to bed quickly before it dragged out too long.

Eventually, the magazine's lawyers agreed to pay £1.5 million and Roger Abbott's lawyers agreed another £500,000.

Danny's lawyer, representing Suzie, agreed to pay the same amount as Roger.

The fall-out was considerable. Roger Abbott lost his job, the magazine went into liquidation and Suzie went into meltdown.

The day after the final meeting with the actor's lawyer, Danny sat at his mother's kitchen table, nursing a cup of tea, while Suzie held her face between her hands, squashing all her features, to give her the appearance of a bloodhound.

Johnny sat massaging his head with open-spread fingers, though instead of moving his digits, he nodded like a madman creating a fan of grey hair with each movement.

"Oh, my God. Oh my God," he kept repeating with each nod.

"Dad. Don't worry about it."

"Danny. How can we not worry about it? We're ruined. Five hundred grand. How on earth are we going to pay that sort of money?" said Suzie through a misshapen mouth.

"Mum."

"I mean, we'll have to sell the house for a start."

"Mum!"

"Where are we going to live? In a caravan?"

"Mum. Stop! Dad. Stop!" said Danny a little louder, which got his fretting parents' attention. "You really don't have to worry."

Johnny stopped nodding, and Suzie removed her face from her hands.

"What do you mean, we don't have to worry, son?" asked Johnny.

"I've got it covered. I can pay the lot."

"What?" said Suzie, sounding a bit like a bicycle hooter honking.

"Come on," said Johnny. "I know you've got a few bob, son, but I think five hundred grand is a bit beyond your means. Unless you've won the pools or something."

"Mum, Dad. I don't want what I'm about to tell you to leave this room."

Suzie looked at her son with her head crooked to one side, doing another dog impression.

"Blimey, he *has* won the bloody pools!" said Johnny.

"No, Dad, I haven't. If you'll just listen. You know I invested grandma's inheritance and made a bit of money?" He looked from his mother to his father, who now both had assumed the crooked dog's head pose. "Well, according to James, who handles my affairs…"

"Who's James?" asked Johnny.

"What affairs?" asked Suzie.

Danny rolled his eyes. "You know. James. James from university."

"Oh, yeah. James. Nice lad. Shared that flat with you and…" A slap on his shoulder from Suzie left the sentence unfinished.

"Go on, Danny," she said.

"Well, according to James, my net worth is now somewhere near £1.5 billion and growing."

This declaration was followed by thirty seconds of silence as his parents sat staring at each other, with 'Did you just hear what I just heard?' expressions on their faces, their heads making little jerky movements like chickens.

The first to react was Johnny. "Ba-ba-ba-billion, with a 'B'?" He started to nod his head between his fingers again, and Suzie looked like her brain had just been sucked out.

"Yep. Billion with a 'B'."

Danny took a few sips of his tea while his parents processed this information.

Suzie was the first to recover her senses. "Jesus, Danny. You've got to stop doing this to us. Didn't you think it might be something you'd tell your mother and father? Why on earth didn't we know about this? I mean, why all the secrecy? You didn't trust us or something? We're your parents, you know? Your own flesh and blood. I can tell you, I'm suffering a sort of déjà vu here. It's exactly like that day all those years ago when Doctor Hanks told me you were deaf."

"I can't really answer that, Mum. I guess I got lucky with some investments and things just moved quickly. The speed at which the money has accumulated and the sheer amount of it made me feel a little uncomfortable. I really don't know how to explain it. This sort of money attracts a lot of attention, and James and I thought it best to remain as anonymous as possible. You have to remember that I also had a lot going on. You know, what with work and so on. I've often thought about telling you, but I just didn't get around to finding the right moment."

"Bloody hell, Danny. It is not like not telling us you've bought a new car or something. You're a bloody billionaire. Did you think we'd be asking you for great chunks of it or something?" said Johnny.

"Johnny, leave him alone," said Suzie. "Whatever his reasons, that's not the important thing now. All I know is, I woke up this morning wondering how I was going to top myself, with pills or by jumping off a bridge – and now I'm probably the happiest person on the planet."

She got up and hugged her son like she'd never hugged him before. Tears streamed down her face.

"Okay, okay, Mum, you're strangling me."

Johnny laughed and shook his head with a look of resignation. "Look, whatever your reasons, do me a favour, son. Just tell me now if you've got any more secrets you want to reveal. I mean, you're not going to strip off your clothes and fly off out the door dressed in some red underpants, are you?"

Danny laughed. "No. No more secrets, Dad," he lied.

Confessing to his parents had been surprisingly cathartic and left him feeling as if he'd been set free of one of the heavy ball and chains he'd been dragging around for a while now, and he left their house feeling light of foot and determined to be rid of the rest of them.

It was time to call Molly.

For two solid days Danny's heart was doing drumrolls in his chest each time he dialled and waited for someone to answer the phone at Simon's house, but nobody did.

He finally decided to try Molly's parents, dialling most of the number and hanging up a few times before a brief self-pep talk and some deep breaths gave him the courage to complete the whole number. He hadn't spoken to them for more than two years.

"Hello," answered a familiar Scottish voice in a flat, neutral tone.

"Hi, Maggie. It's Danny," he said as chirpily as he could.

Five or six seconds passed without any response from the other end of the line.

"Maggie?"

An angry man's voice responded.

"You've got a bloody cheek calling here, Danny. Don't you think our family has been through enough?"

"Dennis, I…"

"Why, Danny? Why couldn't you have stayed out of her life?"

"Dennis, I don't know how much or what you've been told, but…"

"After all she'd been through, Molly was happy at last. She'd found a good man, she had a lovely home, she had even bought a bloody wedding dress, for Christ's sake."

"I know it must be hard, but…"

"But what, Danny? What were you thinking? Did you really read that conversation about New York and all that? I mean, you're not exactly a picture of credibility considering all this business with the actor that's in the papers. Molly told us what you were up to with your Mum. That you were both behind this false story and the lawsuit. What's that all about? We love and respect Simon and it broke our hearts when he turned up here in tears.

"Dennis. Please let me explain."

"Don't bother, Danny. Although we still appreciate all you did for Declan and respect the love he had for you, I think it'd be for the best if you didn't call again."

"But Dennis, you've got it all wrong. You have to believe me. Look, I'd really like to talk to Molly. Is she there?"

"Goodbye, Danny. We wish you well and good luck."

CHAPTER 32

Danny was now the Count of Monte Cristo and, just like his hero, it was time to put his revenge plan in motion. With his money and his contacts, he was going to make this happen. The first thing he did was to ask James to set up a Family Limited Partnership company with four million pounds capital that would give his parents access to the funds.

He then instructed James to buy the media company that employed Simon.

"What are you up to, Danny?" asked James.

"All in good time, James. All in good time."

He then went to see Martin White.

"So, what's this all about, Danny?"

"I suppose you know all about recent events regarding a certain magazine article?"

"You know I do, and it's something I had planned to talk to you about. Danny, it goes without saying that we were aware of your extra-curricular activities with the gossip stories, and, although not entirely happy with it, we decided that it couldn't compromise your work with us. Besides, it made for a good cover story, forgive the pun, and we let you get on with it. Here in MI6 and across the pond we're very pleased with your work, and your contributions to national security matters have been notable."

"Thanks, Martin. Good to know."

"Quiet. As you are aware, there's plenty going on in the world right now that requires attention: Iraq, the Serbia-Kosovo conflict, the Chinese are about to send a rocket into space, not to mention that your friend and ours will more than likely face impeachment this year."

Danny couldn't help but remember Clinton's team's request for his services regarding Monica Lewinsky.

"In a way, this whole affair has done us a favour, and it seems to have been resolved satisfactorily. What's most important to us is your name hasn't been revealed, so all's well that ends well."

"Well, Martin, that's the reason why I've come to you. It has been resolved as far as settling the defamation issue; but, from a personal point of view, it's far from resolved."

Martin sat back and scrutinised his protégé. Danny could almost hear his mind working, trying to anticipate his motive for asking for the meeting. He leant back in his leather chair and clutched his hand behind his head.

"Go on," he said.

"I suppose you also know all about my financial affairs."

"I do. You've built yourself a formidable fortune in just a couple of years. I commend your friend James on his money management skills. It's been difficult even for us to keep a track of just where all that money is and how much there is of it."

"I'll be sure to let him know. Well, you may or may not know that the whole thing was a set-up. Molly... you know who Molly is, right?"

"Of course."

"Well, Molly's husband-to-be, a guy called Simon Smith-Jameson, arranged for two actresses – how he managed to do it, I don't know, but I imagine he paid them – to purposely leak that false story by way of a conversation for me to pick up."

"Surprisingly naive of you to fall for that, by the way."

"Yeah, yeah, I agree, but that's not the point. I'd like MI6 to help me make him pay for it."

Martin's eyebrows did a little dance.

"If you do this for me, Martin, I promise I'll stay on the team."

"Sounds like an ultimatum."

"Let's just call it an exchange of favours."

Martin leaned forward and interlocked his fingers on the desk.

"Okay, Danny, let's say we have a deal. Now just how do you think we can make this Simon pay?"

***

Simon didn't know what hit him. In the space of only four weeks, he was investigated and found guilty of false tax returns, he was sacked from his job, he lost his house, the two actresses confessed to the daily tabloids their part in leaking the story and he was arrested for soliciting prostitution with a minor.

James sat smiling at his desk when Danny came in.

"Well, Danny, old boy. I suppose you're pleased with your handiwork? You're clearly not a man to cross."

"It had to be done."

"Indeed. Revenge is a dish served cold and all that."

Danny let out a long, evil laugh like an arch-villain's in a Bond movie.

"No, seriously, I couldn't have done it without you, James. How much did we pay those actresses, by the way?"

"Let's just say enough to buy a small house each."

Danny smiled. "Worth every penny."

"I have to say your instinct was bang on regarding how the whole actor thing had been a set-up."

"It couldn't have been anything else. After all, the whole conversation was between two actresses, and thinking back over it all, they were damn good at their job."

"The surprising thing was, once they knew how much money was up for grabs, they were pretty quick to confess to my intermediary how Smith-Jameson had approached them and set the whole thing up. The actor story had been his invention. They just had to make sure they acted out the scene in front of you."

"Bloody expensive and elaborate way to get back at me. But I must admit, quite creative and ingenious in its own way."

"Damned Machiavellian, if you ask me; but, Danny, I have to ask you. I know the part I played in all this, but how did you manage to pull off the rest? The tax stuff and especially the prostitute thing?"

"Perhaps it's better you don't know, James." He smiled when he remembered Martin giving him a step-by-step account of the intricate interventions and manoeuvres he had orchestrated with a small OTG team, which apparently stood for 'Off the grid', that involved Her Majesty's Revenue and Customs and a deep-cover vice squad.

"Pretty dammed impressive, I should say. So, what's your next step? To have the poor sod knocked off in jail?"

Danny laughed. "No, I think he's got what was coming to him. I'll take it as closed. Now I want to get in touch with Molly."

He noticed James take a deep intake of breath through clenched teeth. He knew James well enough to know that he only did this when he was about to announce some sort of problem.

"What?"

"Well, that's going to be tough, because she left for Kenya with the charity a week ago."

"What? And you're telling me this now?"

"I only got confirmation today when going over future projects and budgets with John Kenward."

"Bloody hell!" Danny felt his elation instantly evaporate.

"Well, in a way, you can be blamed for that, Danny. After all, it was your initiative with the Kenyan government that got the charity the green light."

His first urge was to get on a plane to Nairobi immediately, but Martin White sent him to the United Nations, along with 'The Russian', Jean-Michelle and his friend Sammy.

There were some important resolutions in play regarding Iraq and NATO. The US and UK governments were interested in getting any information they could about Russia and China's voting intentions.

What's more, a special request from Clinton's office had been put in for Danny to be in Washington for the few days leading up to 12th February, when the senate would vote on whether to remove Clinton from office. The trial had lasted five weeks, and Clinton's team made sure Danny was either strategically placed to pick up private conversations or had him watching surveillance videos.

At times, he felt like he was back with his mother picking up gossip at celebrity functions. He couldn't believe that the Clinton organisation, and much less MI6, would sanction such a frivolous exercise that had absolutely nothing to do with international security. MI6 had already refused his involvement at an earlier request. His own frivolous use of MI6 resources never even entered his head.

He didn't even meet Clinton. He was picked up from his hotel in the morning and either taken to a chosen location where conversations were to take place or to a bunker-like office in downtown Washington to watch live feeds or video tapes.

They needed a two-thirds majority to remove Clinton. Danny's reports went a long way to convince the President's team that the vote would be close to a 50-50 split and would get nowhere near what was required for impeachment. He nailed it.

Danny got back to his New York hotel room at 11pm. Leaving his bag in the corner of the room, he checked his answerphone service.

There were three calls from his mother, each lasting far too long, as she was indifferent to the fact she was having a one-way conversation with a machine. Then Dennis McCracken's familiar voice was pleading him to call. He just wanted to be given the chance to apologise and eat, in his words, a 'ginormous humble pie'.

Danny couldn't help playing the message again with a huge grin. How he'd have loved to be a fly on the wall in the McCracken household when the whole story broke about Simon and how he had set up the magazine. Although the newspapers and news channels hadn't mentioned Danny's name, they would surely have put two and two together.

He sensed a current of excitement overwhelm him, thinking about his impending reunion with Molly.

He ordered a burger from room service and took a shower. Feeling more relaxed and happier than he had for quite some time, he sat on the end of his bed dressed in the hotel's white towelling robe and switched on the TV. He was tired and needed some light distraction after the last few days in Washington.

An interminable advert came on selling a kind of wonder food mixer that apparently and inexplicably did more than just mix food. He flicked through the channels, shaking his head in dismay; rodeos, infomercials touting revolutionary exercise equipment, kids' cartoons, *Knight Rider*, *Bewitched*, infomercials pushing cooking knives, black and white movies, secondhand car lot adverts, and unscrupulous lawyers specialising in personal injuries.

He decided to turn the sound off. Since he'd regained his hearing, from time to time he felt he needed silence. He actually missed it and, although having the faculty of all his five senses was enormously practical, he found that sometimes noise filled every available cavity of his brain, leaving no room for his thoughts or his imagination. Silence was peace.

That was what peace sounded like; nothing.

"Long live the USA!" he said aloud.

He couldn't help musing. If people knew what he'd been doing, and the content of most of the conversations he had picked up in Washington, they would probably never be able to take what was considered the most powerful country in the world seriously ever again. Supposedly highly educated and highly placed government representatives spouting acute examples of hypocrisy, misogyny, sexism and sheer maliciousness.

He finally stopped his channel-hopping on the TV sitcom, *Friends*. He'd seen the episode more than once, but the light, superficial banter was exactly what he felt like watching. Lip-reading comedy was a particularly enriching experience, giving him the chance to appreciate the nuances of the actors' talents.

He was just beginning to feel that he'd found what he was looking for and was anticipating the arrival of his room service burger, when the phone rang. He took a glance at his watch on the bedside table; 11.30pm. Calls at this time of night were invariably bad news.

"Hello?"

"Danny?"

"Martin! What's wrong? Has our friend of Monica had a problem?"

"No, Danny, I'm afraid this is serious. It's Molly."

He could feel his hands start to tremble, and his mouth was suddenly awash with a sharp taste of metal.

"Molly? What about Molly?"

The sharp intake of breath on the other end didn't help to calm his nerves.

"It seems three workers from Molly's deaf charity have been kidnapped from their base in Limuru and..." He exhaled. "I'm afraid Molly is one of them."

Danny sat staring at Chandler hugging Joey on the TV.

"Danny? You there?"

There was a knock on the door.

"Room service."

"Hang on a sec."

"Danny!" said Martin.

In a daze, he dropped the phone, opened the door, let the waiter wheel in his burger, and showed him out without a tip.

"Shit-head," came a shout from the hallway.

He picked up the phone and waited a few seconds.

"Martin. What do you mean, it seems? Just tell me exactly what you do know. I mean, all the facts. Where is she and who has kidnapped her?"

"Now, Danny, we're doing everything we can to get more details. I know this must be extraordinarily difficult for you. You had plans to go to Kenya as soon as this assignment was over, right?"

"Just give me the facts, Martin."

"The deaf charity received a telegram that has originated in Garissa, a small city in the east of Kenya, at 1200hrs GMT today. It stated that a group calling itself 'Adel' had captured a group of charity workers from the teacher training centre based in Limuru. They're demanding two million dollars to be paid in cash and the release of some Muslim militants who were arrested in connection with the Nairobi embassy bombings, who are being held in Mombasa."

"Fuck!"

"They've given seven days to carry out their demands or they'll be killed."

"So who's dealing with them? Have we answered them?"

"Unofficially, we are. Here at MI6 we've answered, telling them to stand by, and we have asked for proof of life."

"How did it get to you?"

"The deaf charity immediately got in touch with the Foreign Office, who in turn informed us. When there's a release of terrorist prisoners involved, we're always brought in. As you well know, since the emergence of Al Qaida, the government is particularly worried about anything to do with Muslim extremist groups."

"So what do we know about this group, Adel? Are they linked to Al Qaida?"

"Absolutely nothing. *Adel* means *Justice* in Arabic. We're in touch with Kenyan Intelligence, who are now investigating and gathering information on the militants named in the demand to see if there are any links."

"So who are we talking to exactly?"

"They've told us we're probably dealing with an independent negotiator and not directly with the kidnappers."

"Have we *any* idea where they are? Do we have that proof of life?"

"We suspect they're somewhere near the Somalian border, but they're probably moving them every day."

"And proof of life? Is Molly definitely one of the hostages?"

"No proof of life yet. It took a few hours, but first we had confirmation from the other charity workers and locals that Molly was among the three people captured. Apparently, a truck with several armed men appeared in the night, stopped outside the small building where Molly and her team of teachers were housed and, in a matter of minutes, were bundling them into the back of a pick-up, blindfolded and with their hands tied. It seems they shot one of the four people in Molly's building during the assault. It's all we've got. As I said, I'm afraid we haven't had proof of life yet."

"Fuck. Fuck. Fuck!"

Danny's mind was racing. He tried to picture the scene at the village and put himself in Molly's shoes. Being deaf, the whole thing must have been even more terrifying, if that were at all possible. And her back? He shuddered and started puffing strongly.

"Now calm down, Danny. We'll get her back, but I'm not going to kid you. It's not going to be easy."

"How can I bloody calm down? Look, I'll pay the money. You know I can."

"Yes, yes, but this has to be handled with the maximum discretion. It's not just about handing over the money and getting them back. This whole prisoner release thing complicates the situation considerably."

"I really couldn't give a damn about the prisoners."

"Danny, I can fully understand how you feel, but this has to be done as carefully as possible."

"Okay, okay, I know. It's just that... So how do we move forward?"

"Listen, Danny. It's best we don't discuss any of the details on the phone. Get on the first available flight back to London and come straight to the office."

"Can I take Jean-Michelle back with me? I'd like to be able to count on him. He can speak the language and knows the region."

"Sure."

"Can you call him and organise the flights? We'll also want flights to Nairobi as soon as possible."

"I'll sort it out. We'll talk about everything tomorrow at the office."

Danny spent the rest of the night pacing around the room. The hamburger went untouched, and he turned the TV off. His heart felt like it had been ripped apart and little pieces of it were running through his veins, each piece still beating. He tried to imagine where Molly was and how she must be feeling at that very moment. The mental images made him feel nauseous and frustrated. The last time he'd felt such impotency was when Declan had lay dying in his arms.

At around 6am, he thought about calling her parents, but decided not to until he had more information. Instead, he called James.

"Danny! Thank God you called. I had no idea how to get hold of you. Something's happened, and all I know is that you were on one of your mysterious trips abroad."

"I know all about Molly, James."

"How?"

"Never mind. What do you know?"

"All I know is what John Kenward has told me. Apparently, it's in the hands of the government."

"Listen. They're demanding two million dollars in cash. Can you get that amount together in twenty-four hours?"

"Jesus! That's a lot of cash. I'll speak to your bank in London."

"Thanks. I'll be back tomorrow. I'll be touch."

"I'm really sorry, Danny. She's... I mean, I know how much..."

"James, just get that cash together."

***

Dawn was breaking and Danny switched the lights off. A faint grey hue of light tinged the room, and he went to have another shower, mainly for something to do. He stood under the hot water in a daze, unable to grab a continuous line of thought. For some reason, he could only hear an imaginary, single finger hitting single keys on the piano in his head. The bathroom filled with steam, and Danny dried himself without being able to see himself in the mirror. The one- fingered piano tune continued to play in his head as if he was in some melancholic arty film.

Dressed and back in the room with a narrow ray of sun dissecting it, he packed his bag and headed off to catch the 8am flight from JFK. A sombre-looking Jean-Michelle was waiting with a car at the front of the hotel, dressed in one of his habitual flowery shirts.

Danny fully expected one of his cryptic fruit analogies, but he just nodded and held the door open.

CHAPTER 33

Molly woke with her head pounding with an intense ring of pain, as if someone had wrapped barbed wire around it. Her mouth and throat were dry, and she tried unsuccessfully to muster up some saliva. Hot and humid air filled her lungs, and tiny rivulets of sweat trickled down her chest and the middle of her back. Her damp cotton T-shirt clung to her like a second skin. Beneath her, she could feel an uneven, packed, warm earth floor. Not only could she feel it; she could smell it. Pungent and peaty. She was blindfolded with a kind of cloth bound so tightly that she couldn't lift her eyelids. Another cloth gagged her mouth, pulling her lips wide and forcing her to breathe through her nose. Her ankles and wrists were tied with what felt like rope, her wrists behind her back. From its rounded shape, she guessed she was sat up against a pole, which, from its slightly rutted, smooth texture, was probably wooden. Her lower back felt like it had a bony knee digging into it.

Deprived of her most important sense, and with the sharp spikes perforating her cotton wool-filled head, her disorientation was considerable if not complete. She turned her face to the left and to the right, her stiff neck making this simple movement painful. Panic began to envelop her as it all came rushing back to her. Short breaths accompanied an accelerated heartbeat and her chest felt as if it had been stamped on. She had been kidnapped.

In the middle of the night, three gunmen had burst into the small, prefabricated hut that housed herself and three of her local trainee teachers. The first thing she knew about this intrusion was when she was brutally jerked to her feet by a strong grip on her arm. Her scream was instantly met with a ferocious slap around the face.

A beam of light shone through the open door, which was enough to reveal the outline of everybody in the room. As they moved through the light, she could see that there were at least three intruders carrying machine guns and dressed in military outfits, with tagelmusts wrapped around their heads and faces.

She was pulled across the room towards the door, along with her room-mates. She was dressed only in a long, pale blue T-shirt and was barefoot. A series of thuds in quick succession resonated in her stomach and chest, accompanied by a white flash coming from the muzzle of one of the guns. Her scream was muffled by a rough hand covering her mouth.

Waiting outside the door was a flat-back truck, its headlights on full beam, which had been the source of the light. The smell of fumes suggested the engine was running. They were roughly bundled into the back and joined by their captors, one of whom banged on the cabin roof to signal it was time to move. Her knees had been knocked on the metal floor, which felt cold and gritty. The last thing she remembered was the cloud of dust that the wheels threw up as they sped off, then a sweet-smelling cloth being held over her mouth as she blacked out.

Behind her, as well as the pole, she noticed the brush of someone's fingertips. Pulling her knees up to her chest and shuffling her back up as close as she could to the pole, she stretched her own fingertips out, wriggling them and hoping for a response. She wondered who her fellow captive may be.

There had been three others who shared the room at the training centre. There was Ruthie, her favourite and most promising trainer. Only eighteen and already a gifted signer, with a deaf mother and two deaf brothers, she had come from a local village to join the programme.

Unlike most of her family, she could hear and was adept in KSL, Kenyan Sign Language, and LAK, Swahili Sign Language. In the short time they had been together, their relationship was strengthened by teaching each other their respective sign languages.

Ruthie had a permanent toothy smile, radiating a happiness that was so contagious that everybody around could not help smiling.

There were two sisters, Moffi and Boffi. Both deaf, they had come to the programme less out of vocation to teach and more out of a need to secure paid employment. At least they were assured food, a roof over their heads, and they could support their numerous family members in the north of the country.

Molly's wriggling fingers were briefly gripped by a hand, then she was aware that her fellow prisoner's fingertips were tapping hers and she took about thirty seconds to realise that it was tactile signing, a way to communicate by spelling out words just using the hands. She then knew it had to be Ruthie, as she was the only one capable of using this method, thanks to it forming part of the training programme and hours spent practising together. It was difficult to decipher, not being able to see. Although Ruthie was still a relative beginner, having to repeat the desired message up to a dozen times, Molly could make out just enough sense of it to learn that Boffi wasn't with them and had most likely been shot when they were taken. Moffi was somewhere in the room to their left, as she had heard her crying.

They asked each other where they might be and speculated on who their captors were. Each exchange took painstaking concentration to transmit and understand, and a conversation that could be had in a few minutes took ten times longer.

Ruthie had heard them speaking Swahili as they barked orders at them. From the heat in the room, they deduced it was some time in the early afternoon.

Ruthie tapped that kidnappings in the region were becoming quite common, but usually involved rich tourists on safari staying at the luxury lodges that dotted the region.

Molly was still terrified and trembling, but Ruthie's company was calming, so much so that she could think a little bit about their situation and possible scenarios and outcomes.

Their kidnappers had surely made some ransom demands, most likely to the charity, and that meant for the moment they were a valuable asset.

The tactile signing stopped for a moment when Molly sensed a change in the room.

A warm waft of air caressed her face, and she felt the presence of other people. Ruthie confirmed this with her tapping. She could hear two voices speaking in Swahili. They were debating how they were going to take a photo of all three of them together and whether it should be with or without a blindfold. Molly was now getting used to Ruthie's rudimentary tapping, and the speed at which she could pick up what she was saying was almost in real time.

Their captors went about getting them together for the photo. This was achieved by sitting Moffi between them and tying her to the same pole, then making Molly and Ruthie shift around until they were in a line. They both felt Moffi's hands trembling, and they gripped her fingers to reassure her; however, tapping was now impossible.

Several minutes later, Molly felt the blindfold roughly removed and light flooded her brain. It took a few seconds to be able to lift her eyelids. She looked to her left and met the blinking gazes of her two companions, their eyes shouting fear, their skin and clothes covered with a film of light brown dust, darker where it was mixed with sweat.

Two men stood talking in front of them. One held the blindfolds and had an automatic weapon slung over his shoulder; the other was holding a Polaroid instant camera. They seemed to have a problem with how to use it, as it was passed back and forth between them, each taking turns to examine it from every angle and press all the buttons, then comically blinding each other with the flash. They accumulated several squares and waited for the photos to develop, waving them in the air to dry and examining them.

At last they seemed satisfied that they were now ready to take their photo. Several discarded images now lay at their booted feet. The flash left Molly with two pink circles in her vision, which remained when she was blindfolded again a few minutes later.

She wondered who the photo was for. The charity? Her parents? Her poor parents. Did they know? Hadn't they suffered enough? She could feel her tears run down her cheeks and it became difficult to breathe as her nose was blocked.

She shook off the tears by changing her thought track and asking herself some more practical questions. If the kidnappers were demanding money, how much would they be asking for? How much were three charity workers worth? Did the charity have millions to rescue them?

There were rumours that the charity's benefactor was a billionaire. That would certainly explain how they had gone from being a small UK charity, with some serious financial challenges putting their very existence at risk, to being an international organisation in the space of less than a year.

Was she afraid to die? Was this where it was all to end? Yes, she was terrified of dying. It was true that there had been moments in her life where she would have greeted death with open arms: when they told her in the hospital about Declan's death, during her long recuperation at her parents' home, and, of course, during the whole ordeal with Simon. But even though it had only been a few months in Kenya, her life had once again recovered a sense of purpose and joy that she thought had been gone forever. She was making a real difference to people's lives.

Her reflections then turned to her childhood with Declan, and soundbites of their experiences together made her well up again, and she tried to swallow what felt like a lodged golf ball in her throat.

It was the good times that came to her now. The classes she gave at the Manchester Deaf Centre, the books she had read, the friends she had made, and yes, Danny. She remembered the day she had met him, their first kiss and just how extraordinarily happy she had been with him and how full of fun their lives had been during the years they had lived together with Declan. What happened? Sitting there, gagged and bound in stifling heat in a remote village in Kenya, she struggled to recover those feelings of resentment and blame that she harboured for so many years and any satisfactory justification for pushing him out of her life. Searching deep inside her soul, she could find none, and that hurt. It had all been so clear-cut and her decision unequivocal. If she were to die, if this was to be the end, she would go with a mountain of regrets, but this was to be her biggest.

Why didn't she get in touch with him when the news broke about Simon and everything fell apart? She had felt embarrassed and confused, but she needed time to gather her thoughts and emotions. Kenya seemed to be the perfect place to do it.

It took quite some time to realise that the three of them were once again alone.

Moffi was still tied to the pole, but Molly was aware that her hands were being tapped. She shifted around to her right to get herself back-to-back with Ruthie and was at last able to make some sense of her tapping.

Ruthie tapped that the photo was to be sent to an intermediary, and they were to be moved to another village that night.

Two hours later, one of the kidnappers came in and removed Molly's gag, allowing her to take a deep breath of warm air through her mouth; and just as her stretched lips were starting to regain their natural form, they came into contact with some type of metal bowl and a warm lumpy liquid was being poured into her mouth. Her head was pushed back by a palm on her forehead. It tasted like thickly floured water and although her initial reaction was to gag, she swallowed the clumpy liquid, glad to lubricate her dry throat.

Her gag was all too quickly retied, the blindfolds on and the three of them were once more left alone with the sounds of silence.

CHAPTER 34

Danny and Jean-Michelle entered the E4 building at 10am. They had come straight from Heathrow. His driver, sent by James, had dropped them off and taken his luggage back to his Barbican flat. He also handed him a black leather bag containing two million in cash.

"Morning, boys," said the receptionist, wearing a black T-shirt with a picture of Miss Piggy kissing Kermit. "Martin's up in his office expecting you."

Danny hadn't slept for at least twenty-four hours, having spent the whole flight dealing with a menagerie of thoughts and emotions. He wasn't in the mood for such chirpiness and just headed for the stairs. They bounded up them, only to pause at their floor a second to exchange nods with Sammy and Shane, who had swivelled around away from their screens.

Sammy mouthed, "I'm so sorry, Danny."

Victor didn't take his eyes off his screen.

They were buzzed into Martin's office and found him sitting behind his desk. A map of Kenya was on his big screen, and two men that Danny didn't know, dressed in dark grey suits, got up to greet them.

"Danny, Jean-Michelle, this is Mr Black and Mr Blue. They're here from head office to help co-ordinate."

They shook hands, and only the circumstances stopped Danny from making a quip about Tarentino's *Reservoir Dogs*. He was also now quite sure that White was not Martin's real name.

"Please take a seat, gentlemen."

Mr Black was the first to speak, which gave Danny the notion that he had seniority over the rest.

"Danny, we've been following you since you were a teenager. I must say you're an impressive young man."

"Very flattering and even more unnerving, but we're not here for a *This Is Your Life* show. Let's talk about how we're going to get Molly back alive. Does the government have any kind of plan as to how we can get her out of there? Because if you don't, with your unlimited knowledge of every aspect of my life, you must be aware that I can easily meet the kidnappers' financial demands and I intend to fly out there personally to deliver it." He tapped the black bag at his feet.

"Yes, yes. If you'd let me finish. We're perfectly aware of this, and we also know all about your history with Molly and we know about your little sideline as a gossip journalist, which Mr White convinced us to turn a blind eye to, and the whole messy incident involving the actor. We also suspect that Mr White here had something to do with Molly's fiancé's meteoric downfall."

Danny and Martin exchanged glances like two naughty schoolboys with a secret.

"So where are you going with this?"

"You've become a productive and useful asset to the division. Your work in China, Hong Kong, Northern Ireland and the UN has been extremely useful, providing us and the government with invaluable information and insight. Your skills are undoubtedly outstanding."

"As I said before, all very flattering, but…"

"What Mr Black is trying to convey is, we can't afford to have you flying out there with a suitcase full of cash on your own and putting yourself at risk of being killed or kidnapped. You're an irreplaceable asset. The Iraq situation is becoming more critical by the day, and we're going to need those skills more than ever," said Mr Blue, employing a more aggressive tone than his boss.

"Well, gentlemen, I'm sorry, but I'm going and you can't stop me."

Mr Black took the reins again. "If you'll just calm down and let us finish, you'll know that we don't intend to stop you. In fact, we're going to help you. Why do you think you're here? As Mr White told you, it's in the government's interest to keep you in our division. However, the government's established a policy of zero tolerance for negotiating with terrorists. The fact that the demands include the release of terrorist prisoners makes it our business. Clinton's people are also eager to give any support that we need to bring this to a successful conclusion."

"What do you call a successful conclusion?"

All three Misters exchanged glances.

"To identify the kidnappers and the organisation behind them and to destroy them."

"Tell me, is Molly's release factored into that conclusion?"

"Absolutely!"

Danny was convinced that it wasn't, and a silence followed as all parties left unsaid what each was thinking.

Mr Blue stood up and approached the large map. "According to our analysts' estimations, taking into account the location of the kidnapping, the roads and tracks around it and calculating the distances it would be possible to cover in the available time-frames we have, we suspect they are somewhere around or in this area."

He produced a red felt-tip pen from somewhere and drew a circle the size of an orange.

"That's encouraging, but that's still a large area."

"We've got a CIA satellite covering the area now, as well as a reconnaissance aircraft. If we can pinpoint them, we'll have them. We can get a joint Kenyan-UK special forces unit in range within an hour. We've been told we can use a base not too far from Nairobi."

"But don't you think an attack would put the hostages' lives in danger?"

"They're already in danger."

Martin put his hand on Danny's shoulder. "Look, Danny, it's no exaggeration when I tell you that our special forces are exceptional; they are the very best, and if we pinpoint where they are, the chances of getting Molly and her colleagues out safely are very high."

"But not a hundred percent?"

Martin shrugged and held up his open palms.

Danny massaged his forehead as if trying to rub any negative thoughts from his mind.

"The instructions are to send one government representative with the ransom money and authority to organise the release of the militant prisoners. He's to stay at the Sarova Stanley Hotel in the central business district and will be contacted by someone representing the kidnappers."

"And that'll be me."

"Yes. Yes. That'll be you," said Mr Black.

"Good! Can I take Jean-Michelle? He was with me in Nairobi on the last trip and he could be very useful."

Jean-Michelle grinned.

"Absolutely, but he'll travel separately on a commercial flight and check in independently. He'll be your eyes and ears in Kenya, but he will not be at your side, so to speak. Jean-Michelle, we'll give you instructions and your brief before you go. Okay?"

Jean-Michelle grinned and held up a skinny thumb.

"And how am I getting there?" asked Danny.

"On an RAF transport plane that will take off from our Northolt base in West London. Easier to get you into Nairobi with a bag full of cash without any unfortunate incidents. We've already briefed Sammy, one of your colleagues, who will be your direct contact with us and our local agents. They will be no further than a hundred metres from you at all times. All communication will be limited to lip-reading. You only have to mouth messages to Sammy and receive instructions by the same method."

"Ingenious, yet at the same time quite obviously simple," said Danny, pleased that his closest friend in the unit was going to be with him in Nairobi. He'd been happy to see him on the way up the stairs. They must have flown him back from New York.

"How are the kidnappers' representatives going to make contact with me?"

"They'll approach you in the main lobby of the hotel. You're to sit at one of the tables until you're contacted."

"And how will I know it's them?"

"You'll be asked if you prefer coffee or tea."

"Oh, very subtle. Is that straight from the MI6 book of sophisticated code words? And what am I supposed to reply? I mean, just in case I happen to be approached by someone who has a genuine interest in my taste in beverages?"

"No need to be facetious, Danny," said Martin, sternly.

"I'm sorry. I'm just feeling a bit edgy about the whole trip."

"We understand perfectly," said Mr Blue. "Your answer will be coffee in the morning and tea in the afternoon."

Danny went to speak again, but Martin shot him a glance that could kill.

"You'll get a further briefing on the plane, but from the moment you enter the hotel, Sammy will be your only point of contact. One of our teams will always be within fifty feet of you."

"That's reassuring."

"So, Danny, take your bag of cash, and there's a car waiting for you downstairs that will take you to the airfield. We wish you luck, and let's hope that the next time we see you will be to celebrate a successful conclusion."

Danny stood up and shook all their hands.

"Thank you, gentlemen, for your support and everything you're doing. I really appreciate it."

On the way down the stairs, he crossed with Sammy on the way up. They hugged briefly and Danny mouthed, "See you on the other side."

The car took him right up to the enormous plane's steps. On entering the rear door, he was fully expecting the interior of the plane to resemble what he had seen in WW2 films: rows of inward-facing seats lining the sides. Instead, he found himself in what appeared to be a normal charter flight aircraft with hundreds of rows of dark green seats that only lacked the logo headrests, hovering air hostesses and glossy flight magazines.

He was greeted by a man who introduced himself as Paul Green, middle-aged, bald, with steel-framed glasses, whose only remarkable feature was conspicuous by its absence: he had no discernible chin or jawline. He reminded Danny of his school maths teacher.

He was invited to sit in one of the empty rows at the front. He placed his bag on the seat next to him. Paul hovered around in front of him like a worried parent.

A few moments later, a dozen shaven-headed men dressed in army fatigues, with automatic weapons slung over their shoulders, boarded the plane, and each one nodded at Danny as he passed to the back of the plane in silence.

Danny raised his eyebrows as a way of asking who they were.

"Special Ops," said Paul Green, almost as a whisper.

"Of course," said Danny. "They look like they mean business."

"I can promise you, they do. Do you want to go over the brief now or would you prefer to sleep a little? It's a long flight."

Just hearing the word sleep triggered an extreme need to do so in Danny's head. He was exhausted, and his mental and physical batteries were on empty.

"If you don't mind, I'd like to sleep."

He was passed out before the plane had even taken off.

Several hours later, he was woken by some gentle shoulder shaking and saw that Paul was sitting next to him.

"Coffee?"

His neck was stuck in forward position, and he had dribbled on his shirt. He hadn't had a chance to put the seat back, he had passed out so quickly. His first thought was coffee and his second was to remember to buy his own plane. He sometimes forgot just how much spending power he had.

The rest of the flight was taken up by Paul going over the plan again and again and a long visit to the bathroom to wash, shave and change clothes. He was given a pair of beige cotton trousers and a pressed light blue shirt that somehow MI6 had managed to provide at short notice.

They landed at an airstrip surrounded by a rocky, arid terrain dotted with low thorny shrubs. A pale blue, cloudless sky gave no clue to what time of the day it was. He hadn't adjusted his watch since he'd been in New York, so the two o'clock it was showing meant nothing at all.

From his window, Danny saw four jeeps approach the plane. The lack of any visible buildings made him wonder where they had come from. He watched three of them head for the rear doors which, now open, were letting warm air pass through the cabin as if someone had opened an oven door. The jeeps were soon full of his flight companions and headed off out of sight.

Danny and Paul descended the front basic metal steps that appeared soon after. The fourth jeep was awaiting them with a Kenyan uniformed driver. Danny felt his lungs cooking as he crossed the few yards to the jeep.

Paul Green got in with him. Beads of sweat were already streaming down his forehead, which he constantly dabbed at with a white handkerchief. He tapped the driver on the shoulder as a signal to go.

"Now, just to go over the basics again. We'll take you to a civilian Land Rover and you'll be driven into Nairobi to your hotel. Remember, you're to check in as any guest would. You may spot your colleague Sammy in the lobby. He'll be the only one of the local team you'll see, but I can assure you everybody will be in place and no further than fifty yards from you. As soon as you're settled in, go down to the lobby lounge and wait. Find Sammy and he'll relay any instructions or information to you via lip-reading. Rather impressed, by the way. I understand you can read lips at a considerable distance."

"Thanks, but what sort of distance are we talking about?"

"Oh, I don't know. As I said before, shouldn't be more than fifty yards."

Danny nodded. He had once participated in a test that the division set up to see from just how far away he could read lips. He managed to relay perfectly at sixty yards in English and around twenty in Mandarin.

"Should be okay if I get a clear view, but I know that Sammy can't manage more than thirty yards, so he'll have to get within that distance to read mine."

"All under control," said Paul Green.

"So it seems. Anything else?"

"You'll find a suitcase with a few changes of clothes in the boot of the Land Rover. So, don't forget to tell the bellboy to get it."

It took them almost half an hour of driving through the dry and sparse landscape on a straight, dusty track to get to any kind of civilisation. The appearance of acacia trees, with their flat crowns and ever denser green, leafy shrubs, ushered them through to a tiny mud-hut village shaded by clumps of high palm trees. Barefoot children and barking dogs chased their jeep. Five or six similar villages later, each a little closer to the next, they arrived at a mass of thousands of shanty sheds with the familiar and ubiquitous rusty corrugated iron roofs that Paul told him was Kibera.

They pulled up behind a Land Rover and, after a businesslike handshake with Paul, he was soon ensconced in the back and was driven through Kibera until its amalgamation with Nairobi. The appearance of taller buildings no less shoddy signalled their entry into the capital and he was soon on the same pot-holed streets he'd been through on his first visit.

He hugged the leather bag full of cash closer and watched the seemingly unsustainable mayhem and chaos of everyday life in Nairobi pass by. He felt a lot more vulnerable this time around as he had no armed convoy surrounding him, but at the same time he felt strangely exhilarated. It was as if the closer to danger he was in, the more excited it made him feel. With the prospect of what lay ahead, he felt more alive than at any time he could remember, with the exception of living with the woman he loved – and he was getting closer and closer to her.

He shook his head in disbelief as he wondered at how fast things can change. Only a few days ago he was in Washington DC, reading politicians' lips, and now here he was in Africa, about to enter a life-and-death scenario.

"You okay back there?" said his driver into his rear-view mirror.

"What? Oh, yeah, fine." He must have been muttering his musings to himself out loud. "How much further to the hotel?"

"Should be there in about ten minutes."

He sucked up as much air as he could through his nostrils and let it out slowly.

They passed some children playing football with what looked like a ball made of newspapers bound with string. The scene triggered a memory in the not-too-distant past and it occurred to him that if those kids in Manchester hadn't hit his head with a ball that day, perhaps his whole life and indeed the lives of all the people he knew would have taken a very different path and he wouldn't be on his way to rescue Molly from international terrorists.

They pulled up in front of the Sarova Stanley Hotel. A bellboy went to the boot and removed the government-provided luggage and held out his free hand to take Danny's leather bag.

"It's okay, I'll take this. It's not heavy."

The foyer wasn't overly crowded, and he crossed the black-and-white chessboard, polished marble floor to the reception desk, passing a big Chesterfield circular sofa. There sat Sammy reading a newspaper. Without looking up, he mouthed, 'Welcome to hell. All set. Jean-

Michelle is also in the hotel. Come down to the lounge bar you can see on your left at 1200hrs.'

Danny looked at the clock behind the desk as he handed over his passport and told the black-suited receptionist that Mr Valentine-Rocker had arrived and had a reservation. It was 10.30. He looked at his watch. It said four o'clock, and he adjusted it while they checked him in.

He was shown to a comfortable room on the third floor at the end of the hallway. He put the suitcase onto the bed and took the cash bag with him to the bathroom. Taking full advantage of the hotel's complimentary sanitary bag, he took his time to have a leisurely shave and shower to restore himself to feeling a little more human. Sometime later, and wearing a white towelling robe three sizes too small, he lay on the bed and stared at the ceiling.

He needed to mentally prepare himself for what was going to be a complicated day, but his bodily systems had other ideas, and he lost consciousness within seconds. All his thoughts disappeared down a black hole inside his head like the last grains of sand in an egg timer.

CHAPTER 35

He woke with a start. Air was stuck in his windpipe, and he sucked hard to get a bit down to his lungs. His heart was thumping and, while he regained normal breathing mode, he checked his watch. 11.45.

"Fuck!" His hands shot out on both sides, feeling for the cash bag. It was there, safe and sound.

He got up and dressed in his government-issued khaki chinos and a pale blue shirt that could have done with an iron if he'd had time. He got the lift down to the lobby and luckily nobody joined him, so he was able to take several deep breaths before the doors opened. Another check of the time. 11.55. Sammy was still sitting on the circular Chesterfield, studying a tourist map with apparent concentration. Without looking up, he mouthed, 'Take a seat at one of the tables in the centre of the lounge. Our people are all in place. Good luck, my friend.'

A quick scan of the people milling around the lobby and he was unable to spot anything or anyone out of the ordinary. Just the same mix of tourists and businessmen he'd seen when he'd arrived. He was relieved to spot an empty table perfectly placed for its occupants to be in full view from anywhere in the room.

He took a seat and immediately caught sight of Jean-Michelle walking with a newspaper under his arm to take a seat at a nearby table. It was the first time he'd seen his colleague dressed in a simple white shirt.

'Here we go,' he mouthed.

He sat with the bag on his lap, and seconds later a waiter approached and he ordered a sparkling water. One last check of his watch: 1200hrs – and when he looked up, he found two men standing at his table.

"May we sit?"

Danny was a little surprised, as for some reason he had expected to meet only one intermediary and that he would have an Arabic appearance; but here were two people who were clearly black Africans.

Both were dressed in grey off-the-peg suits, white shirts and black ties. Despite their identical attire, they couldn't have been more different. They were like an African version of Laurel and Hardy. The one who had spoken was extraordinarily slim, with a narrow face, wearing large, black-rimmed glasses and whose suit hung off him like a coat hanging on a broomstick. Meanwhile, his companion was a large, overweight man with a face like a football, who looked like he had never worn a suit in his life. His white shirt collar came nowhere near circumnavigating a bull-like neck. His tie knot hung in the middle of his chest.

"Yes, go right ahead."

The slim one sat and crossed his bony legs. His long fingers rested interlocked on his knee.

His companion squashed himself into his chair with some effort, his strained suit jacket opened to give Danny a glimpse of what was quite clearly a gun holster.

"Do you prefer coffee or tea?" asked the slim one in an African accent.

Danny felt a barrage of emotions overcome him in an instant, ranging from an urge to burst out laughing at the surreal absurdity of the whole scene playing out in front of him, to trembling with fear and nerves. He almost forgot the reply.

"Erm. Coffee in the morning and tea in the afternoon."

The slim one smiled and leant forward.

"So?" he said in a lowered voice, and hesitated for Danny to lean forward to hear him better. Leaning in to hear better wasn't something that Danny was used to, but he felt it would be wiser to do so.

"I presume you have the money?" the man said, nodding at the bag. Instinctively Danny clutched it a little closer. "May we see?"

Danny opened the bag just enough for them to appreciate that it was full of bundles of dollar bills with $10,000 written on the bands holding them together.

They both leaned forward simultaneously and nodded.

"Do you have the list of prisoners to be released and the authority to release them?"

"Of course I do, but I must insist that there will be no prisoner release and certainly no money until the hostages are safe. I only have the money here to prove that we are acting in good faith. Do you have a proof-of-life photo?"

His two new friends conferred, their heads closed together. Danny couldn't pick up what they were saying, so they were probably communicating in an African dialect. Danny looked over to Jean-Michelle, who had a decent view of their faces, and he was delighted to see that he was almost simultaneously mouthing in English what was said.

"*It was to be expected. Okay, let's just go with the plan.*"

"*We could always just take the money now.*"

"*Don't be so ignorant. First, do you think he's alone? And second, our priority is the prisoners.*"

"*Show him the photo.*"

The thin one smiled.

"Okay, Mr...?"

"Names are not necessary. The photo?" Danny held out his hand as the fat one took out a square Polaroid from his inside pocket. It was a little creased, and the image was quite dark, but he could clearly see three women sat in a row on a dirt floor in some kind of hut. Their eyes were pink and their expressions serious. Their mouths were tightly shut. In the middle of the two African girls, a pale face framed with familiar unruly curls stood out like a beacon. Danny felt like his breath had been taken away for an instant, and he tried not to show it while taking a large swallow of nothing.

"How do I know this is recent and that they're still alive?"

"If you turn it around, you can see the date that the camera printed on the back at the time of taking."

3.15-15-2-1999

"That was the day before yesterday."

"I'm afraid it's the best we can do."

Danny looked over at Sam for indications.

'*It hadn't been anticipated that there would be more than one intermediary. This might be a game changer. You need to get them conferring. It's our best chance to get some useful information that might help us pinpoint where the hostages are being held.*'

Danny remembered the Special Forces team that had accompanied him to Nairobi and wasn't sure about facilitating any kind of rescue scenario which could endanger Molly's life. He honestly thought they were going to do it by the book and follow instructions.

'*Really?*' he mouthed.

"What?" enquired the skinny one.

"What?" said Danny.

"You were saying something."

"Just thinking out loud." He kept Sammy within his vision as he answered.

'*HQ's instructions,*' mouthed Sammy, then sneaked in a subtle, '*Yeah, I know, but they're insisting,*' in ASL.

"Okay, so how do we do this?" Danny asked the skinny one.

"We had anticipated this, so we propose to meet again at a remote location only accessible by helicopter. We will make sure the hostages are there and we can complete the transaction simultaneously. You will arrive alone and when we present the hostages, you will hand over the money and give the order to release the prisoners. Once we have received news that the prisoners have been released, we will hand over the hostages and each party will depart in their respective helicopters."

"I see you've thought of everything. How do I know that I won't be ambushed for the money on arrival?"

"My honourable friend, I can assure you that our prime objective is to get the prisoners released."

"Okay, I hope you forgive me, but that isn't the most reassuring guarantee that I won't end up in the middle of nowhere with no money and no hostages."

"It's the best we can do."

"Where and when do you propose this meeting?"

His table guests put their heads together and had a whispered exchange. Danny wasn't sure if he was glad to see that this question was one that needed some conferring, and he held his breath with anticipation, wondering if Jean-Michelle could pick something up.

'*How far are the hostages from the meeting site?*' the thin one asked in the language that Danny was unable to read.

'*They are being moved once again tonight across the border to Kolbio. From there we could have them at the site in five hours by truck, but it is a rough ride. There are only tracks on the route and, as you know, it is on a plateau surrounded by jungle. They are just waiting for the green light from us.*'

Danny glanced over to Jean-Michelle for any sign that the whispered conversation had revealed what they had been hoping for. He was sure he saw the briefest of toothy grins appear on his colleague's face.

'*Bingo*,' he mouthed. This confirmed something that Danny himself had picked up when the two men were conferring. A flash of anger showed in the eyes of the thin one.

"Let's say 3pm tomorrow. We will send you a messenger with the exact co-ordinates just one hour before, for obvious reasons," said the slim intermediary.

"Okay, gentlemen. I'll await your message and arrange for a helicopter to be ready to take me to the rendezvous."

"Any sign that you are not alone and we will abort, and your charity people will be executed. The transaction will not be complete until we have had notification all the prisoners have been released."

"And any sign of an ambush and I personally will destroy the money on the spot."

"I trust in a successful and peaceful conclusion, and everybody will get what they want. I'm sure your people will now try to follow us, but it will be in vain, as our part in this operation is complete, and we will now go our separate ways. If either of us is apprehended, the charity people will be immediately executed."

They stood, shook Danny's hand, and walked straight out the front door.

Danny sat back in his chair and breathed a sigh of relief, although he felt more than a hint of uneasiness about events to come. Now they had an approximate location of the girls and, if his colleagues could pinpoint the plateau, an idea of the meeting point, what was to happen next?

As he had originally thought and desired, perhaps just following the intermediaries' instructions would be the best plan. All by the book. He'd exchange the money for the hostages and the prisoners would be released. But what if what was surely MI6's preferred choice to try a rescue attempt didn't work out and the girls were executed? He really didn't care about the two million dollars or if the prisoners were released or not, but he knew the government's policy to not negotiate with terrorists, and 'by the book' was not going to be an option. Sammy mouthed that he should go back to his room and wait. The Special Ops team had already been mobilised.

CHAPTER 36

Molly felt her tummy rumble as they were roughly led into another room. This time her feet detected a rough concrete floor. She was totally disorientated, not knowing if it was day or night, morning or afternoon. She doubted that she had been able to sleep more than an hour at a time. Her neck and back ached, her wrists were sore from the rope, and her mouth was dry and tasted of the cloth that gagged her.

It had been a long time since they had last been hand-fed the usual watery, lumpy gruel from the metal container. They hadn't removed the blindfold since the photo session, and different coloured dots danced in front of her eyes. She could feel the grime on her skin and was acutely aware of her and her fellow hostages' pungent body smells.

Between houses had been the same knee-crunching flatbed truck on which they had helplessly bounced around without having hands to steady themselves and no sight to prepare them for the bumps, which were many.

Molly was relieved that their captors had now finally sat them back to back as they had been in the first house. She stretched and wriggled her fingers, desperately hoping to make contact with Ruthie's. At last, she felt them, and she could feel the tears welling up behind her blindfold when she could finally communicate.

They tapped frantically, each explaining their aches and pains and how hungry they were and how little they had slept. Molly speculated that the fact that they were still alive and being moved meant that an imminent death wasn't going to happen and that somebody must be doing something to meet their captors' demands.

Ruthie tapped that she had picked up some snippets of conversation that confirmed Molly's instincts. They had talked about their brothers soon being released and that the UK government's representative had arrived in Nairobi with the money. This information sparked a glimmer of hope somewhere inside her and spread throughout her body, re-energising her spirit. All her aches and pains faded, and her anxieties dissipated as she felt like she had plunged into a cool pool on a hot summer's day.

Molly and Ruthie tapped for as long as they could. The mental concentration needed to read each other's tapping was enormous; even more so given their circumstances, having to repeat their messages over and over again just to be understood. Molly became aware that at some time Ruthie had stopped tapping and had probably fallen asleep. She soon followed suit and for the first time in days she slept of her own contented accord.

***

Back in London, Mr White, Mr Black and Mr Blue finished their meeting with the team of MI6 analysts who had been poring over maps and satellite images. They promptly despatched orders, and two teams of Special Ops based at a site just outside Nairobi boarded Chinook helicopters, one team headed to Koike and a smaller one to the pinpointed rendezvous site just in case.

Danny remained seated when the intermediaries had left and ordered a pot of tea. He noticed that Jean-Michelle had disappeared, but Sammy had stayed on the circular Chesterfield. He relayed that as soon as the analysts at HQ had identified the rendezvous spot and studied the satellite images of Kolbio, the Special Ops teams would be deployed.

He should now go back to his room and await the messenger.

"But if I'm in my room, how am I going to know what's happening?"

"You've got a phone in the room, haven't you? We'll call if it's absolutely necessary. Right now, it's best that you stick to the plan and follow instructions."

"What are the chances that the Special Ops teams are successful?"

"No idea, Danny, but you can be sure that these guys are the best in the world at what they do."

"That's what they keep telling me. I still don't know why we don't just hand over the money and release the bloody prisoners."

"Government policy and all that. No paying ransoms and no negotiating with terrorists."

"Yeah, right. You and I both know that they do both. If we hadn't picked up that information, that's exactly what we would have done, right?"

Sammy nodded.

"So all this has been a sham? The intention was always to give priority to a rescue and destroy mission."

"If you hadn't got that info from them, we would have probably had to go through with the exchange as MI6 still hadn't located the girls. But Special Ops would still have mounted an operation at the exchange point."

"Great, that's just great. I've possibly just instigated Molly and the other girls' death warrants."

Danny went back to his room, taking his now apparently superfluous bag of cash with him. He was in for one of the most restless nights of his life.

***

Molly was woken by Ruthie's hands frantically shaking hers. Then she felt the thuds in the air. She recognised them as the same thuds the automatic weapons had made the night they were kidnapped. She tried tapping, but only found shaking, wriggling fingers. This wasn't a case of them being moved again; this was very different. She sensed a lot of movement and activity in the room, then she lost contact with Ruthie's fingers. Her nostrils filled with unfamiliar smells and dust. She felt her wrists come free of the rope, and her blindfold lifted only to leave her just as blind, seeing those dots and splashes of colour. There was little to see anyway as the room was dark and full of moving shadows.

A hand gripped her upper arm strongly and lifted her to her feet, which had also been released from their bindings. Her legs were stiff and unsteady as she was guided through the shadows. Molly removed her gag herself and spat the pasty dust out that had accumulated in her mouth. She tried to speak, but she was never going to hear an answer. The thuds continued to reverberate through her senses.

Once out of the door, she caught glimpses of what was going on around her as sweeping torchlight beams highlighted soldiers' uniforms. The strong grip on her arm belonged to one of those uniforms and she briefly spotted Ruthie and Moffi in front of them, each accompanied by their own escorts.

They were led down a dark, narrow lane. Small stones dug into her feet, but she couldn't feel them. She wasn't so much being led as pulled, urging her to pick up the pace.

Pure adrenaline allowed her to do so, as physically her body was weak and only running on back-up mental energy. In what seemed like an eternity, they found themselves in an open space. She could feel a blast of air as if a strong wind had picked up, and the ground under her feet was now some kind of short vegetation.

In the torch beams she could make out Ruthie and Moffi ahead among five or six uniformed soldiers. Red and green flashing lights invited her towards them. Beacons of freedom.

Molly could quite clearly make out that these lights belonged to a large helicopter. Her guide lowered her head and helped her climb on board with an unceremonious shove on her backside, and she was shown where to sit. In a very dim orange light she could make out that Ruthie and Moffi were sat opposite among more uniformed men. The faces of the men were painted black, making them look like menacing panthers with the light reflected in their eyes.

"Well, that was an unexpected experience. Are you okay?" she signed to Ruthie.

"Wow, oh my God, I honestly thought we were all going to die. I'm a bit in shock still, but I seem to be all in one piece. You?"

Molly found it hard to express how she was. *"I feel... I feel incredible. Whoever these guys are, they've just rescued us. Of course, this might all be a dream and I'll soon wake up tied to that damn pole."*

"Where are they taking us?" signed Moffi.

"Home, I hope," signed Molly.

Two more soldiers climbed on board, the helicopter took off, and they were soon high above the dark terrain below, which Molly could see highlighted by the moonlight through the still open door. She was surprised how smooth the take-off had been, only feeling a slight upward lift.

She could see Ruthie trying to speak to one of the soldiers without much success until she was handed some headphones. Her arm was around Moffi, who had moved to sit next to her and was now resting her head on her shoulder while they spoke. They were all given water, which they eagerly gulped down.

After some minutes, Ruthie relayed in sign the gist of their conversation. He was the commanding officer and his team was UK SAS, a special operations group, and they were now on their way to a base just outside Nairobi, where they would be debriefed and given medical attention.

"He thinks we'll probably be taken to the British embassy from there."

"How did they find us? I thought the charity was negotiating our release."

Molly waited for Ruthie to ask the soldier.

"It seems that while negotiating with the kidnappers in Nairobi, an MI6 agent picked up our location by means of lip-reading."

"Lip-reading? He did say lip-reading, didn't he?"

"He says it was a stroke of luck, and the original plan was to pay the ransom and release some prisoners, but who knows how that would have worked out?"

Molly nodded. She knew all about lip-reading, and for a moment she thought of Danny.

"He says the operation went smoothly except for the fact that they were supposed to capture at least one of the terrorists for interrogation, but, unfortunately, they all had to be eliminated. Their team suffered zero casualties."

The helicopter took about an hour to reach the base, but to Molly it had seemed like minutes, as, despite all the adrenaline pumping through her veins, her exhaustion took over and she fell asleep.

Once landed, they were taken to the medical unit, where they were thoroughly checked out. Their numerous cuts and bruises were attended to, and they were given a small serum IV drip.

Next was a hot shower, which Molly swore she would never take for granted again, and they were given identical green army fatigues that surprisingly fitted their small frames. Only the sandals were slightly too large for them.

Molly was now halfway to feeling human and more than a little overwhelmed by the transition from being tied up, blindfolded and gagged only a few hours before, to being led across to the base canteen in the orange and pink light in which the recently risen sun was painting everything.

Molly, Ruthie and Moffi walked arm in arm, and Molly felt close to tears with emotion when the enticing smell of bacon filled her nostrils. They were each given a tray and joined the line of soldiers loading their plates with bacon, sausage, eggs and beans. Despite being told to go easy on the food as their shrunken stomachs were not prepared for it, they sat at a table with their trays loaded and a large mug of tea. They were soon joined by two officers and a man who introduced himself as Mr Green, the UK government representative.

They were then debriefed on their experience, starting from the night they were kidnapped to the recent rescue. Ruthie relayed everything in sign, and Moffi began to cry when describing what had happened to her sister.

Molly once again asked about the circumstances that led to them being rescued, and Mr Green repeated what the soldier had informed them on the helicopter. He added that he had accompanied the extraordinary young agent from London that had played an active part in negotiating directly with the kidnappers' representatives and discovering their whereabouts.

"*I'd love to meet him and thank him personally.*"

"*I very much doubt you'll get the chance. MI6 secrecy and all that.*"

He told them they were to be taken to the British embassy in Nairobi, where Molly's repatriation would be organised. Ruthie and Moffi would later be taken back to their families.

A soldier approached the table and informed Molly that she had a call from a Mr John Kenward in the administration building and that he would accompany her.

"A phone call? How am I supposed to take a phone call?"

"I'll come with you, Molly," signed Ruthie.

The two of them were led to the base's communications room, where Ruthie was passed a large, chunky satellite phone. She'd never seen anything like it and held it at arm's length, as if scrutinising what could be a dangerous animal.

"Hello?" said the concerned voice on the other end. The soldier who had accompanied them took her hand holding the phone and gently guided one end up to her ear.

"Hello, hello."

"Hello, it's John. Who's that?"

"It's Ruthie, John. You of all people should know that Molly can't use a phone!"

"Ruthie! Am I glad to hear your voice! My God. How are you?"

He didn't give her a chance to answer and continued, "Yes, I know Molly can't use the phone. I was hoping you'd be able to help out. Is Molly with you?"

"She's right here next to me."

"Oh, thank God for that. You've had us all worried sick. It must have been terrible, *terrible*, what you've been through. Are you okay? Did they hurt you?"

"John. Calm down. Everything is okay now. We're safe and being well cared for."

Molly was frantically signing.

"John. Molly wants to know if her parents know she's safe and how they are doing."

"Well, you can imagine they've suffered a lot, been phoning me every half an hour for days now. But we got the good news a couple of hours ago and we are all relieved and delighted."

Ruthie signed his reply to Molly.

"She says that if you speak to them now, tell them she's fine and she'll be home soon."

"Okay, and Ruthie, don't worry about a thing. The charity will help and support both you and Moffi with whatever you need."

"Thank you, John."

"Before I go, just tell Molly that she might like to know that our mysterious charity benefactor is in Nairobi now, and he was, in fact, the

276

person who took the ransom money to negotiate your release directly with the kidnappers. She may just meet him at the embassy."

"Okay, I'll tell her. Speak to you soon."

When Ruthie relayed the conversation to Molly, she was momentarily confused. Mr Green had said that an MI6 agent had been actively negotiating their release, but the conundrum only occupied her thoughts for a second as Ruthie immediately threw her arms around her and started jumping up and down with excitement. Then she signed how John had promised to take care of both her's and Moffie's needs.

They were shown to some bunks and told they had until 4pm to rest and sleep before a car would take them to Nairobi.

CHAPTER 37

Danny had been trying to get to sleep all night without much success. The hands of his watch moved agonisingly slowly. Every time he checked, only half an hour had passed.

He was awake at 12, at 12.30, 1, 1.30. The last time he looked, it was 3.30, and he thought, if everything had gone well with the rescue, he would hear very soon, and decided not to try to sleep any more. The next thing he knew, the phone was ringing, and it was 5am. He nearly jumped out of his skin. He grabbed the receiver, which flew into the air and was left dangling on its cord.

"Fuck! Fuck!" He pulled it back up to him. "Yes?"

"Danny, it's Sammy. It's done. The girls are safe and on their way to the base."

"Really? Oh, thank God for that. Everything went well? No casualties?"

"All went as planned. No casualties."

"That's brilliant. I thought I was going to go crazy waiting for news."

"They'll be brought to the British embassy some time tomorrow. You can meet them there."

"Thanks, Sammy."

"Now get some sleep."

Danny hung up and jumped off the bed, punching the air with joy. He then paced around the room, not knowing how to vent this immense elation he felt. He was jigging in front of the bathroom mirror when the phone rang again.

"Yes, hello?"

"This will not be forgotten. I would watch your back."

The line went dead.

"Fuck!"

The phone rang again.

"Danny, it's Sammy. We just heard the call. I think it's best if we get you to the embassy right now. Be downstairs in the lobby in five minutes and you'll be escorted."

He didn't hang around to pack, he just grabbed the money bag and headed for the lift. His mind, as he watched the floor numbers count down, was in a million different places. His emotions were so numerous he struggled to settle on one as they battled each other to gain total mind dominance.

Sammy, flanked by two burly men dressed identically in jeans and black t-shirts, was waiting outside the lift doors. No words were necessary. Sammy gently pushed the small of his back, guiding him across the empty lobby, out through the main entrance and into a waiting Land Rover.

Darkness still shrouded Nairobi's streets as they bounced along mostly empty roads to the embassy. The only lights were the odd white fluorescent tube flickering and providing intermittent purpose to a swarm of moths.

Danny was the first to break the silence.

"Well?" he asked Sammy.

"Well?"

"We did it, eh? Saved the girls and killed the bad guys."

"We sure did."

"Now what? Am I going to have to spend the rest of my life looking over my shoulder?"

"You can be rest assured, Danny, that when you do, you'll see me or one of the team. Anyway, we think it's highly unlikely you'll be in any danger once out of Nairobi."

"Well, that's only mildly comforting and not exactly what I wanted to hear."

Sammy shrugged in the darkness.

Danny turned his attention to the passing scenery, which was now mostly office blocks and large, ugly administrative buildings. They were now on a smoother dual carriageway with streetlights. A kind of grey tinged the cement and trees as dawn began to encroach on Nairobi.

He thought about Molly and he could feel an all too familiar knot forming in his stomach.

"Do we know what time Molly will be arriving at the embassy?"

"Not sure. Probably around early evening, I'd guess."

Danny sucked in some air and held it for a few seconds before blowing it out slowly. The knot was getting bigger.

"Does she know I'll be there?"

"I'm pretty sure that she doesn't. Having said that, they may have told her she'll be meeting the president of the charity."

Danny chewed his bottom lip.

"I honestly don't know how she's going to react when she finds out it's me."

"What do you mean?"

"I mean, the whole trust thing, the thing about lying to her. It's what broke our relationship up in the first place. When she realises I've been hiding the fact that I'm the mysterious benefactor all these years, who knows? Let alone working for MI6. That's going to be a tricky one. I mean, how much do I tell her? Do I tell her all about how I set up her fiancé to go to prison as an act of pure revenge?"

"Listen to me, Danny. You're overthinking all of this. Whatever her reaction is, whatever you decide to tell her, she must realise sooner or later that you are hugely responsible for her and her colleagues being alive today and, what's more important, that you are an exceptional human being."

Danny was now chewing his top lip. He could feel tears trickle down his cheeks. Both physical and emotional exhaustion were now overwhelming him, shutting down all his systems.

"Well, I've waited years for this moment, Sammy. Let's hope it's sooner rather than later."

He passed out.

Sammy placed a reassuring hand on Danny's knee while his friend slept until the Land Rover turned into a drive and was waved through the security gates and stopped in front of two big glass doors, tinted orange by a rising sun.

***

Molly, Ruthie, and Moffi were shown into a large office with dark red leather sofas and armchairs, oak wood panelling and bookshelves, and a large Persian rug. An oil painting of the Queen hung on the wall behind a huge, highly polished wooden desk.

The ambassador, Mr Green and a Kenyan army officer welcomed them with handshakes.

"Please, take a seat," said the ambassador, indicating the sofa. "First, I'd like to congratulate you on your safe return. I trust your journey here was not too uncomfortable."

Ruthie relayed in sign.

The door opened behind them, and the ambassador announced Danny's entry.

"May I present you all to the president of the charity."

Mr Green's face scrunched up in confusion.

"But I don't understand. That's that extraordinary agent I flew to Kenya with and who was mainly responsible for your release. The one that I mentioned."

The girls turned around.

"Mr Valentine-Rocker," said the ambassador.

Molly's face froze, her mouth wide open.

"*Hello, Molly. Surprise!*" he signed.

Molly's arms were flapping and spinning as she tried to sign her reaction.

"*D, D? D!*" was all she could manage.

She ran over and flung her arms around him and they embraced in silence for some minutes. The rest of the people in the room stood, perplexed.

Now was not the moment for questions and explanations. They eventually stepped back and watched each other's eyes fill with tears as they simultaneously made a fist, held it to their chests and drew circles around their hearts.

Lightning Source UK Ltd.
Milton Keynes UK
UKHW011847250820
368813UK00003B/110